PRAISE FOR HOOPS

In her timely novel, Gillam pits Hillary against a villain who plays by his own rules to preserve a way of life he's obsessed by. Thought-provoking and filled with suspense!

Linda Townsdin, Author of *Spirit Lake Mysteries*

Another intense Hillary Broome adventure, a tale of what a woman faces today: success at her job, concerns about her past, and the biggest job of all…keeping her daughter safe.

Robin Martinez Rice, Author of *The Blue Clay Pot*

Praise for previous Hillary Broome novels

HOUSE OF CUTS, BOOK 1.

House of Cuts builds towards a powerful climax, reminiscent of *Silence of the Lambs*. Susan Rushton, Author of *And Another Thing... Reflections from My Small Town*

HOUSE OF DADS, BOOK 2

Another successful woman leading the way through career and family issues. This story is close to reality and will leave you wanting more. A. K. Buckroth, Author of *My Diabetic Soul - An Autobiography*

HOUSE OF EIRE, BOOK 3

Hillary Broome's struggle to work through her own conflicts, her dedication to the causes she believes in, and her compassion for those she loves make the danger gathering around her all the more threatening. Ann Saxton Reh, Author of *Meditating Murder*

HOUSE OF HOOPS

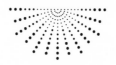

JUNE GILLAM

Gorilla
Girl Ink

Dedicated to Gianna Bryant, "Gigi," 2006-2020,
An inspiration to so many basketball players

PART I

CHAPTER ONE

"We Got Next"
1997 WNBA slogan

HILLARY TAPPED HER STEERING WHEEL TO THE ROCK BEAT of Queen's classic fight song. The pounding lyrics voiced the grim intentions of ill-fated young men determined to overcome the odds. Her daughter's basketball team had adopted the four magic words of the title as their mantra, boosting their energy to make it big in basketball. Hillary was on her way to another of their home games this late autumn afternoon.

As the light turned green, the music stopped.

We interrupt with breaking news of an active shooter at Mercury High School in Thousand Oaks, fifty miles west of Los Angeles. Two students are known dead with a possible five wounded. More later as the story develops.

Hillary's jaw tightened. Her first thought was her daughter, but the past came roaring into her consciousness. As a journalism student, she had covered tragedy with a heavy heart. Back in the late eighties, everyone was stunned by the Stockton schoolyard shooting. Hillary still had nightmares of the carnage and the shocked faces of the survivors. Her college newspaper editor had assigned her to drive the fifty miles south to cover that Cleveland School massacre. Five students were killed and more than thirty injured. Now, as a mother, dread poured through her veins. Last week there was an active shooter drill at Sacramento Jr. High. She had to rush to see for herself that her daughter was safe today. Nothing else mattered at the moment.

"We Will Rock You" screamed its ear-blasting finale as Hillary ran a stop sign and squealed into the school parking lot. She hopped out of the car, looked around and up. Everything looked calm, the cloud cover overhead holding back its rain. She was probably just overreacting.

Inside the junior high school gym, the game was in progress. Relief washed over her. She focused on the youngest player on the court. Her daughter, Claire, ran point guard, zigging and zagging, dancing away from defenders, shoes squeaking on the worn hardwood. Dribble, sprint, take it down the floor.

Shrugging off her navy peacoat, Hillary took a seat behind the home team's bench. She nodded to Stacy, always there early, red and tan streamers clutched in her fingers. "Thanks for saving me a place."

A broad smile smoothed the wrinkles from the older woman's cheeks. "It's no never mind, honey."

"It took longer than I planned, getting Kampus Klothes to sign on as a sponsor."

"They're lucky to have you for PR. When the Center opens, it'll be better times for our girls." That was Stacy, always with the support for young people and basketball.

Sunlight broke open the clouds and shot through the high windows of the old gym. The light illuminated Claire as she bounce-passed the ball to a teammate who thrust it up. It arced high and swooshed into the basket.

A woman at the score table flipped over a card to show the Tasmanian Devils ahead 20 to 16.

The opposing coach called a time out. Within seconds, dark clouds shuttered the sun and threw the place into shadow, leaving the young athletes standing in the gloom. The fear always hovering nearby settled on Hillary's shoulders like a dark cape, even heavier today. That news flash stirred some kind of panic within her.

What would it look like this afternoon down in Thousand Oaks? In her mind's eye she pictured TV images of tear-streaked faces, of candles, flowers and teddy bears after school shootings. Eyes narrowed, she surveyed the spectators, a practice begun years ago when she was a cub reporter. What if some madman burst in and sprayed these innocents with bullets? Her icy hyper-vigilance took over. She scrutinized each person in the crowd, her mind focused like a sniper in wartime.

When action resumed on the court, her attention returned to the game. Stacy's granddaughter pounded down the floor, reached out and blocked a shot. She grabbed the loose ball, pivoted and raced the length of the court to leap up and slam dunk it, leaving the old iron hoop quivering from the assault.

Hillary high-fived Stacy. "Keisha's looking better than ever."

"Teamwork." Stacy gave a nod, crediting all the girls. "They giving it up for Coachie."

"Tiffany's the best coach in California," Hillary said. She and Stacy always sat right behind the bench, concentrating on the coach and her eager young players.

Coach Tiffany called a time out and huddled with the girls. "Shooters, control your dribbling. Keep the ball low and close to your body, so they can't steal it."

Claire led the way back onto the court.

Hillary stiffened as the gym doors banged open and the principal strode in, his face a fish-belly white. He bent to whisper in the coach's ear. She nodded and signaled timeout to the closest referee, a gangly high school boy. The players ran to their benches.

Mr. Hagerty picked up a microphone from the scorer's table. "Ladies and Gentlemen, Sacramento Jr. High is going into a lockdown. Students, you know what to do. Parents, follow their lead. Questions will be answered after we move to the designated locations."

Adrenaline poured through Hillary's veins. She texted her husband.

lockdown SacJrHi know about it?

He answered immediately.

will check if related to SoCal shooting

On the sidelines, mothers clutched purses and looked around wild-eyed. Students hefted backpacks and clambered down from the bleachers to join the teams. A tall redheaded player had tears rolling down her cheeks.

Hillary helped Stacy gather her things. They followed the players into the girls bathroom that served as a locker room. The small space was crammed with students and parents from both schools.

Coach Tiffany began speaking in a low and measured tone. "Everybody stay calm. This is not an active shooter drill, like last week. Mr. Hagerty said the office received a threat on the phone, so the school must be searched. We will be leaving as soon as it's safe."

Her voice was soothing, thought Hillary. Maybe that was one of the qualifications nowadays to work at a school—the ability to handle emergency situations. Mother of God, let this threat be some kind of sick joke. Hillary pinched the tiny Mary medal hanging from her bracelet.

A father she knew from elementary school days called out, "What kind of threat? Who was it?"

"We haven't been told," Tiffany said. "But when we learn, you'll be informed. Check with the school website when you get home."

A pair of uniformed officers edged into the crowded room. "Gather your belongings and leave in single file," one of them commanded. Hillary recognized the other man. It was Walt, her husband's partner back when they worked as deputies for San Joaquin County. Walt was retired and picking up occasional work now.

Keeping an eye on Claire, who was ahead of her in the line, Hillary moved along toward the hallway leading to the parking lot. As she neared the door, she whispered to Walt, "Is this related to what happened in Thousand Oaks?"

He huffed in disgust. "That killer turned his gun on himself, so doesn't look connected. Our secretary got some kind of phone call. A guy asked who pays for the basketball program."

Hillary shook her head.

Walt chewed on his bushy mustache for a few seconds. "Takes all kinds. Some taxpayer off his nut, my guess. Hard to keep track of 'em all." His face looked puffy. Hillary felt a pang of worry. They should have him over, give him a healthy meal, poor man. No family. Must get lonely. What did he do to keep himself busy?

As she left the building, she texted Ed:

safe on way home

talk at dinner

Hillary threaded her way through the parking lot and hit the remote to unlock the car, letting Claire get into the back of the Rav4. "Will this keep us out of the Reno tournament, Mother?"

"You had one more game than the minimum," said Hillary, recoiling at Claire's use of the word *Mother* instead of her special and sweet *Maa* from childhood. Her twelve-year-old daughter's mood changes were hard to keep up with. "As long as you play next week, you should be okay. You and Keisha both. That game will be at the high school, so if they don't get any threats, all should be fine."

Claire buckled her seat belt, sat back and chewed on her thumbnail.

"Take your nail out of your mouth," said Hillary.

"Can Keek spend the night?"

"Sure, if it's all right with Stacy. Text her that we'll follow them and pick her up from her house." Hillary had to laugh at how the name of her daughter's friend got shorter and shorter as they became closer and closer.

Claire had started out calling the tall bronze center *Keisha*, her name on the roster at Hoops for Girls camp the summer before last. The two girls' hustle on the court was obvious. Hillary wasn't surprised the Most Valuable Player award went to Keisha while Claire won the High Basketball IQ honor. The girls shared a single-minded obsession to become professional players. Once they realized they had potential, they became their own peer support system. Claire began calling her friend *Kee Kee* and sometimes, like today, even the one-syllable, *Keek*.

Hillary thought back a few years to when they'd become like family. Since she and Ed moved from their Lodi vineyard for the new jobs, Ed's office with South-bridge Private Security and her Singh Development office were both near the downtown arena hosting those youth basketball camp sessions. They'd been able to duck in to watch the girls, get to know their families. For Hillary, it was another public relations opportunity for the still-under-construction Ans Botha Community Center a few blocks away from downtown commons.

One lunchtime, she'd taken Keisha's grandmother over to Sauced BBQ & Spirits for some of their famous brisket. Over a craft beer, Stacy explained she was raising her granddaughter Keisha. "My daughter, Tamika, she couldn't stay on her meds. One minute lay on the bed all day, next you know out on the street. Bad mood swings. Ran off, still don't know where. Have to make it up to my Keisha, she be no motherless child."

Hillary nodded with sympathy, but withheld that she'd grown up without a mother. "I worry some about Claire and how changeable her moods can be. I've read it's common though for girls between childhood and teens. Keisha seems more stable, from the little I've seen of her."

Stacy nodded emphatically. "Girl takes after her father, must be. Wish I knew what her mother is like nowadays. When Keisha's at school, I been watching that show Long Lost Family. You ever seen it?"

"I've heard of it but not taken a look." Hillary's stomach clenched at the thought of looking for family, and she put down her fork, unable to take another bite.

"I've toyed with trying to find Tamika, you know?"

"You're a fabulous grandmother, better than many mothers I've known." Hillary felt her heart soften. "In a way, you remind me of my good friend Sarah, who was like a grandmother to Claire." Hillary downed the rest of her beer. "She lived on our vineyard in her own little cottage back some years ago before we moved up here."

"What happened to her?" Stacy was almost done

with the brisket. "This barbecue's not bad, reminds me of my pop's."

Hillary pushed back from the table. "It's a long, sad story. Let's save it for another day and get back to watching our girls, setting records for their ages."

"Mighty proud of them both," Stacy said, "and glad to get knowin' Claire's good mama."

A flush crept up Hillary's cheeks. This woman was a hundred and eighty degrees opposite from Hillary's own mother, if that woman who abandoned her could even be called a mother. It was Hillary's deepest desire to be the good mother Stacy had just called her.

AFTER SHE PICKED UP KEISHA AND DROVE HOME, HILLARY put a loaf of French bread in the oven and got the table set while the girls practiced their shooting at the basketball hoop in the driveway. They came in ravenous and chowed down Hillary's done-to-perfection slow-cooker beef stew.

Ed cleared his throat. "So you girls haven't heard what happened down south?"

"What?" Keisha stopped, holding her empty plate on her way to put it in the sink.

"Down near L. A. There was a shooting at a Thousand Oaks high school."

Claire jumped up, wide-eyed. "Near Mamba's?" she asked.

"No, several miles away from Kobe's Academy," Ed said. "But two students were killed and six others wounded. Before he turned his rifle on himself, the shooter was yelling that guns take care of mix-ups."

"Mix-ups? Was that phone call at our school connected?" Claire bit her lower lip and finger-combed her short blond hair toward her cheeks.

"We're working on it with the police. No one is sure if the two are related. So, if you see something, say something," he urged.

The girls nodded, wide-eyed, standing silent and still for a few seconds before they headed out for pickup basketball down at the end of the street.

Hillary fixed a brandy and soda for herself and one for Ed. Out in the living room, he stacked up a couple split logs and started a fire. Hillary took a long pull at her drink as she settled near the fireplace. "So, do you have your guys at Southbridge working the threat we got today?"

Ed nodded. "City has us bumping up patrol around the arena, they're putting more resources on the schools. Caller had a thing against sports."

She shook her head. "How much danger were our kids in?"

Ed frowned. "School had a recorder on the phone, thank God. He was ranting about solving problems the right way. Thinks sports ruins young minds, says schools should focus on history and math."

"Holy Mary." Hillary shook her head. It hit her again how some people were so ignorant of how academics and athletics complement each other. Rubbing the gooseflesh rising on her arms, Hillary clenched her teeth and nodded for him to go on.

Ed swirled the ice cubes in his glass. "Said he knew his call would make everyone run through what he said was their 'well-rehearsed security scripts'."

Hillary dragged her fingers through her hair. When she'd met Ed, he was the lead detective on a murder case down near Stockton. He'd always tried to protect her at the same time he worked to prepare her to face danger. It was still the same now that he'd taken the job with a private security firm hired by businesses to bulwark the protection provided by the local police. "What else?" she asked.

Ed took a long swallow of his drink before he continued. "Ugliest part was, he ended with 'Next time there will be no call.'"

She slapped her thighs. "I'm going to have to do a better job checking at the kids' games."

He shook his head. "What happened in Thousand Oaks is a ticking time bomb for copy cats. Got word of an unstable guy had to be fired from one of the private schools this morning. Our contract is for downtown, but I'm asking Southbridge to let us keep an eye on the schools, too."

Hillary stared into the fire. "Walt was there today, at the lockdown. He doesn't look healthy. Reminds me of a sad Pillsbury doughboy."

"He's at loose ends with retirement, misses our days as deputies. I hired him for side jobs, helps us and keeps him busy."

Ed pressed his lips flat and sat silent a few seconds before he carried on. "Don't get mad. I've had Walt poking around, trying to find your mother." He cleared his throat. "You said you were going to look for her when we got home from Ireland and had to bury Grannie Sarah. That's been five years now, and I've not seen anything in that direction." He waited for her reaction.

Hillary felt her stomach twist. "I thought about it off and on, yes, after Sarah died, but I've researched cases like this, and there's no guarantee of a happy ending. I think going with Claire to the Day of the Dead celebrations every year helped and now basketball with new friends and interests.

"Even if I found her, she might reject me again… don't you see how hard that would be? Don't you?" She grabbed a tissue from the box on the coffee table and blew her nose. "Why is it so important to you, anyway? We are good parents, aren't we?"

Ed's face looked as grim as Hillary had ever seen him. "Claire has been asking about her, or I wouldn't have done it."

Hillary's mouth fell open. There it was. The question she dreaded hearing from her daughter. "What? When?"

"Just last week. She asked why we don't have any pictures of her." He waved at the fireplace mantle and its framed photos.

Frowning, Hillary walked to the mantle, moved aside her favorite shot of Ed and Claire as a baby and looked around at the other pictures. "Holy Mary, you're right." She noticed the picture of Sarah out in front of the cottage on the Lodi vineyard was gone. "Where's the picture of Sarah?"

"Claire told me she took it into her room."

Hillary's pulse raced. There was a photo of Hillary and her father the day she graduated with her degree in journalism from Sac State. But not any of Hillary's mother.

Ed stood and pointed to a picture of a wiry old couple outfitted in hiking gear. "They took me with them one week backpacking along the Pacific Crest Trail. When school was out for summer, he taught me to fish the Sacramento River when the Striped Bass were running." He sighed. "Now they're gone and my parents killed in that train wreck. It's not right for Claire to have no grandparents on either side."

Ed set the photo of his grandparents back on the mantle. "I told her she'd have to ask you about a picture of your mother. Guess she's picked up on it being a taboo subject."

Hillary bristled. "I've already told her my pictures got lost when I moved to Columbia for my masters. She knows that."

"I'd like to have Walt continue looking for your mother. What could it hurt?"

Hillary paced the living room. "She could be a raving maniac, a drug addict, maybe even a killer. She is probably dead by now. Even if she's still breathing, there's no way we have a clue whether she would be a blessing or a curse in our life." What hovered as an inchoate thought was, what if I found her and she refused to see me.

She shook her nearly empty glass at Ed, the ice cubes rattling. "Isn't it enough to focus on real problems we face, like violence at school helping Claire live long enough to make her dreams come true?" She set her glass on the mantle, picked up a poker and stabbed at a burning log until it broke in half and sent sparks flying.

Ed sighed. "Walt did get some information..." He paused.

"What? He's already found something, and you didn't tell me? What is it?"

"He thinks your mother might go by the name of Paisley nowadays."

"Doesn't that sound like an egomaniac calling attention to herself?" Hillary hooted. "Paisley! Talk about a self-centered artist type." She shook what was left of the ice cubes in her glass. "Get back to here and now, would you. The scare at school's made me even more anxious for the Center. What is Southbridge doing to really protect people at the arena? And all of downtown commons?"

Ed sat silent, nodding his head and staring at Hillary. "Ok. The metal detectors are as much for show as security. What we really watch for, and keep dogs trained on, are people loitering, not getting into the lines to go through the detectors."

"Have you had any suspicious guys lately?"

"We brought in a man for questioning last week, learned he was involved in that Capitol Park riot couple summers ago."

"And?"

"Calls himself a true believer, whatever the hell that means." Ed snorted. "He wasn't with the supremacists, and he says he's not Antifa, either. An odd duck. The

Capitol's got their share of those flying around. He got injured back then at the park, caught between the two groups."

Hillary frowned, jumped up and gestured toward downtown Sacramento. "But how about a couple blocks away from the capitol? Where Sunny's Community Center is going up? As Public Relations Director, I have to keep a lid on my fears in public, but the building's vulnerable, in the last stages of construction. Does Southbridge give it any attention?"

"Don't you worry. We are on top of it, Chickadee." He stood and ran his fingers lightly along her cheek.

Hillary couldn't help but laugh at his old nickname for her. *Chickadee*.

She would have to trust the law-and-order locals bolstered by the company that hired Ed to run their capital branch. Besides, there'd never been a mass shooting here. Nor a bomb, either, since way back when the Unabomber left one at a Sacramento computer shop. She was just fifteen years old and had been excited and alarmed to cover it for her high school newspaper.

But that was long ago, another day. She opened her arms and embraced her husband.

CHAPTER TWO

ALLIANCE, n. In politics, the union of two thieves who
have their hands so deeply inserted in each other's
pocket that they cannot separately plunder a third.

-Ambrose Bierce, *The Devil's Dictionary*

CHARLIE ZIPPED UP HIS BROWN LEATHER JACKET, BAGGY ON
him since the chemo treatments, positioned his black
cap on his bald head and looked in the mirror. Almost
perfect. But he missed his red LA Angels baseball cap.
Had to move it to the back of the closet after Trump
adopted the red cap look. Ended up winning the elec-
tion, too. Another damn developer, trying to take over
the world.

Out on the porch, Charlie clutched the gift for his
daughter Tiffany's birthday. His other hand took hold
of the wooden banister that had come to feel like a
friend, keeping him from a fall.

He descended the stairs of his vintage Victorian near downtown. Tiffany and her husband waited in Sunny's Denali SUV to take them to dinner at the Firehouse Restaurant in Old Sacramento.

He reached up and yanked open the rear door of the huge vehicle.

From the driver's seat, his son-in-law looked over his shoulder and called out, "Would you like some help with that, Dad?"

"Nah, piece of cake." Charlie gripped the handhold and heaved himself up to the platform step of the Denali. He settled onto the luxury vehicle's bench seat and ran his hands across the smooth black leather.

Charlie couldn't understand what had come over his daughter to marry a foreigner in a Hindu wedding at a San Francisco hotel. Crazy. All those colors. Under a tent, with prayers that had to be translated into English.

The man had already figured out how to dip his fingers into the taxpayers' treasury and claim that his downtown projects were for their good. Now Sunny was putting pressure on Charlie to sell his house and get the whole block cleared for a high-rise.

"Nice truck," Charlie said.

Dark eyes flashing, Sunny turned to grin at Charlie. "Gets me around to my building sites. I'm going to leave you and Tiff off at the restaurant and go park under the arena."

That basketball arena. Charlie's gut tightened. Five years ago, the city's backing of it had set the tone for growth. He swore it was the biggest waste of public money in recent history.

"Tiff could play in that arena if they would bring back the women's game," Charlie said. "Be a professional again."

"Dad, you know I love coaching the middle school girls. It gives me time to help Sunny downtown, too."

"Humph," Charlie replied. He didn't want to upset her on her birthday but there was plenty wrong with the way his daughter was going about her life.

He kept quiet for the short ride until Sunny left them off at the restaurant. Charlie pushed open the frosted glass doors and led his daughter into the saloon-style entry. The restaurant occupied a large brick building, transformed from the first firehouse in the state during the gold rush days. Charlie's parents had taken him there to celebrate his tenth birthday back in 1960, the year the restaurant opened for business.

Walking by the long sweep of mahogany bar, Charlie took note of who was seated at the barstools, which faced a massive framed mirror that doubled the apparent width of the entry.

He soaked in the feel of the place—the gold accents and crystal chandeliers. A server led them to a forest green leather banquette, the sides angled to place diners in a semi-circle and facilitate conversation.

Charlie slid himself into the middle, took off his jacket and folded it, placing it between himself and Tiffany, who'd seated herself on his right, facing the bar. She flashed her bright smile, and once again Charlie thought how those braces had been worth the cost. As a teen, his daughter had shot up to nearly six feet and taken to basketball with zest. He'd always been proud to support her choices. Until her choice of a husband.

She tucked a few strands of her long black hair behind her ear. "I haven't been here for ages. I love these red walls—and the black spiral staircase is so mysterious—did you ever learn what's up there?" She leaned back and allowed a hovering waiter to place a white napkin on her lap.

Charlie switched the subject. "Did you notice Judge Herring sitting up there at the bar?"

"No." She looked toward the entry. "Wasn't he the one who…"

Charlie followed her gaze and saw his beefy son-in-law coming in and nodding with a smile as he passed by the judge.

"Yes," Charlie continued, "Herring got thrown off our case after he let it slip he'd encouraged his wife to sign our petition."

"What petition?" Sunny slid into the seat on Charlie's left, blocking his view of the bar, unfolded his napkin and placed it in his lap before the waiter could get to him.

"The one that would have let us citizens," Charlie said with a frown, "vote on whether or not to finance that arena."

"Ah. That. I read you were involved with that attempt to stop progress. That was quite some time back, before I met the love of my life." Sunny blew a kiss across the table at Tiffany.

"Not that long ago," Charlie said. "Our petition got thrown out, and we lost our lawsuits. Now the city's in hock for years, paying for that fiasco, we couldn't stop. Wanted to keep life simple. Used to be," he waved in the general direction of his nearby neighborhood, his voice rising in volume, "on summer evenings we'd walk to the creamery for strawberry ice cream, take it home and eat it on the front steps."

Charlie slapped the table so hard ice rattled in the water glasses. "Frozen berries in it, this big!" He punched the air with his thumb and index finger a couple inches apart. "Creamery's gone now, replaced by your high priced, packed close, houses." He fanned open his fingers. "And now you want to put up a tower!" He glared at his son-in-law.

"Calm down, Dad." Tiffany nodded toward the menu, a strained smile on her face. "This is my birthday, remember. What sounds good to you?"

Several waiters stood nearby, alert and at the ready. In the ensuing silence, one approached the table and described the specials in a low, clear voice.

At the mention of roasted loin of venison, Charlie's mood quieted and his appetite perked up. He hadn't tasted venison since the years when his father hunted deer in the Sierra and shared game meat with his neighbors.

The appetizer of raw oysters, accompanied by his favorite local Ruhstaller beer, sent a flow of happiness through Charlie. The venison was seared dark at the edges of thin, melt-in-your-mouth-tender slices—and in keeping with the diet advised by his oncologist.

He beamed watching his daughter's eyes light up as the crème brûlée was set in front of her. A blazing candle pierced the middle of the burnt sugar crust and "Happy Birthday Tiff" was scrawled in a fancy chocolate script across the lower edge of the service plate.

Later, after the table was cleared and with as much pleasure as he felt anymore, Charlie handed Tiffany her gift.

She opened it with care. "Oh, nice! A new book on Alkali Flat." She fanned through it, looking at the pictures.

"Our house is in there." Charlie adjusted his John Lennon glasses and pointed. "Can you spot it?"

She flipped through pages more slowly. "No." She turned to the back of the slim volume. "And there's no index."

"It's also in the library's 'River City' collection." Charlie sat up straight, proud as if he were the author himself. "It features our district in the triangle of land between the Sacramento and American rivers."

"Good to have history documented and safely stored," said Sunny, "before it gives way to the future." He laughed, showing his gleaming white teeth, a stark contrast against his deep bronze skin. "Can't hold onto things forever." He patted Tiffany's hand. "Remember the Ganesha festival."

Charlie shot her a quizzical look and Tiffany said, "Got to let go of stuff, Dad. Every year the Hindus make a paper mâché version of their elephant god Ganesh and drown him in the closest body of water to show that his spirit doesn't live in material things."

Charlie pursed his lips and pulled at his chin where

the goatee used to grow before the chemo. He could relate. His after-dinner glow faded.

Sunny leaned forward. "We've sketched an exciting vision, Dad. The Community Center will open in a couple months. Our tower could add hotel rooms for events like an all-star game and also offer millennials the housing they're desperate for. We'll give you more than a fair price for your place if you'll reconsider."

Charlie pressed his fingertips to his temples, his head pounding at the reference to his son-in-law's latest proposal. How could the man bring this up at a birthday dinner?

Tiffany set the book down. "I'll look for the photo of our house later. Now, I'm requesting a different kind of birthday present." She handed Charlie a white envelope.

Still trembling over Sunny's audacity, Charlie opened the envelope and unfolded two letter-sized sheets, printed in purple and black with small, square QR codes at the top. "What the devil?"

"Courtside seats to the basketball game tomorrow. Bring cousin Justin." Tiffany stretched out her arm beside the table and mimicked dribbling a basketball. "You and Justin will be kings for the day."

After all this time, his daughter still didn't understand his viewpoint. "Kings, huh! Don't count me among those crazy cowbell fans."

Tiffany picked the sheets off the table, folded them in half once and half again, lifted his jacket from the banquette and slid the tickets into his pocket. "Come early for Women in Sports Night before the game. I'm on the panel." She mimed shooting a basketball up toward the crystal chandelier. "That's the best gift you could give me—celebrate women in sports breaking the glass ceilings!"

Charlie couldn't help but laugh at her antics.

Sunny stirred his after-dinner coffee and took a sip of the black brew. "Let's go check out the arena on the way back to where I'm parked. It's an easy walk through the tunnel under the freeway, settle our food."

Charlie frowned.

"Besides," Sunny continued, "I discovered last week that tunnel is lined with exhibit cases showing California's history."

"Humph," Charlie said. "Those half-baked historians got some of their stories wrong, they did." He stood and headed for the men's room, giving himself time to consider his daughter's tickets for tomorrow's game.

He made his way along the hallway. Hanging in a prime spot, a framed and signed photo of Governor Reagan beamed his charismatic smile alongside other political figures who'd been feted at the Firehouse. The pictures underscored the fact that traditions of the past were still honored, at least here in this landmark establishment. They soothed his mood.

Okay, fine. He'd be a good father and go see Tiffany, help to honor women in sports tomorrow. Make up for her mother gone, run off to Seattle last year with that billionaire.

. . .

IT WAS DARK WHEN THEY LEFT THE RESTAURANT, SATED BY the meal. They walked the plank sidewalks of Old Sacramento, moving past weathered brick buildings.

"This all," Charlie gestured at the streets around them, "was known in the eighteen-hundreds as 'gateway to the goldfields.' Now, it's gateway to Golden 1 Center. That place gets promoted like a promised land, but you ask me, it just gilds the pockets of the already wealthy." Charlie's steps slowed as a portly man strode toward them with a matronly woman on his arm, the pair headed for the Firehouse Restaurant.

The man tipped his hat at Sunny, who nodded back with a smile.

Charlie frowned at his son-in-law. "There's your pal on the city council," Charlie grumbled. "The builders' buddy." He stabbed an accusing index finger toward the distinguished-looking pair and exclaimed, "It's people like them who are to blame."

Tiffany took hold of his shoulder. "Daddy, can't you let it go? Come see downtown commons. We call it DOCO. It used to be a slum. Now it's thriving!"

Charlie couldn't help himself. "Thriving? Haven't you seen all the people on the streets, no place left they can afford to live. There was nothing wrong with the old basketball arena, built out of town like made sense!" His head was pounding.

"Golden 1 is an entertainment center, too," said Sunny. "Entertainment and Sports—known as an ESC." He vocalized the three letters separately. "It benefits everyone."

"Entertainment, my ass," said Charlie. "ESC. Escape from the tyranny of big shots ruining the town."

He gave Tiffany a quick hug. "Happy birthday." He nodded curtly at his son-in-law. "Thank you for the dinner, but I'm in no mood to go witness that arena tonight."

Ignoring his daughter's tug at his jacket sleeve, he walked off in the other direction, throwing both hands into the air and calling over his shoulder, "Don't worry about me, I know these streets like the lines in the palms of these hands." He turned towards Alkali Flat, the weathered setting for the classic Victorian his great-grandfather had built back in the 1860s, hugging to himself his memories before Interstate 5 cut Old Sacramento off from his beloved neighborhood.

He wouldn't be 70 until next year and was cocksure he could still find his way home on foot, going under the freeway by the old railroad museum. But he wasn't sure he could stomach going into that arena tomorrow. Even for his darling daughter.

CHAPTER THREE

LAND, n. A part of the earth's surface considered as property, subject to private ownership and control...if owned by A, B and C, there will be no place for D, E, F and G to exist.

-Ambrose Bierce, *The Devil's Dictionary*

BY THE NEXT DAY, CHARLIE HAD REASONED IT THROUGH. He had mixed feelings about her being on that women-in-sports panel in the basketball arena. He considered the arena had been a starter spore for nearby construction projects rising like fungus after rain. But he realized there would be a Q and A session at the end of the panel. He could ask when the women's professional game would come back. Give his daughter something better to do than coach little girls and shill for her greedy husband. He could trust Justin to come along into this den of thieves with him and not get carried away with the false glitter and glamour of the arena. Justin had been orphaned when he was three years old, adopted by Charlie's parents and raised like a brother to Charlie. Justin had agreed to meet him in front of the arena.

On his weathered front porch, Charlie tipped his head so the brim of his cap blocked out the afternoon sun. He furrowed his brow. Slabs of concrete soared up toward the setting sun a few blocks to the West, new roads turning into enterprises of all kinds built over the abandoned rail yards.

Never mind the conniption fit Mother would have thrown, what about the cost to taxpayers? What about the damage to the neighborhood?

Charlie strolled his block, carrying a book. He nodded at his neighbors, children and oldsters living together in extended families, renting places in Victorian houses divided into flats.

He turned toward the library to return *Black Sunday*, the Thomas Harris thriller focused on a plot to bomb the Super Bowl. The book had been recommended by his friend Victor Ramirez, the son of a former student of Charlie's. Now a history professor at Sac State, Victor had the information and connections, might be able to help stop the overdose of new development the way Charlie hoped his cancer had been halted by the surgery and treatments.

It might be too late for Charlie, burdened with his diagnosis, but not for this town, his birthplace and life-long object of his affections. His warm sentiments included his daughter, of course, despite that developer she'd become infatuated with and married.

Charlie placed *Black Sunday* onto the lip of the library's book return box and pushed the handle closed. He loved the ponk of the book hitting the rest of the returns. Books were solid objects you could count on to last over the years. It warmed his heart that people still appreciated the library, a classic building in the Italian Renaissance style, sheltering the wisdom of the ages. It had been restored, not torn down and replaced.

He turned in the direction of the arena and crossed the street to where a stocky middle aged woman was pounding her fist on a parking meter. "What's the trouble?" Charlie tipped his cap.

"My quarter's stuck in the slot. Can't push it all the way in or grab it out." She stared wide-eyed at Charlie. "Last month, same thing, these meters. Fees doubled and tripled. Want to grab our money, forget about making it easy to come downtown."

Charlie pinched her quarter with his fingertips and wriggled it around but no luck. He shook his head. "Damn shame, what they've done in the name of progress."

The woman blinked back tears and stomped the few steps to her green Hyundai. "Last time I'll try and use this library, you betcha." She got into her car and edged her way back into traffic.

Progress, my ass, thought Charlie. Motorists now had to circle for blocks, looking for rare and high-priced parking spaces.

Across the street in Cesar Chavez park, men and women arranged shopping carts, raggedy blankets and bedrolls into what would pass for bedrooms, the frigid winter sky as their ceilings. More homeless all the time. Now *there* was a cause *Suttertown News* beat the drums for, finally starting to get some government attention. But fat chance these poor souls would ever get anything from the developers who'd taken a wrecking ball to affordable housing. It would drive some of them into a life of crime—their survival would demand it.

He walked on toward the arena, his gut aching as he passed a vacant shop that once was a thriving bookstore. Decades before, the owners had commissioned tiles painted with colorful books and set them into the sidewalk. Now it was out of business, and the niche coffee shop that replaced it was just a memory, too, witnessed by a faded latté menu taped inside the old bookstore window.

In the alcove of the shop's narrow entry stood a gaunt black man, unsteady on his feet. He was pointing to a fat white woman sitting on a tattered cushion that once upon a time might have been the corduroy liner of a basket chair.

"Sho betta, know betta," the man yelled. "Gotta feed him." He bent to stroke the fur of a scrawny dog that looked to Charlie like an aging toy poodle mix gone gray.

Charlie kept his breathing on the shallow side, trying not to inhale the vapors of stale urine.

The woman rattled a big purple plastic cup. "Got change?"

Charlie didn't believe in giving money to the homeless, on principle. It postponed the day when local leaders would be forced to face the problem, and really do something about it. He'd read that every night, nearly 4,000 people were homeless in Sacramento County, far more than in 2015. The downtown development had a lot to do with that.

Charlie glowered at the tiny dog dancing on the sidewalk. The dog jumped over the purple cup, pivoted and jumped back. "He's a show dog," the woman said, with a toothless grin in Charlie's direction.

With a quick nod, he reached into his pants pocket, grabbed his loose change and dumped it into her cup.

"Bless you," said the woman.

With a scowl, Charlie headed toward the arena. Golden 1 Center had started it all. Golden—where did they come up with that name? Dull gray metal, aluminum if anything, towering sixty feet into the air, metal and glass surfaces askew in jutting triangles, as if it could collapse at any moment.

Charlie thought it looked like a mammoth aluminum can someone had stepped on to crush and flatten. In his heart, he yearned to flatten it himself like the stadium was destroyed in the novel he'd just returned to the library. The book was based on real life, the tragic Olympics hostage crisis where middle eastern terrorists took Israeli athletes hostage and killed them.

Violence was not the best problem-solving option in real life. In fiction, maybe. He would keep on writing his fantasy novel about bombing Staples Center, warning people against creating another L. A. mess up here in Sacramento, try getting this anger out of his system.

Charlie headed on toward the arena, his mind a hot jumble.

CHAPTER FOUR

It is hard to be brave, said Piglet, sniffing slightly,
when you're only a Very Small Animal.

-A. A. Milne, *Winnie-the-Pooh*

ON THE LOOKOUT FOR YOUNGSTERS IN COSTUMES, OUT
early for trick or treating, Hillary adjusted her rear view
mirror and glanced at the battle taking place in the back
seat. Head bent low over her cell phone, Claire pitted
her fantasy NBA team against that of her friend Kee
Kee. The young athletes sat side by side in the Rav4
rear seat.

Hillary jerked her head in the direction of the girls,
absorbed in their shared virtual reality. "Look at them,"
she whispered to Stacy, next to her in the front. "Crazy
for NBA Live 17. Will there ever be a WNBA video
game? At least we get to honor women athletes this
afternoon."

Stacy pursed her lips and picked at her hair. "Appreciate you picking us up. Got to keep our girls gettin' ready for when their chance comes."

Hillary narrowed her eyes and focused on Oak Park's faded lane markings. "Ed's working security tonight, so I left a bowl of candy on our porch with a 'Please take one' sign."

"That might work in your part of town." Stacy shook her head. "Not on my street."

Hoots erupted from the back seat as Keisha shouted, "Beat your ass again! When you gonna learn the game?"

"Language, girl," chided her grandmother.

"Getcha on the way home," Claire told Keisha and reached forward to tap Hillary on the shoulder. "Will Ruthie be on the panel, Mother?"

"It said so on the website, honey." Last summer both girls had attended a youth camp where the highpoint was getting coached by Ruthie Bolton, a former Olympian and player on the Sacramento Monarchs. They'd won the national championship back in '05. But that team got the axe in '09 from the previous owners. It made Hillary heartsick every time she thought about it.

"Ruthie was the best point guard ever," said Claire.

"Nuh-uh, she was a shooting guard."

As the girls argued, Hillary felt the familiar pang of sorrow over the death of women's professional basketball in the area. The panel tonight was scheduled to take place before a game pitting the Kings against another NBA team. She knew the panel was a nod to female athletes, but it meant little unless ownership decided to bring back the Monarchs. The arena itself had cost the public-private partnership nearly half a billion dollars. The city's part of the investment was to be paid back from parking fees spread out over the next thirty-five years.

Surely the modest cost of a women's team was manageable? Maybe even raise private funds, as some had been raised for artwork in and around the arena.

Everyone had been shocked by the exorbitant price for the sculpture of Winnie the Pooh's friend Piglet, soaring eighteen feet into the air outside the arena's massive glass front doors. An affluent family in town had donated the eight million dollars for the controversial artwork, constructed of polished stainless steel layered with transparent color. The artist had said the sculpture was part of his "Coloring Book" series of figures appealing to children and the child in everyone.

For Hillary, the phrase produced a sick feeling in the pit of her stomach. This would be the first time she'd see the sculpture in the afternoon sunshine.

"Maybe Piglet will be all sparkly," Claire shouted from the back seat. "I'm going to squint my eyes and see if that makes him look like he's colored outside the lines."

Hillary's stomach did flips at this comment. As a child, her daughter was the rambunctious sort. As a youngster, she'd loved scribbling on the walls when there was no paper handy.

Keisha said, "We never read that story, did we, Bibi?"

"We missed that one, girl. Got to check out Piglet at the bookstore next week."

Hillary visualized the small character she'd identified with when she was young, growing up the only child of strong-willed parents—her mother a petite and hot-tempered artist envious of her award-winning journalist father. "You know, Piglet is pink in Winnie the Pooh books," said Hillary. "But the sculpture of him in front of the arena has chunks of blue and orange and yellow. 'Course I've never seen that sculpture in the daylight, only at night games."

"I heard he's like a mirror," said Keisha. "We might see our own colors instead of Piglet's." The girls laughed and high-fived.

"I don't care what we see," said Hillary, changing the subject, "as long as there's a chance for girls to play at Golden 1 Center someday."

"Women," said Claire.

Hillary corrected herself, amused at the know-it-all tone her preteen daughter had recently adopted.

HILLARY PARKED UNDER I-5 NEAR THE RAILROAD Museum. Claire and Keisha dashed up the wide stairway to the plaza fronting the arena, followed by Stacy, who gripped the handrail as she climbed. Hillary kept a few steps behind, with an eye on the older woman but not worried. Stacy was wiry and strong. Hillary scanned the crowd, a habit from her days as a reporter. Nearby was a slightly built man wearing a black cap and John Lennon glasses who reminded her of someone, but she couldn't place him.

When Stacy reached the plaza, she turned and called to Hillary, "There's that pig," pointing to the 18-foot tall sculpture,

Hillary stepped up onto the plaza. The girls were circling around the sculpture's concrete platform, stopping every few seconds to toss imaginary basketballs up at Piglet's gigantic shining legs—one turquoise blue and one hot pink.

Suddenly feeling small, Hillary moved toward the massive figure, then stopped and gazed up at it, holding her breath, her fists clenched.

Keisha knelt for Claire to jump onto her shoulders, and when the tall girl stood with Claire on her shoulders, they reached halfway up the height of Piglet. "I'm on stilts!" cried Claire waving her hands as her friend took a few steps. The pillar of girls seemed to wobble in the air.

Hillary watched as Piglet's shimmering surfaces spread across the sky. In the setting sunlight, the metal flashed against her mind like a hall of mirrors to the past.

She was transported back inside her ten-year-old self, a pink crayon pinched between her fingers and thumb, coloring with care inside the lines of Piglet, her favorite page in the Winnie the Pooh color book, a gift from her teacher for being a good student. Feeling soothed inside her project, she hadn't heard her mother coming to peer over her shoulder. Suddenly her mother reached down and clamped her hand over Hillary's.

"Let yourself go free!" Her mother pulled the pink crayon from Hillary's fingers. "Don't be so rigid." Her voice was high and lilting. "You're too much like your father." With the crayon in a pincer grip, she scratched in zigzags from the top to the bottom of the page as if cutting the paper into pink slivers. In paralyzed silence, Hillary watched her mother throw the crayon onto the floor and seize the coloring book. "How many times must I tell you?" She ripped the flimsy book in half. "Let yourself go free!" She threw the book into the waste basket. "Use the sketch pads I got you!" She stormed out of the room, leaving Hillary frozen in place, her orderly boundaries shattered.

Seconds passed. Hillary stood motionless on the arena plaza. This was why Walt had to stop searching for that woman. Paisley indeed! Her name was Joanna. Didn't deserve the name of Mother. Even before she ran out on Hillary, she wouldn't have been anyone's idea of a good mother. The kind Hillary was determined to be.

Stacy tugged at Hillary's sleeve. "You okay, hon?"

Hillary shook her head and brushed at the front of her coat, as if to whisk away the memory. She folded her arms across her chest and cleared her throat, searching for her voice. "Yes. Yes. Amazing, isn't it? What artists can do."

She motioned the girls away from their lurching, double-decker circuit around Piglet. Claire jumped to the ground, out of breath. It hit Hillary that in spite of her mother's insistence, she had never tried it herself. Coloring outside the lines.

Near the security checkpoint, a tall man Hillary

pegged as an undercover officer shot a frown at the two chattering girls. He kept a tight hold on a leashed pair of German Shepherds, his eyes on the body language of dogs and humans, both.

"Open your bag," a chunky security worker shouted at Hillary. "Cell phones in your purses," he yelled to others waiting in line. She unzipped her tote and set it on the conveyor belt for him to rummage through while she stepped into the open framework of the metal screening system.

She raised her hands, elbows out at her sides as the staffer directed, while he waved a wand screener up and down the length of her body. She was relieved not to hear any beeps that would halt her progress. An old saying crossed her mind about the guilty fleeing when no one was pursuing.

No reason for her to feel guilty, she reminded herself. All that trouble was in the past. She wasn't even going by Hillary Broome anymore. She was here as Hillary Kiffin, to do her job in public relations for Sunny Singh Developers. Sunny had arranged for her to be on the Women in Sports panel to promote his Community Center opening on New Year's Day. The Center was designed to focus on helping youth in the region. It should be an easy pitch to these sports fans in the arena this afternoon.

She fingered a charm hanging from her black bead bracelet. The day Sunny hired her, he handed her a little box that held a tiny four-armed elephant crafted of silver. "Ganesha's my culture's way of bringing good luck to new ventures," he said. "He's been known to clear away obstacles."

Hillary put Ganesha on her bead bracelet right next to her Mary medal. It was exciting to be part of the renewal of her hometown and ready for plenty of good luck.

CHAPTER FIVE

Public humiliation comes to us all, and never so surely
as when we're just a little bit pleased with ourselves
and feel, just for once, that everything is going
our way.

-Kate Reardon

As they entered the cavernous lobby, Hillary
spotted a few fans wearing Halloween masks of famous
NBA players.

"Kobe!" screamed Claire. "It's Kobe Bryant!"

"LeBron!" yelled Kee Kee.

Hillary led the way across the concourse toward a
thin man in a purple pin-striped suit who was waving
at them. "Welcome to Women in Sports Night," he sang
out, his words nearly visible in capital letters of enthusiasm. He spread his arms wide to showcase the lobby,
decorated with blue glass orbs the size of bowling balls

strung together in swaths hanging high above escalators leading to the upper levels.

The man in stripes pointed in the direction of a stairway leading down to the arena's lower bowl. "Sit where you please. The event starts soon."

"I'm on the panel," Hillary said, "but I want to get my friends settled first." She started down the stairs toward the court. Stacy followed, one hand holding the railing bisecting the stairs, and the girls trailed behind. When Hillary turned in at the row right next to the court, Stacy said, "These seats must be for VIPs."

Hillary laughed. "These are for the panel. Our seats for the game are up there." She pointed back toward the concourse. "Ed doesn't get a discount on anything. No one does."

Stacy sat a few seats from the aisle, nodded at her granddaughter and patted the seats on either side of her. The girls plunked themselves down like a set of parentheses around Stacy.

"Break a leg, girl." Stacy reached forward to high-five Hillary, who left for the tunnel, feeling confident and energized.

In the media room, Hillary touched bases with Janine Ramsey, a local TV talk show host she'd been meaning to catch up with. She had known Janine since they'd started out together as young reporters at the *Sacramento Bee*. Janine waved a list of panelists in the air, giving the names and affiliations of all the women she was to talk with on the panel. "I see you're down as Hillary Kiffin in PR," Janine said.

Hillary felt her fair skin take on a slight flush of guilt

over why she was no longer a journalist. "Well, you know, the money's better here, too." She laughed but felt like such a hypocrite. She loved reporting, didn't care so much for the money. But her lapses had come out in an article in Columbia's student newspaper. She was identified as a plagiarist even though the story got little play beyond the campus.

"Why going by Kiffin, now, though?" asked Janine.

Hillary's skin crawled. "Just wanted to keep it in the family, now that we've got our little Claire. All Kiffins. Kind of old fashioned." Her mouth went dry with the lies she found herself telling to cover up her ethical faux pas. "Got to grab myself a water. Can I bring you one?" Janine waved her off holding her own bottle.

Hillary felt like she was hiding her true self. Like it was a life or death matter for her to succeed at this new role in life, building public support for a cause. It almost didn't matter what cause it was, just that she would do a good job of it. Plus, the Center was going to help Sacramento thrive. She was born and raised in a suburb of Sacramento and felt genuine enthusiasm for the exciting new developments downtown.

Claire's basketball coach, Tiffany, waved at her from the far end of the room and hurried to join her. "Our Devils are doing so well, and soon we'll have the fabulous Center to showcase our young phenoms! Next thing you know, Kobe will be bringing Gigi and the Mambacitas up here for competitions, just you wait and see."

"Let's go ladies," shouted Janine and led the way back

out of the tunnel to the basketball court. The women mounted several steps to a platform, set a few feet out on the hardwood. Hillary waved at her daughter and positioned herself between a white-haired woman wearing an Olympics jersey and the Tasmanian Devils' coach, Tiffany.

"Look!" shouted Claire. "Ruthie!" She and Keisha jumped up and joined in the applause as the women took their places on high stools. "There's Tiffany, too!" The girls flashed double thumbs up on recognizing their coach among the famous athletes.

Standing to the side of the athletes was Janine, who introduced herself and the women sharing the platform. "Welcome. Please join me to honor these women, champions in so many realms."

Janine moved from woman to woman asking questions about their sports. Yvonne Baker stepped off her stool and raised her Olympic gold medal high while she described the thrill of being on the Women's Track and Field team back in the 90s. "I was quick and strong, and kept it up. My twin granddaughters are runners out at Sac State." She gestured for two young women in the audience to stand.

Hillary noted Claire and Keisha clapping in affirmation. When Janine moved to the next two athletes, their coach Tiffany and role model Ruthie leaned their heads together toward the microphone and joined forces in describing their time as professional basketball players for the Sacramento Monarchs. "The thrill of winning it all in 2005 will never be forgotten," Ruthie crowed. The audience stood and applauded. "And we got rings!"

Ruthie waggled her fingers, flashing her diamond-encrusted championship ring.

Ruthie pointed up to the white and gold championship banner hanging from the rafters, along with a banner for their coach Jerry Reynolds. "Tiff here," she elbowed Tiffany in the arm, "she might not have a banner, but we couldn't have done it without her, being the string bean center that she was."

A man stood, waved his black cap in the air and yelled, "Best center the women's game ever had! Bring back the Monarchs!" Hillary felt a faint stab of recognition. Who was that man?

Tiffany blushed, twisted her championship ring around her finger, and spoke about what she'd learned from her high school coach about never giving up. She added, "Although the team was dissolved in '09, let's hope in this new era, we see a revival." Dozens of people rang cowbells and shouted, "Go Monarchs!"

The man with the black cap stood ramrod stiff, his lips set in a proud and determined straight line. He reminded Hillary of an elderly Sean Connery. Where had she seen him before? Janine moved next to Hillary. It was her turn at the mic.

The man sat, his expression shifted to a sneer, he elbowed a man sitting next to him and then took off his cap and ran his hands over his bald head.

Memory struck Hillary with force, and time stood still. He was that awful English professor, the one who shredded everyone's confidence—red ink on the papers and black insults in class.

Her palms grew sweaty. Damn him, he deserved the

poor grade her father gave him in the *LA Chronicle* series ranking state college professors. The next year, the man had been dropped from the tenure track.

"Hillary Broome Kiffin, here…." Janine nodded at Hillary, who panicked to hear Janine add in her maiden name, but realized it wouldn't mean much to this crowd. Claire and Keisha gave her googly eyes, making Hillary laugh and relax. "…will conclude our panel telling about an exciting new development for women in sports here in Northern California."

Hillary stood and gestured toward the arena's front doors. "A few blocks away," she said, her voice loud and clear, "is the nearly completed Ans Botha Community Center. It's named for an Olympic coach in South Africa, a 75-year-old great grandmother passing her wisdom on to the next generation. She shows that both women and men can excel at every age and place, which is our goal for the Center, too. Its four floors will feature sports courts and project spaces to build athletic skills, academic powers, and job-related practices. At our website, SunnySinghdotcom, you can download free tickets to the New Year's Day Grand O—"

"You witch, you don't belong on this panel with these Monarchs!" The wiry old man jumped up. "Owners got to bring back the women's game and you got to get off your broomstick flying high," he waved his arms, fingers pointing to the arena's upper levels, "promoting more damn buildings nobody needs!"

Hillary's spine stiffened. She shot back, "We've got major sponsors supporting our vision of raising each young person as high as—"

The man shook his fists and yelled, "Don't think you can shill for the greedy builders, take over our town and make it sound like a blessing!"

Hillary recognized his insults as echoes from long ago, in the days he'd held students paralyzed with fear. But she was a grown woman now. She sucked in a deep breath and called, "We'd love to tour you around the Center, show you the ways it will serve the city."

"I'd like to tour you out of town, witch!" He wheeled and started up the stairs, grabbing at the hand rail and followed by a man in a gray suit.

Yvonne Baker jumped off her stool, waving her gold medal frantically. "Our youngsters are our future!" she shouted as he fled up toward the concourse. "You can't push back the ocean, you old fart!"

Nodding agreement at this motherly woman taking up her cause, Hillary stood silent, feeling suddenly paralyzed inside her own skin, voiceless.

Janine came to the rescue, repeating the Center's website information and thanking everyone for coming to celebrate women in sports as outstanding examples for young players.

Hillary was last to step off the platform and join the girls gathered at the edge of the court, taking selfies with the famous athletes on the panel. Hillary reminded herself that the old man hadn't won in the past, that her father's articles in the *LA Chronicle* had stripped him of his tenure track and sent him packing in humiliation. That broomstick comment. Had he recognized her and launched into a vendetta against her? The presence of these strong women in this iconic arena soothed

Hillary's spirits, calmed her down a notch and loosened the hold the virulent attack had had on her. "That man," she said to Tiffany. "I feel shocked. I had him as a professor at Sac State, and he was always on a rampage back in the classroom."

"I'm sorry." Tiffany wrinkled her nose in dismay. "Believe it or not, that's my father."

"No." Hillary was stunned. How could such a horrible old man have a great daughter like Coach Tiffany?

Tiffany nodded. "He was always an old curmudgeon, but now he seems demented some of the time. He has this obsession against development in our town. He's battling brain cancer. I have no control over him. You know how it is with parents."

Hillary nodded but she was lying. No. She didn't know how it was. Her own mother had walked out on her when she was only ten years old. Her father died before she met Ed. How was it with parents? She felt rattled. That old man was Tiffany's father? A foe of improving the downtown and now adding a personal vendetta against her? This event had turned inside out from what she'd expected. She tried not to let him ruin the evening.

Aglow with excitement, the girls snapped selfies with the famous Ruthie Bolton. Impatient workers started taking the platform apart and hauling it off the court while players from the two NBA teams loped onto the hardwood for warmups.

Finished with selfies, Claire got Coach Tiffany to stand next to Ruthie Bolton and position their hands to showcase their WNBA championship rings. Hillary admired these visible signs of success.

Working to transform her wounded feelings into righteous anger, Hillary stood to the side like a spectator at a game where she wasn't sure of the rules. She'd call and ask to get on Janine's TV Show. It would give her a chance to explain the Center in detail, defend it, and encourage the public to get tickets for the New Year's Day opening celebration. Why would that man be against such a great project his own daughter was helping her husband build?

Hillary looked up the stairs and through the broad doorway to the concourse. She studied the blue glass orbs in permanent and full-bodied floatation hanging over the escalator. Another giant work of art. This arena —bigtime success. What would it take to make certain the Community Center would open as a success? Make her feel like she'd overcome the shame still clinging to her from what she'd done in those panic attacks. She twisted the tiny medals hanging from her bracelet, feeling her confidence shrivel, like a week-old helium balloon.

CHAPTER SIX

POLITICS, n. The conduct of public affairs for private advantage.

-Ambrose Bierce, *The Devil's Dictionary*

CHARLIE STORMED OUT OF THE ARENA AND CROSSED THE plaza, without waiting to see if his cousin Justin was following. When he reached the sidewalk, he stopped to stare at traffic inching forward on *L* Street. Once Justin had caught up with him, Charlie pointed at the cars. "Looking for parking, poor fools," he said, still breathing hard. "Only going to get worse, the more buildings they put up."

Justin took Charlie's elbow and turned east. "Take it easy. I'm on your side. Let's walk down to my office, and I'll show you what I'm doing."

As he followed his cousin's lead, the pressure in Charlie's head built. "I despise that damn cheerleader. I recognized her. Daughter of the hack reporter who ruined my career. She's nothing but a lackey for that developer. Acts like it's all for the kids." He turned to glare at Justin. "And I didn't get to ask about bringing back the Monarchs." His voice came quick and shrill. "Give Tiffany the platform she deserves instead of being stuck coaching middle school and shilling for that greedy man she married."

Justin nodded. "In fairness, you could have waited to ask about the women's game before you stomped out of the arena."

"Humph!" But Charlie knew his cousin had a point. That was Justin, calm and centered. Charlie breathed easier as they walked along L Street. His temper had cooled by the time they passed the state capitol, lit up and glowing under its golden dome on this late autumn evening.

On their side of the street, he stopped to admire the Roman arches fronting the restored Hotel Senator and cast his glance up the side of the nine-story Italian Renaissance-style building. "Now this is the right way to treat our treasures," he said. "Keep them alive as part of our heritage, not just photos in a book. Remodel when it's needed over the years."

Justin offered his square-jawed smile. "They call it 'repurposing' nowadays."

Charlie adjusted his wire-rimmed glasses, annoyed at his cousin's sophistication. Justin led the way up the wide marble steps and entered the courtyard-styled lobby.

"Look at this place." Justin waved to indicate the

ornate lobby. "There was a bar here back in the hotel's heyday. Writers like Saroyan and our cousin Ambrose mixed with political power brokers, holding court during cocktail hour."

Charlie nodded with appreciation. Ambrose Bierce, his hero. Charlie had written a few short stories in that stream of consciousness vein. And his fantasy novel was serving well as an escape valve for his anger.

Justin hit the elevator button for the third floor. "Bar's gone now, but lots of us are still here, attending to politics." The sign outside his office said it all.

Justin Bierce, Esq.
Environmental Law

He unlocked the door. "That woman you found so upsetting? Hillary Kiffin? She plays just a minor part in Sunny Singh's global landscape." He waved Charlie into the office.

Charlie stood perfectly still out in the hall. "That woman! She's not only Hillary Kiffin. She's Hillary Broome Kiffin, didn't you hear how she was introduced? She's the smart-ass daughter of that big time *LA Chronicle* writer, got me pushed off the tenure track at Sac State!"

"Let's stay in the present, where we can make a difference." Justin nodded in the direction of a couple young people bent over their computers. "My staff is so dedicated, idealistic," he murmured as he led the way into his private office. "Let me give you the full picture of Sunny Singh and his big ideas. He calls our region shockingly underdeveloped, with great potential."

Charlie gave a hollow laugh. "Underdeveloped? Structures paid for by so-called public-private partnerships shot up all over the place since that arena was built, looking like some mammoth alien space ship. What happens if a disaster hits, empties the buildings, leaves them hollow shells. What kind of investment will tax money spent on them look like then?"

Justin touched a flat screen and brought to life a map of Northern California counties, dotted with a half dozen gold stars. "Look. Each star is one of Sunny's proposals. His urban homes are in full swing, a purely private project. Then the Ans Botha is public-private partnership for the community benefit. A couple of them are actually great ideas, environmentally ahead of the times. Similar to the arena, which is solar powered for one thing. You could give 'em a chance." He raised his eyebrows at his cousin.

Charlie was irritated with Justin's broad focus. "What I care about is my neighborhood," Charlie said. "Preserve it. I would think you would care more, being raised there yourself."

Justin zoomed in on Sacramento's downtown neighborhoods. "I've got an Environmental Impact Report in the works to save your block from Sunny's tower, a purely private enterprise, that one. But a law pushed through to get the arena up fast might let Sunny avoid a lengthy EIR process."

Charlie paced the floor. "I'll be damned if I'll sell, but I can't convince others on my block to refuse

Sunny's offers. I don't want my house isolated on a corner like old St. Paul's church, surrounded by that Convention Center. Being designated an official Historic Landmark saved the church. The Preservation folks would never listen to my applications. I worry Sunny will try to get my place by eminent domain, the way that Macy's Men's store was forced to sell to make way for the arena. You remember that."

Justin shook his head. "That was different, it was a public-private partnership. Sunny's hotel tower coming up soon is just a private project. The city is not in the practice of using eminent domain for private projects."

"But they do have the power to approve or deny private projects. I need to wake up my neighbors and the public to what's being stolen from them."

"Be patient. Good things take time," Justin said.

"Horse shit," Charlie spat out. "If we don't stop this, our time will be up, and the new generation will never know what they lost."

Justin switched his computer to a government website. "Take a look at what's on the planning commission agenda—a key vote on Sunny's Alkali Flat tower proposal. If you would come into the twenty-first century and get a computer, you could keep track better of when these decisions are to be made."

Charlie scowled. "Don't want those things in my house."

"Could use the computers at the library, close to your house," Justin suggested. "Read the minutes, keep up with the schedules, give public comments."

Charlie's shoulders slumped. "Your plans are too

slow…" He sat down and rubbed his temples. The pressure in his skull—was it real or imagined? "Head's killing me," he whispered.

Justin pulled out his cell phone. "Let's discuss this later. I'll get Uber to take us home."

"Call a Taxi," Charlie protested.

"Uber provides income for people on the edge," said Justin, "and takes care of some parking issues, as well."

Charlie let his cousin talk him into giving Uber a try. Charlie had to admit, it was a good alternative, yet what about those poor hoodwinked idiots who still wanted to find a good place to park downtown at a decent price?

CHAPTER SEVEN

All women become like their mothers.

-Oscar Wilde

As if pulled by an unseen hand, Hillary led the others up the stairs to the arena's concourse, then onto the escalator lifting fans up three levels during Kings games. They strolled the upper level, pausing at the Sierra Nevada Draught House lounge for a view of the court below where pregame warmups were in full swing.

"There's Richaun Holmes!" Keisha cried out. She turned to Claire. "Love his tats. Bibi's making me wait 'til I'm 18."

"Let's get our faces painted," said Claire. The girls ran off.

Hillary and Stacy stood gazing down at the men on

the court tossing up practice shots at both ends of the floor. The platform for the women's panel had been taken down quickly, vanished as if it had never been there. The aroma of beer and hard liquor filled the air, but Hillary feared having a drink while she was still so unnerved. She got water in a bottle printed with the bright purple Kings logo.

Stacy ordered a draft beer. She raised her cup, took a long swallow, and licked her lips. Nodding down toward the court where the verbal assault on Hillary and the Center had taken place, she said, "Good thing that man didn't have a snootful before he went off on you and the Center. Coulda been worse."

Hillary looked around to be sure the girls weren't nearby. "Did you know that man is Coach Tiffany's father?"

Wide-eyed, Stacy huffed, then said, "Oil and water, those two. Man better not show up at our girls' games."

Hillary hadn't even considered that. Awful idea. Him disrupting the Devils.

Downstairs, they found the girls. Keisha's face sported a tiny white and purple Kings logo, while Claire had convinced the artist to give her one in Lakers gold. They strolled around, surveying the Farm to Fork offerings—and agreed on tacos you could dress with your choice of toppings. Hillary piled on shredded red cabbage, chopped cilantro, and guacamole, pleased with the look of the salad she'd achieved. They ate standing at one of the open counters scattered along the wide concourse.

"So cool to see that Olympics track star—I want to be on team USA basketball," said Keisha. "Bet you coulda played in the Olympics, Bibi."

Stacy tucked a cilantro leaf into her mouth and shot her granddaughter a warm smile. "We played in high school gyms until title IX. Women didn't get in Olympic basketball until 1976."

"I loved that gold medal woman yelling at that old man," said Claire.

Hillary warmed at her daughter's support.

After the others were done, she led the way through cowbell-toting Kings fans crowding the concourse, as if she were swimming through people.

Their seats were a quarter of the way down the lower level, directly across from the home bench. Hillary saw to it that Stacy got the aisle seat, while the two girls sat between them, leaving Hillary next to a plump woman who held an open cup of beer in her hand.

"Sit right down," the woman greeted Hillary, and hoisted her beer in the direction of the upper level seats. "We were at the Paul McCartney concert that opened this arena right after it was built." The woman raised her beer higher. A few drops sloshed over the edge and ran down her arm past the bend in her elbow, wetting the edge of her purple Kings tee shirt. "Up there."

Hillary turned away from the woman's beery breath and craned her neck to look where the woman was pointing as she carried on her loud rant.

"Can you believe it? A woman in the row above us

fell onto folks in the row below. Those poor dears ended up leaving in wheelchairs before that adorable Paul even started to sing."

Hillary nodded.

"Cheaper seats up there, but dangerous, let me tell you. The owners gave us comp tickets for down here tonight, to keep us from suing their asses." The woman warmed to her subject, and Hillary again appreciated how management was balancing various demands in striving for success, something for her to emulate in getting the Ans Botha Center ready to open.

The game got underway. Fueled by three-point shots and ferocious dunks, the home team built a lead and tribal ecstasy energized the crowd, clanging cowbells to juice up their players. The fans' euphoria filled Hillary and her public humiliation faded away.

At halftime, an announcer stepped to the middle of the court, microphone in hand, his voice lusty. "Our guys are on *fie-yer*!" He pointed to the scoreboard. Fans waved giant foam fingers and screamed with elation at the numbers showing the Kings ahead 55 to 40.

When the crowd quieted, the announcer waved to a couple of black iron rings set up on the court, one large as a hula hoop and one half the size. "Speaking of being on fire, we've got athletes of a different size now to show you their hoop magic."

Three Border Collies ran onto the court, their eyes focused intently on their trainer running ahead, a young woman dressed as a circus ringmaster in a black top hat, red jacket and carrying a wand instead of a whip.

As she waved her wand high in circles, the dogs jumped one after the other through the large hoop, took a couple steps on the hardwood and then jumped through the small hoop. The trainer ran to the other end and reversed the order. The dogs had no trouble flinging their furry bodies through the smaller hoop first and easily jumping through the large one to get a reward. The trainer gave a stay command and streaked back to the other end. Before she could raise her wand, the hoops burst into flames.

The audience gasped. At the lift of her wand, without hesitation, the dogs leaped through the set of burning hoops. The young woman took bow after bow to the cheers and clanging cowbells of the fans.

Buoyed by the animals' performance, Hillary nudged Claire. "Those dogs are fearless," she said. "That's the way to play any game." Claire nodded with a grin.

Hillary vowed to ignore obstacles like the old man's fiery outburst and keep herself pointed toward a perfect New Year's Day opening for the Center. A celebration the whole city could be proud of.

After their terrific first half, the Kings came out cold in the third quarter, struggled in the fourth, and lost the game. Shaking their heads, dejected fans filed out of the arena. Hillary matched their down mood. Witch. Broomstick. Had that old man recognized her, known her name had been Hillary Broome? Or was it just a clichéd Halloween reference?

. . .

ON THE WAY HOME, CLAIRE HAD THE POSTGAME SHOW blasting loud on her phone from the back seat. She and Keisha were arguing with the local broadcasters' analysis of the players, the coach and the slim chances for a winning season.

In the front seat, Hillary felt it would be a good time to run her thoughts by Stacy. "You know that old guy who called me a witch in front of everyone? Coach Tiffany's father?" At Stacy's vigorous shake of her head, Hillary carried on. "On top of that, I had him in a class back at Sac State. English professor. 'Professor Poison' we called him. 'PP' for short."

Stacy laughed. "I know that kind."

"If we answered when he threw out questions, he would rip us up with his words. Finally we kept quiet and then he hammered us as passive dummies. Slashed our papers with red ink."

"Sounds like what I went through," said Stacy. "Dropped outta college over it."

"Where did you go to school?"

Stacy looked over her shoulder at the girls still shouting disagreements with the sports radio talk show host. She continued in a soft voice, "Community college." Hillary leaned toward her to catch her low tone. "Most essays came back a red mess I couldn't even read."

Hillary waited for more.

"I kept at it though," Stacy said getting louder with each word, "even after one old teacher said he couldn't start class until all of us girls crossed our legs so the gates of hell were closed."

Hillary's jaw dropped.

Stacy continued. "But them teachers and them red pens saw to it my grades hit the ground."

"I got my first and only F from Professor Poison," Hillary said, reignited by the memory of today's indignity. "And in an English class! My best subject."

Stacy shook her head. "Kill the spirit, they do."

"My father exposed him in a newspaper series on bad professors, got him kicked off the tenure track back then. The man wrote letters to the editor for years against my father's articles, course they stopped running them in the paper pretty soon. But you could see, the man jumped right on to attack me." She hit the brake at a yellow light. She turned and frowned at Stacy. "Given his spiteful nature, I wouldn't be surprised if he was plotting against me."

Stacy nodded and sighed. "Some folks never give up."

HILLARY DROPPED STACY AND KEISHA OFF AT THEIR HOUSE and invited Claire to sit in the front seat, but her daughter said she was fine in the back. The postgame show ended and Claire turned off the streaming radio. Hillary glanced into the rearview mirror and caught her daughter glaring.

"What's up, Princess?" said Hillary. Claire was no longer a young and precocious child, but Hillary's nickname for her popped out every so often. Especially now that Hillary miscarried in the years after Claire's birth. Now she would always be an only child, front and center of Hillary's striving to be a good mother.

"I just was thinking," started Claire, then she fell silent.

"Thinking what?"

"Well, you know, Kee Kee and her grandmother."

Hillary's stomach did flip flops. She'd been wondering why it had taken so long for this to come up. Claire was plenty smart, so much so she'd skipped third grade.

Silence filled the car until Hillary broke it. "What about them?"

"How much Stacy is like a mother to Keek. What happened to..." Claire said, then paused.

"To..." Hillary prompted, holding her breath and slowing her speed to make time for this conversation before they reached home.

"To Keek's mother."

Hillary exhaled in a rush. So Claire was not going to ask about Hillary's mother after all. She glanced in the mirror to see a deep frown on her daughter's face. "Didn't Keisha say her mom had drug problems? Ran off? They couldn't find her anymore?"

"Yes, but," Claire's voice grew soft, "what happened to *your* mother? Was she on drugs, too? Why don't I have a grandmother?"

Hillary's stomach bucked. She coughed, took a swallow of cold coffee from her car cup and searched among her scattered thoughts for something to say. A few years ago, her widowed friend Sarah had come to live in a cottage on their Lodi vineyard and become part of the family. Claire would put cookies in a basket and take them and her Rapunzel doll for tea parties at Sarah's, announcing her glee at not having to go through a dark woods like Red Riding Hood to get to grandmother's house.

Hillary and Ed had taken them on a family vacation to Ireland, but in a tragic turn of events, Sarah died over there and her ashes had been flown home. Claire grieved over the loss of her grandmother figure, who had urged her to cut her long blond hair after it got caught under the seat on the flight to Ireland. In honor of Sarah, Claire had donated her hair to a charity that made wigs for children with cancer. From age seven on, Claire kept her hair short, in memory of Sarah.

Ever since Ed's mother and father were killed in a hit and run accident last year, Hillary had worried about Claire bringing up this question.

Now in response to her daughter's plea, Hillary was stunned to hear the words coming out of her own mouth: "My mother was a hot-headed artist who deserted me and my father. Even if I could find her, you wouldn't like her."

She waited, but Claire said nothing. Hillary glanced into the rear view. A tear had blurred the painted-on Lakers logo on her daughter's cheek.

What else could Hillary say? She sped up and pulled into their driveway.

Claire jumped out of the car and ran into the house, her question reverberating in the cage of Hillary's mind, like a trapped animal.

. . .

HER PULSE RACING AND FEARING MORE QUESTIONS, Hillary got herself a glass of milk and drank it before she went in to say good night to Claire. She was already in bed as Hillary as bent to kiss her cheek.

"Fun to see Ruthie and Coach," murmured Claire as she drifted off, "with you, Maa."

Hillary felt warm and comforted by her daughter's lapse into using the name from long ago and spent several minutes gazing at her sleeping child. Her bed looked half-empty without her old friends.

Last year, Claire moved her stuffed leprechaun, his orange beard nearly worn off, and her Rapunzel doll, her golden locks shorn leaving a few blond patches, onto the top of her bookshelf. The old toys sat next to an orange paper lei Claire saved for Day of the Dead. Hillary noticed the picture of Sarah that had been on the fireplace mantle now stood next to the orange lei. She breathed heavily for a few minutes. That was good. Help Claire keep the memory of Sarah's love close this way.

Their yellow labs, Daisy and Darius, were hunkered down for the night in the huge dog bed that mother and son shared under Claire's window. Part of their family, the dogs kept Claire company, too. And safe.

ED WAS STILL DOWNTOWN. HIS WORK FOR SOUTHBRIDGE Protection Services went on even after the game was over. The house was quiet. Echoes of that humiliating outburst at the arena brought a flush to Hillary's cheeks. The old professor ranting, still out of bounds just like back in the classroom. Was there anything more to the man than verbal abuse? Had he ever actually done anything? She'd not followed Sacramento politics much while she lived down in the Stockton area until a few years ago.

She googled around and discovered he'd been very active in the Sacramento Taxpayers Opposed to Pork, with a clever acronym and logo showing a pink pig lettered with black block STOP on their flyers and other materials. They wanted to block the downtown basketball arena and had nearly been successful in halting the publicly subsidized arena by taking the project to court more than once. They claimed the project and others like it would take money that otherwise would go for police, street work, parks, libraries, and other basic services. But they'd failed in the long run. Now they still kept a Facebook page going, Hillary realized. But she didn't see Bierce posting there. Maybe he was too old fashioned for Facebook or even computers and didn't have a clue about what she'd done at Columbia.

Still, trying to discredit people and projects had been Bierce's goal even after he left the university, Hillary realized. Now he seemed focused on her personally. And with so much passion, like the mission he was on had set her at the center of his bulls eye. What if somehow he found out what she'd done so long ago? It wasn't too likely, of course, but still there it sat in the *Columbia Spectator*. That article five years back, ensconced in the archives. Her heart raced. It would ruin her credibility in public relations. What could she do to stop him if he uncovered her shameful secret?

How could she silence him beyond the public censure that ended his academic career? She didn't need to pull up the archives on the *Chronicle*'s website to visualize the headlines: "Grading the Profs." Entered for a Pulitzer, the series ranked the best and the worst faculty in the Cal State system in the early '90s. In Jake Broome's critique of Professor Charles Bierce, her father had cited the students' nickname for him, "Professor Poison." Yes, the man was pure poison, still.

But she remembered charges against Bierce that never got into the newspaper. In the spare room she used as her home office, Hillary looked through her files under P, for professors and poison. Where were her father's notebooks she'd saved after he passed away? She could picture his square block print, penciled onto those long skinny, spiral bound pages.

She couldn't find anything under the Ps and searched through other sections of the files without any luck.

Had it really been almost fifteen years since he suffered that deadly heart attack? She missed him and his pride in her career as a reporter. Her cheeks grew hot. He would be ashamed of what she'd done, lifting a line from another writer for her articles on bad mothers, all because of her panic when writing stories about bad mothers. She'd sullied her father's Broome byline but he'd passed away before he ever heard the horror story of it. She'd had to take to ghostwriting without using her byline at all and now this public relations work using her husband's last name. It just happened twice, but she'd only got caught when it happened at Columbia. She knew one day she would have to confess and make amends.

"Maa," cried Claire, standing in the doorway, arms flailing.

Hillary's head jerked up, her heart racing. Claire was wearing that old paper chrysanthemum lei.

Claire didn't normally speak when she was sleep-walking. She would just head straight toward the basketball hoop out in the driveway.

"What, honey?"

"Is it time to go see Sarah? Where's her picture?"

"You're dreaming." Hillary stood. "Let's get you back to bed." She guided her daughter down the hall to her room. As Hillary started to lift off the lei, Claire clutched it to her chest. Hillary tucked her into bed wearing the lei.

Claire's wiry frame relaxed into sleep, and Hillary brushed the orange paper flowers with her fingertips. Saturday was Day of the Dead. They would make their annual visit to St. Mary's Cemetery. Hillary pictured the marble Virgin Mary standing tall in her dark blue alcove along the cemetery wall. Spread out in front of the virgin stood an altar crowded with orange flowers celebrating *Dia de los Muertos*. They would place a picture of Sarah on the altar and march in the parade through the cemetery to the veteran's section, where Sarah's ashes were buried in the plot she shared with her husband.

Hillary thought about Day of the Dead. Did

Hillary's mother have a grave somewhere? Had she thrown away her dead father's notes? Hillary's losses welled up inside her, and she couldn't hold back the tears.

CHAPTER EIGHT

Some of us think holding on makes us strong; but
sometimes it is letting go.

-Hermann Hesse

*An elephant floated through the wine cellar door, extended
his trunk and tickled under her chin. She shook her head
violently, her hair whipping her face. The elephant slid his
trunk past her shoulder, and parted her long copper locks.
He wound his trunk around her hair, lifted her and flew out
the door of the cellar, dangling her high above grapevines
growing in rows below.*

HILLARY WOKE DRENCHED IN SWEAT, AWASH IN DREAM
images. It was dark outside. She could picture the roots
of vines they'd planted slumbering away, mere twigs in
their winter dormancy. But the wine cellar was in Lodi.

This house they'd moved to a few years ago had just a basement, home to an old furnace.

She lay still, relaxing her jaw, sore from grinding her teeth in her sleep. When she felt calm, she stripped off her damp nightgown and put on yoga pants and a tee shirt.

Standing on her mat, she stared out the window, fingering her bead bracelet, the Virgin Mary medal dangling against the tiny silver Ganesh.

Last month, Sunny had bussed Claire's team down to his main Silicon Valley headquarters for a Ganesh festival, done the Mumbai way, full of color and music and celebration. The Hindu tradition of honoring the elephant-headed Ganesh was similar to *Dia de los Muertos* in Hillary's mind. Orange flowers and exuberant marching were central to both traditions, but instead of ending with a Mass, the Hindus drowned a paper mâché replica of Ganesh. It was their reminder to let things go.

Letting go was something Hillary struggled with. She was good at covering things up, storing them in the cellar of her soul. But now she was having nightmares of that drowned-every-year elephant god. She still felt drowned herself, shouted down last night by that angry professor.

She would call Janine and get on her community affairs show as soon as possible. The TV show was a good venue to build enthusiasm for the Center. She could counter the attack by Professor Poison.

The soothing strains of voices chanting Shri Ram filled her senses, and she stood straight and tall in the mountain pose, feeling like a warrior, the way she had years ago in karate. After moving through a few more basic poses, she stretched for a couple minutes before she tiptoed out to the kitchen, grateful that Claire slept on.

She'd barely had a sip of French Roast coffee before the bundle of energy that was her daughter came running into the kitchen. "Mother, how long before tryouts?"

So it was "Mother" again. Hillary had googled around on "tweeners," girls between childhood and teenage. They could be moody like this, hormones flooding their bodies.

Hillary lifted a paper calendar off the wall, set it on the table and turned the page over to November. "Today is a game after school." She looked at her daughter and pointed to November 2. "And tomorrow is Day of the Dead march at noontime."

Claire gave a sharp nod. "I hung up the orange paper lei to let the wrinkles fall out." She dribbled an imaginary basketball around the kitchen then tossed it into an invisible hoop above the fridge. "Got to get to school early this morning. One-on-one with Kee Kee before first period." She yanked open the fridge and pulled out a half gallon of milk.

Hillary continued. "Then an away game next week. The scores from today and next week have to be turned in to the committee to make sure you Devils qualify for Reno."

Claire shook Wheaties into a bowl and poured milk over them. She studied the Olympic Gold Medal athletes on the front of the cereal box. Her finger traced the circles of the five intertwined Olympic rings.

"Wouldn't it be wonderful," Claire said, then fell silent and munched away on her cereal, tapping on one ring after another.

With a start, Hillary realized how the rings looked like intertwined basketball hoop rims. She refilled her coffee.

"It's stupid, I know." Claire frowned. "But…"

Hillary blew on the hot black brew and waited.

"If someday after college, I could play at…" She spooned up the last of her cereal, chewed slowly and swallowed. "That arena downtown."

She stared out the window with a half-smile on her face. "Now that Dad is there so much, it seems more believable." She stuck out her chin and nodded. "I mean, play there when they bring the Monarchs back."

"Sacramento getting back into the women's game is only a fantasy right now. Let's take one team at a time, focus on the Devils."

"Sarah would be proud of me."

Hillary felt a jolt to her heart and changed the subject. "Don't get distracted. There'll be time later for the big leagues for you, and Keisha, too."

"Kee Kee is so talented. I'm scared I can't keep up with her."

"Keisha's good," Hillary agreed. "But don't forget, she missed a year of school when she was out with that anemia, so she's older and bigger. For point guards like you, it's better to be small and quick."

"Yeah, like Kobe and Gigi." Claire's eyes narrowed

and she resumed shooting the invisible ball into the invisible hoop over the fridge.

Hillary rubbed her Ganesh charm. It was going to take all the good luck from anywhere and everywhere to make Claire's dreams come true.

CHAPTER NINE

The suspicious mind believes more than it doubts. It believes in a formidable and ineradicable evil lurking in every person.

-Eric Hoffer

BACK HOME FROM DROPPING CLAIRE OFF AT SCHOOL, Hillary chopped up carrots, potatoes, celery and onions and tossed them into a slow cooker along with a couple pounds of stew meat and a few leaves from the bay laurel tree out back.

She set the slow cooker on low heat. The stew would cook all day and be perfect that evening, opposite from how her mother used to start dinner late, set her crockpot on high and forget it while out painting in her studio. With orders not to disturb her mother when she was painting, Hillary would eat ice cream to soothe her growling stomach while she waited for her father to get home after putting the "paper to bed," as he called meeting his *Chronicle* deadline. The inedible, dried-out mess in the crockpot would infuriate him, and he'd take Hillary out for pizza, just the two of them.

In cooking dinner as in everything, Hillary worked to be different from her mother and to hold her family together.

She thumbed through her contact list and called Janine, who anchored the Sactown Saturday noontime TV show. Hillary counted on Janine's support for local youth and the Center.

"I was just about to phone you," Janine shouted after she said hello. "Great to see you last night."

"You handled the panel so well. I'm hoping I can get on your show in a week or so and give an update on our Community Center."

"You were trained as a journalist, Hilly. You know we can't cover the Center without providing the opposing view as well, not after that confrontation last night. I recognized him, a guy named Charles Bierce. He was in that STOP group that tried to take the arena to a vote."

"Yes, I googled him after his outburst in the arena."

"Well, Sacramento Taxpayers Opposed to Pork started back in 2012 and they still post to their Facebook page. I wouldn't put it past them or at least Bierce to push hard against your Center as an emblem of urban renewal and gentrification hardships. They want to get future projects halted, not always to save themselves the taxes but for ideological reasons. They're a committed bunch, often have supporters who work behind the scenes."

"Can't you just showcase what our Center will offer for the region? We're adding art workshops plus a tutoring service."

"We can't run a puff piece, not since Bierce took you on in public. Not a chance. That makes it a bigger story. If we have you on, we have to invite him, as well. I'd love to get you in tomorrow since the two of you are practically breaking news." She laughed. "In a Sactown kind of way. I'll reschedule the Sutter's Fort folks. The controversy there is on the back burner."

Hillary wished she'd waited to call Janine. The woman was like a shark seizing on chum in the water. "How about the following Saturday?" Hillary suggested. "That would work better for me."

"Want to get you on while you're hot news, girl. I'm slotting you in now. It's true there's no such thing as bad publicity except your own obit," Janine said.

Hillary sighed. "See you tomorrow and thank you."

She paced the floor. How would Claire take to missing the *Dia de los Muertos* march?

HILLARY HAD A FEW HOURS BEFORE CLAIRE'S GAME WOULD start. She drove out to call on Speedy Soles, a midtown shoe store, to enlist another sponsor for the Ans Botha Center.

"I love what your center will bring to town," the businessman said. "Be lots of shoes of all kinds wanted and needed. But we're just one shop, with a tight budget. We can't afford to help out."

Hillary set her chart on his desk in the back store. "We've got a level for every outfit in town. Say when." She traced her finger along a series of price points.

He laughed and watched her. "There." He tapped the spot she'd stopped on. "Speedy Soles is proud to sign on and support Ans Botha by that amount."

Within an hour, she had a farm-to-fork restaurant lined up as a major sponsor. Their chef was going to offer culinary training classes in the Center, as well.

She stopped by *Suttertown News* and checked in with a columnist about his op-ed piece endorsing the Center's value to underserved youth, despite what the managing editor saw as unsavory cooperation between business and local government. Pretty standard for alternative media to be opposed to public-private part-nerships as crony capitalism. It took all kinds.

Under a cloudy sky she drove over to Sac Jr. High. The Devils were playing against the Boy Wonders again. Hillary admired the way the school district had set up the competitions. It helped strengthen the girls' game to play against the boys, who'd often had more years of experience at the game.

Settled at courtside next to Stacy, Hillary began a visual survey of the place, checking for anything suspi-cious. Strangers. Tennis racquet cases.

The Tasmanian Devils were ahead by six points when the Boy Wonders' coach called a time out.

Flushed with excitement over the girls' lead, Hillary again scanned the bleachers lining both sides of the gym. At least the school had a gym even though it had just three rows of bleachers, and creaky old wooden ones at that.

One of the metal doors to the gym slammed open, and a tall, bald man she'd never seen before strode in, a black guitar case slung over one shoulder and a blue backpack over the other.

"Who's that?" she whispered to Stacy and nodded in his direction. Since her eye surgery last year, the older woman often saw things Hillary missed.

Stacy thrust out her lower lip, staring from under her sparse eyebrows. "New music teacher." She scowled. "But Keisha said he supposed be teaching drum not guitar."

Hillary watched the man climb the few steps to the top row. He sat and faced her from across the floor, his guitar case vertical and leaning against his knee. Hadn't someone carried a shotgun in a guitar case into a school last year? Hillary's glow froze into fear.

The timeout was over.

With her phone, she snapped a couple pictures, as if merely capturing the action on the court, and texted the photos to Ed.

check out this guy

She twisted her bead bracelet around her wrist while she kept an eye on the man and waited for Ed's response. Mentally she reviewed the moves she'd learned in karate years ago.

Stacy stood, waving her streamers and shouting,

"Go, Devils!" Hillary admired the older woman's unselfconscious passion, her warmth and connection to the young players. The Devils, thanks to their signature spin moves and three pointers, were trouncing the Boy Wonders in this game, which was preparation for the Reno tournament.

Hillary cheered, shook her fists in the air and screamed, "Beat those Boy Wonders!" The fall after Claire turned nine, Ed had introduced her to playing basketball and it had become her life. When she wasn't playing she was watching YouTube videos of players young and old. She followed Kobe Bryant on Twitter. She idolized his daughter Gianna, who had caught the imagination of the sports world.

"Atta girl, Kee Kee! Go Claire!" Stacy sat down and elbowed Hillary. "Our girls. Like Mutt and Jeff." She cackled. "You're too young to know them funny papers, honey."

Hillary's heart skipped a beat at the memory. "My father read them to me from the Sunday comics back in the day." She nodded agreement at Stacy's comparison of the two girls: Keisha, the granddaughter Stacy was raising—already six foot, two inches at thirteen, a center on the team, her black braids flying as she ran—and her own Claire, a twelve-year-old point guard at five-foot-one, her blond pixie a neat cap as she passed the ball to her teammates.

Hillary studied the stranger with the guitar case on the other side of the court. The man pulled a bottle of water from the side pocket of his backpack, took a long drink, and wiped his mouth with the back of his hand.

He screwed the cap back on and stared straight at Hillary.

She turned back to the game.

Claire controlled the ball, her eyes darting to find an open teammate. Tiffany was gesturing and screaming "Let's go! Let's go!" Claire bounced a pass to Keisha who tossed it up for a lay-in, moving the Devils ahead by ten points.

As she ran by, Keisha shot a thumbs up to her grandmother. "That girl," Stacy said turning to Hillary, "always with the love." A grin lit up her face. Over the past year, she'd shared more details on how she rescued Keisha when her mother abandoned the toddler, to run off with a drug dealer. Hillary admired the older woman and envied her relationship with her grand-daughter. Why couldn't she and Claire be close anymore? A distance had grown between them over the last few years ever since Claire had reached puberty.

Ping. It was Ed.

school dist id'd the pic. transferred music teacher. talk later

Hillary showed her phone to Stacy, who studied the message, her eyes narrowed. "I pegged him. Kee Kee wants take up drums next year. New music teacher. But good thing you got an in with 'the man.'"

The man. Her husband Ed was a law and order guy, yes. She was proud of him, getting this new position with Southside Protection in Sacramento after he retired as a deputy sheriff and they moved off the Lodi vine-yard. He was a perfect fit for these new responsibilities with Southside, a respected private contractor to supplement city police. There was so much violence these days. People got enraged when life didn't go their way. Hillary preferred the cool comfort of reason and following the rules.

AFTER THE DEVILS' WIN, SHE AND STACY MADE THEIR WAY to the girls' bathroom, which doubled as a locker room in the old building. Sacramento Jr. High School, its name carved into a stone archway over the front doors, was built before they started calling them middle schools. Here the hallways were dotted with buckets to catch occasional leaks from the roof, the floors buckled a bit around the edges, and everyone was grateful the basketball hoops still clung to the cracked backboards.

COACH TIFFANY GATHERED THE GLEEFUL PLAYERS INTO A circle and gave a strategy talk for the game coming up next week. "The winning team will get a basketball court named after them in the new Center when it opens downtown. Playing on a court named after your team will look impressive on your highlight videos." She finished with high fives all around. "Great job today!"

The coach turned to Hillary. "My husband appreciates the way you're getting sponsors for the Center, so we can improve things for these kids. They deserve it."

Hillary smiled. "Thank God for Sunny's vision. Who knew someone from so far away would help out over here?"

Tiffany blushed. "When I met him on that NBA tour of India, we had a magical connection." She laughed and twisted her wedding band. "Just like that, he proposed, we got married, and he expanded his business to Northern California. He wants to help us mirror India's advance as the next big thing in basketball."

Stacy reached her arm around her granddaughter's waist in a hug. "For girls, too, right?"

Tiffany smiled. "For sure. He's working on getting the WNBA back here." Tiffany let out a sigh. "It would be like the good old days." She gathered her things and joined some of the players, leaving in small groups with their mothers, headed for the parking lot.

Keisha turned to Claire. "Want to stay over and go with us to Underground Books tomorrow? There's a noon talk by Angie Washington."

"Who?"

"You know, she wrote *Motherless Girls Bounding Around*."

Hillary held her breath. This could substitute for missing the Day of the Dead march.

"Sounds good, but Mom and I," Claire smiled up at Hillary, "we'll be dancing in a procession blessing the four quarters of St. Mary's cemetery and laying flowers on my Grannie Sarah's grave."

Hillary swallowed. "Well, out of the clear blue sky," she said, glancing out the narrow windows near the ceiling, "or really, out of the cloudy gray sky," she cleared her throat, "I've been summoned by TV queen Janine Ramsey to be on Sactown Saturday. It's at noon tomorrow."

"Noon?" Claire frowned, her gray eyes boring up into Hillary's face. "That's when we get to her grave. You know that, Mother." She clutched at her jersey, as if pulling on the paper lei she wore in the march.

Flooded with regret, Hillary nodded. "I'm so sorry. Being on the TV show is for the Center, for all of you."

"Sarah will think we've abandoned her," cried Claire.

"We can make it up to her, go another time."

"We won't be marching and blessing. It won't be the same." Claire stamped her foot. "It won't!" She glared at Hillary.

"Come on, you'll like seeing Angie," said Keisha. "You know you loved that book, too."

"And Underground Books sometimes has basketball players dropping by," Stacy said, nodding. "Ruthie even came by once to promote her book." She high-fived Keisha, and Claire raised her own hand to take a hit from Stacy.

Hillary raised her hand for high fives from Stacy and Keisha, but Claire ignored her mother's open palm. Hillary brushed her hand down over her bobbed hair as if it needed smoothing.

Arm in arm with Keisha and Claire, Stacy went out to the parking lot, leaving Hillary standing alone, her navy peacoat bare protection against dark clouds starting to let go of their rain.

CHAPTER TEN

Sticks and stones may break my bones but names will
never hurt me.

-old adage, 1862

HILLARY FACED CHARLIE, ON THE OTHER SIDE OF A COFFEE
table set with KRAN TV mugs filled with water. This
morning, Professor Poison didn't seem so intimidating
as at the arena last week. In fact, he looked like a nice
old man, glasses perched on his nose. No one to fear.

The TV camera light turned red. They were live on
the air. Janine flashed a bright smile. "Welcome to our
lunchtime chat about what's happening in your
community. Today we're presenting the latest on the
Ans Botha Center, under construction downtown. Most
responders to our survey have been in favor of this
latest public-private project but there is some opposition, as some of us saw just a few days ago at the down-

town arena. Our viewers will have the opportunity to hear both sides today at noon."

A series of architectural drawings of the structure as it would look when finished appeared on the TV monitor. Its four-story glass facade mirrored a parklike setting.

"Sactown Saturday," Janine fanned out her fingers, gesturing toward Hillary and old man Bierce, as Hillary had started to think of him, "is delighted to welcome Hillary Kiffin, representing Sunny Singh, the energetic newcomer on our urban development scene, along with Professor Charles Bierce, who was known to many of you for his work with STOP, Sacramento Taxpayers Opposed to Pork." She nodded at Bierce. "And at the basketball arena downtown last week, you expressed opposition to the still-under-construction Ans Botha Community Center." She then turned back to Hillary. "Please remind viewers of the ways Mr. Singh's Community Center will benefit our region?"

Hillary sat forward and smiled at the camera. "We're thrilled over the contribution the Center will make to prosperity. It will give educational and professional opportunities to people of all ages who may have been left out before. Our programs are patterned after outreach efforts around the globe, such as the popular Basketball Federation in India." Hillary paused as images flashed on the monitor, showing a giant sports complex in Mumbai, dedicated to Junior NBA camps and tournaments, part of the international Basketball Without Borders movement.

"Here in Northern California," she continued, "we

will offer not just a venue but transportation to it. There'll be coaches, trainers, counselors and other health and well-being experts to bring people to their best state possible to thrive. In all kinds of sports and—"

"Dreamers!" shouted Bierce. "Ripping off the poor and middle class, stuffing money into greedy developers' pockets. Wants us to become Los Angeles north."

"So, Mr. Bierce," began Janine.

"It's Dr. Bierce," he interrupted. The camera zoomed in and exposed his pale blue eyes, peering through wire-rimmed glasses. "History shows downtown's no place to bring people. Look at the failures ever since the I-5 interstate freeway went through."

He thrust a photo toward the camera, picturing the derelict downtown mall that had been torn down a few years before to make way for the arena and other urban renewal projects. "Outsiders come in and think they can rip off the people. Forget about it! We won't be stopped at the ballot box nor in the courtroom. This greedy grab at public money is out of control, ruining the downtown, demolishing historic old neighborhoods nearby."

Hillary didn't wait for Janine to bring her into the conversation. "There is relatively little public money involved in this center, and it will more than pay a return on the investment in human beings. You should be on our team, sir, as is your daughter, Tiffany." Hillary turned to Janine. "Doctor Bierce is Tiffany Singh's father. You've had her on the show as one of the former WNBA stars who's agreed to play in our New Year's Day opening game, showcasing talented young athletes alongside famous all-star players. Dr. Bierce of all people should be supporting this project."

"Why bring up my daughter?" Charlie scooted to the edge of his chair. "What about your own father? Why are you called Kiffin now? What happened to your proud byline? Daddy Broome died and left you hanging?" He grabbed at his throat, gasping as if being hanged, his eyes bulging.

A hot flush rose in Hillary's cheeks. She reached for the KRAN TV mug and took a swallow of cool water. She felt small, a motherless child again, her father leading her to become a calm and cool collector of the facts, a disciplined and objective reporter. She'd colored inside the lines, controlled, observing others and their dramas, concealing her own. But those dreams at night…

How long had the air time been empty? Had Bierce been carrying on and she hadn't heard? Silence was forbidden on TV.

She pointed at him and spoke as if the words were bullets. "Think about your daughter, the basketball coach for our young women. You should be working with us to strengthen this effort but instead your answer is to attack my deceased father whose articles ruined your career as a college professor!"

"So," Janine nodded to the camera, "we've got clear opposition to the Center." She turned to Charlie. "Thanks for being with us this noontime," she said and smiled at the camera. "Stay tuned over a short break for a peek at what's coming to Golden 1 Center for the winter holidays."

Barely waiting for the camera's red light to go off, Hillary jumped up, her five foot, eight inches flooded with outrage, her hands showcasing Charlie. "This man is a rabble rouser, a hater with unreliable information, using insults instead of facts."

Janine looked up at her. "You know, he's got the right to his views. We're here to show all sides."

Hillary countered, "He's unstable, always has been, kicked off the tenure track at Sac State for character assignation, he's not fit for public forums."

Charlie got to his feet and leaned over, eyeball to eyeball with Hillary. He jabbed his finger at her and flashed a big smile. "You and your Center haven't seen the last of me, lady."

She fantasized knocking those John Lennon glasses off his grinning face. But she had to be the professional, keep her cool. She let him gather his things and leave first. The man was more than an old curmudgeon. Who knew how far his warped mind could take him now that Ans Botha was his target and she was the bull's eye?

CHAPTER ELEVEN

PLUNDER, v. To take the property of another
without observing the decent and customary reticences
of theft.

-Ambrose Bierce, *The Devil's Dictionary*

AFTER GETTING IN THE LAST WORD AGAINST THAT WITCH,
Charlie was loaded with adrenaline. He drove home
and parked in the narrow garage at the rear of his property. The very soil of the place was dear to him as was
the fragrance of his mother's rose garden, planted a few
years after the house was built by her father. Tending
what was already established, that was what counted.

He was hoping Tiffany would be on duty as
weekend hostess in Sunny's model homes nearby. If his
powers of persuasion held, getting his stubborn
daughter back on his side would be a big step forward
in protecting the legacy of the past.

Charlie walked by his neighbors' houses. The Macfarlanes had already moved out, leaving their drapes drawn and front porch devoid of its rattan furniture. How could James McFarlane have let Sunny get to him like that, sell his birthright to make way for a high-rise tower?

Two blocks over, the latest section of Sunny's housing development was under construction, nail guns hammering like machine guns.

Charlie nodded at a couple workers taking a smoke break. "How you guys doing?"

A burly bearded man saluted Charlie with his thermos cup. The rest of the guys ignored him. Charlie understood. They weren't to blame, had to earn a living somehow.

In Charlie's mind, this project was a perfect example of gentrification. He had read these tri-level homes had roof-top views of the Sacramento River. They featured geometrical patterns, industrial materials and sleek lines.

There was no way low-income people could afford living here anymore. Renters were being evicted by landlords as often as they could pin some petty offense on the tenants.

He was relieved to see Tiffany playing the role of hostess in the sales office today. She'd grown up to tower over him, but she was always the baby girl he'd fallen in love with when his wife first handed the wrapped infant to him. He strode in.

Tiffany, dressed in a flowing white top over a black

skirt, rounded her desk with open arms. "Welcome to our gorgeous homes, Dad," she sang out, leaning to dust his cheek with a kiss. "But, I wish you hadn't made such a spectacle of yourself during the sports panel."

It looked like she hadn't seen the noon TV show. Just as well.

Charlie scowled. "I've seen your name linked to this in the paper." He rolled his head in a semi-circle to indicate the block of houses. "You know what these have done to the cost of rentals?"

Her eyes sparkled. "We've boosted employment like you can't believe. Many of our construction workers are earning more than they ever did."

"They still can't buy at these prices," Charlie snapped.

"Signing up on our wait list can hold today's prices for the next release." She held out a clipboard with a pen attached.

"Why would I want to move?" He rubbed his fingertips over the bare skin where his white sideburns used to fill out the hollows in his cheeks. "My house was good enough for my grandparents, and it's good enough for me." He scowled. "It was good enough for you to grow up in, too. You should be trying to talk Sunny out of what he wants to ruin next." He stabbed his index finger in the direction of his house. "Our whole block!" He took a deep breath.

"True, Dad, but we're building for what's needed, for people working downtown, empty nesters and retirees like you."

Girl thought he'd retired. Doesn't know that no one wanted to hire him anymore. Grounded freeway flyer.

"We'll offer personal elevators in the new releases." She glanced at his legs. "For when those knees and hips start talking back."

"Nothing wrong with my knees," Charlie barked. "Got 'em well-oiled from patrolling neighborhood watch."

"And the Ans Botha Center nearby will give opportunity to young basketball players in our whole region," Tiffany said. "Come for dinner next week. It's Sunny's birthday. He'd love to explain the details."

Charlie's head throbbed. His own daughter saw the malignancy here as a thing of beauty. "No, thanks. I'm fighting to stop this growth like I fought to stop the arena. It's wrecking our downtown, the parking's a disaster and more homeless are taking to the streets."

She shook her head. "There are plans for the homeless, Dad. You need to be patient—it's going to take time. The Center will bring a bright future. You might even see your grandchild compete there someday."

He shot her a questioning look.

"No bun in the oven." She patted her flat stomach. "Yet."

His frame trembled with a brief spasm. She was trying to bribe him with the lure of a personal connection to these changes, a living legacy. He wouldn't let her trap him.

Pulling his black cap down tight, he gave a quick wave, pushed open the plate glass door and left the model home office, neither too old nor too weak to protect his city. Not yet, anyway.

It was clear he couldn't count on help from this daughter he thought he'd raised the right way.

CHAPTER TWELVE

ADMIRATION, *n.* Our polite recognition of another's resemblance to ourselves.

-Ambrose Bierce, *The Devil's Dictionary*

CHARLIE DROVE OUT TO CAL EXPO. MAYBE THERE WOULD be something at the gun show, something useful for his novel. Writing was keeping him sane, a catharsis, a way to vicariously prune the dangerous overgrowth of his town, return it to the good old days.

Hovering at the back of his mind was the line from *Black Sunday* complaining how hard it was to get explosives. Maybe he could find something—something small but powerful. For his novel.

The smells inside the exhibition hall were energizing, the pungent aroma of gun oil permeating the air. As a boy, he would watch his father clean his deer hunting rifle, rubbing the metal with rags to wipe off excess lubricant, its sweet, faintly licorice smell filling their narrow garage.

Charlie inhaled deep and opened his mind to the array of dazzling weapons, new and antique alike. He wandered around, picking up grenades and sniffing at boxes of gunpowder set out on vendors' tables.

A sudden slap on the back got his attention.

"Hey, buddy!"

He turned and recognized an old friend, Robert Wickham, from their years together in the Alkali Flat Neighborhood Association. Robert viewed the group the same as Charlie, a bunch of high-minded do-gooders who never accomplished much for the neighborhood. After Robert's Craftsman house was approved for the California Historical Register, he sold it at a profit and moved up to the Nevada side of Lake Tahoe, to better indulge his hobby of hunting game.

"What the..." Charlie stuck out his hand to shake Robert's. "I miss you, pal. How's life up in the Sierra?"

"Nevada is heaven. Got myself a pronghorn antelope last year. Grateful to escape your Golden State taxes sucking me dry." Robert guffawed. "We're down here for my mother-in-law's birthday, and I couldn't pass up this show. Sure hate what I read's going on down in the valley." He gestured toward downtown. "That damn arena fucked up your lives big time, already cost the taxpayers a bundle, more to come."

Charlie's shoulders slumped. He felt guilty for failing to stop the stampede of developers. "Yeah, well, some of us haven't given up yet."

Robert picked up a shotgun shell from a box on the

table and rolled the metal-capped red tube around in his fingers. "What do you mean?"

"I'm not sure but seems like something needs to be done. I'd love to hear your thoughts."

"I go to the Bay Area every other Wednesday morning—how about I come by your place one of those days?"

Charlie nodded. "I'd be glad to see you, pal."

"Great, you got the same phone number?"

"You know it."

"I'll call you. Got to go now. The wife and grandkids are waiting for corn dogs." He nodded in the direction of a far wall, lined with food booths.

As he watched his friend leave, Charlie's chest swelled with pride. It was like discovering readers for his novel to be running into friends like Robert. People who appreciated him.

Charlie made his way past booths selling mortar launchers and automatic rifles, most vendors sporting a sign quoting the Second Amendment to the Constitution about a well-regulated militia. Of its own accord, a fantasy began playing in Charlie's head.

Wouldn't it be wonderful if his cancer was really in remission? He could muster a small militia and lead them to vaporize what had no place standing in his town.

Out in the parking lot, a lone protestor paced back and forth, her sign calling for a ban on assault weapons.

Charlie let go of his imaginary return to the past. Best to limit that sort of strategy to the land of fiction—

keep reality non-violent, the way Justin always counseled.

But his utopian daydream floated in the back of his mind.

CHAPTER THIRTEEN

Holy Mother, Where are You?

-Eric Clapton

IN THE CATHEDRAL OF THE BLESSED SACRAMENT, HILLARY gazed at people lining up to take communion. For years she'd denied herself the sacrament because of her secret shame, the panic attacks when she was a reporter, writing articles about mothers. The plagiarism. She couldn't bring herself to talk about it even to a priest in the privacy of the confessional. Saying it out loud could magnify the harm she'd done to her father's legacy, to his Jake Broome byline.

It was soothing to sit in this holy place. The church was neat and contained. She tried to shape her life into that kind of structure to give herself comfort. She and Claire had gone to church with Ed who always went to mass after a Notre Dame win, lit a candle and gave thanks. Claire had taken first Communion when she was eight, but this was the first time Hillary had seen Claire light a candle, too, alongside Ed.

In the tradition of his late father, Ed carried on a life-long love affair with Notre Dame. His mother's passing last year increased his religious fervor and caused him to plan a family trip to South Bend for a pep rally in the Grotto next year. Claire was thrilled at the chance to visit the campus where she yearned to play college ball.

In a sonorous tone, the priest was making an announcement. "…invited to a series of rosaries for the purification of souls," said Father Chris.

Rosaries. Hillary's heart felt as heavy as the storm clouds outside. The Rosary, with its Hail Mary…*blessed is the fruit of thy womb* refrain, and its sorrowful mysteries about the mother of God. Hillary had tried the meditative practice of rolling the smooth rosary beads between her fingers and thumb, but each round hard bead felt like holding that color crayon just before her mother yanked it out of her hand that awful day. Hillary wore a bead bracelet instead, outfitted with a Mary medal and now a Ganesha charm, too.

She winced as lightning cast a shadow play against the church's stained glass windows and thunder cracked a split second later. Again, lightning and thunder shook the building. As the priest carried on about the rosary series, a single tear slid down her cheek. Ed put his arm around her shoulder, pulled out his big white handkerchief and slipped it into her hand.

On the way home, Hillary appreciated neither Ed nor Claire mentioning her not taking communion—it was understood that was her way. Nor did they say a word about her tears. It was best to keep things like this buried, stuffed down with whatever was at hand. Today all it took was a lunch of left-over crockpot stew and pop-in-the-oven Pillsbury biscuits.

Full and satisfied, Hillary picked up her plate, wiped clean by her second buttered biscuit. This was no time to diet. On her way to the sink, she reminded Claire to clear the rest of the table.

Claire wadded the used paper napkins into balls and tossed them into the tall trash bin she considered a makeshift hoop, one more avenue for practice.

Ed smiled at Claire's antics. "Get your homework finished, and we'll rerun the Notre Dame women crushing Indiana."

Claire went to her room. Hillary never ceased to be impressed at her daughter's focus, keeping up her A-plus average, essential for the barest prayer of someday getting into Notre Dame.

A FEW HOURS LATER, THEY GATHERED DOWN IN THE basement den. The video opened with a shot of the Golden Dome atop Notre Dame and zoomed in to a statue of the Virgin.

"I lit a candle at church, Maa. Prayed for Sarah to forgive us missing the Los Muertos march."

Hillary's heart warmed. "That's wonderful, Princess."

They watched the ND women mount their historic 108 to 40 win, coached by the famed Muffet McGraw.

Ed and Claire danced up and down, screaming "Go Irish!" until victory was a sure thing halfway through the game.

Ed grabbed a basketball and bounce-passed it to Claire, who caught it and pivoted for a behind-the-back return pass to her father. As the lopsided college win neared its finish, he waggled his eyebrows in a Groucho Marx style at her and then the screen. Claire doubled over in laughter. Ever since their daughter was a toddler, Ed had known how to connect—playful then and playful now. At the game's finish, highlights came on.

Ed nodded at the TV. "Whatcha think? March Madness isn't that far off. Irish women going to win the whole thing?" He passed the ball to her.

"I have a feeling," Claire pulled the basketball to her chest and heaved it up into a rainbow pass, elbows out at the sides and thumbs pointed down toward the floor, "a feeling they'll make it to the top!" She laughed. "I can't wait to get there."

Ed thrust his chin toward the TV screen where the game's high-scoring athlete was being interviewed. "She looks like your friend Kee Kee," he said and turned up the volume. A tall black student bent down and rubbed cheeks with a smaller and older version of herself. "I give credit," said the player, "to MawMaw who raised me."

"That's what Kee Kee always says about Stacy," said Claire. "But she calls her 'Bibi.' Such a cute name." She looked over at Hillary and asked, "What would I call your mother?"

Ed stared at Hillary. Rain pounded sideways at the high basement windows and panic flooded her. All she could say was, "I have to go to the bathroom."

She ran up the basement stairs and found her way into her bedroom closet, staring up at her mother's pink sewing basket at the back of the top shelf. She got it down, opened it up and bent to take in the scent from inside the satin lining.

Nothing. She inhaled deeply. Nothing. Over the years her mother's spicy smell had faded away. Hillary rubbed the bumpy surface of a Winnie the Pooh iron-on patch and smiled, remembering the few times her mother had sewn what Hillary asked for instead of those gaudy hand-painted paisley scarves that embarrassed her as a child.

Hillary reflected on Claire's question. What would my mother be called? If I could find her. She must be in her late sixties now. What if I wouldn't even recognize her? Hillary lifted packets of rick rack and needles to uncover the small photo she'd kept. It was from the days when her mother was one of the flower children of the late 60s. Hillary's father had met her at a rally on the state capitol steps while he was writing a series on antiwar demonstrations.

Jake Broome disposed of all pictures of his wife a few months after she ran off, but Hillary had hidden away this tiny black-and-white photo. She hadn't looked at it in years. The snapshot showed a slim and laughing young woman dressed in a gauzy patterned dress, her long blond hair topped by a circlet of daisies, her hand outstretched offering a flower to a stern-faced cop.

Hillary felt a shock of recognition—Claire looked so much like this young woman, whose hair was blond not dark copper like Hillary had inherited from her Irish ancestors. And those hands. Her daughter and mother both had large, strong hands.

Is she still an artist? What happened to the man she ran off with? Hillary let her mind drift as questions formed, questions she'd worked to suppress. Who would watch Claire if I went looking for her? Will it trigger Stacy to go searching for her long-lost daughter? Too many questions. If only—

Claire dashed into the bedroom. "It's hailing, Maa!" yelled Claire. "Let's go catch some!"

Relieved, Hillary put the sewing basket away and followed her daughter out to the driveway. They opened their palms to catch hailstones, squashed them into balls and tossed them up into the basketball hoop fastened above the garage door.

Hillary turned to see Ed watching from the living room window, his face wreathed in smiles. What a good choice she'd made, saying yes to that man so long ago. He was not only a wonderful husband, he was the kind of father she'd hoped her child would have. She flashed back to how close she was to her own father, even before her mother ran out on them.

Then in later years, he would take her to his Sacramento Bureau downtown, into the cubicle with his computer and his files. She could wander the office and learn how the reporters worked, when they were stuck they prowled the place, jawing with each other over one point or fact. It was a fraternity, women allowed in, as well. Looking for the best ways to offer the truth to the readers. And after they filed their stories with the LA office, they'd slip over to places like the old barge on the Sacramento River for hamburgers and drinks, Shirley Temples aplenty for Hillary. She grew up knowing she belonged. Until she made those mistakes. She shook her head. That was then.

She waved at Ed. He joined them out on the driveway, the three of them shrieking with laughter and pelting each other with the melting hail.

As the hail changed back to rain, they headed into the house. Ed announced he'd been called to run downtown and check on a problem in the arena security system.

"Can I come, Dad?"

"Only if you keep yourself from hopping all over the place. They're laying out the court for Tuesday's game, so you need to stay off it. But you might get onto the practice floor if none of the players are there."

"Can we take Kee Kee?"

"Okay, that girl always knows what to do."

Hillary said she'd stay home and work on promotions for the Center. "You run along, you Golden 1 fans."

Alone in the house, the only sound the muted roaring of the basement furnace, Hillary nursed a brandy and soda, some public relations work spread out before her on the dining room table. Here, she was unavailable as a target for that awful old man. She gazed out the window at the side yard. The rain poured, nourishing the dark soil of their garden, planted with two short rows of zinfandel grapes. The black fruit would become rich red wine, maybe blended into brandy, both drinks a sort of medicine for her hurting soul.

She recalled Claire's question. Yes, what would her mother be called? And why was Claire asking about her so much lately?

Chilled, she turned up the thermostat. Heat rose from the vent at the base of the wall. She let herself consider starting to look for her mother—still an artist? Hillary felt like a match just struck into a flickering flame.

CHAPTER FOURTEEN

Bitterness is like cancer. It eats upon the host. But anger
is like fire. It burns it all clean.

-Maya Angelou

CHARLIE WAS ALWAYS ON TIME FOR HIS APPOINTMENTS,
and this Friday afternoon was no exception. He scowled
as he hunted for a spot inside the poorly lit Medical
Center parking structure, but the damn place was so
crowded, he had to go all the way to the roof, open to
the sky.

Gray clouds mirrored his mood as he waited at the
elevator. He didn't use stairs anymore except at home
where he was familiar with his front porch steps.
Surgery and chemo to shrink his tumor had not affected
his speech, but he made sure to take care when walking.

He got off at the second floor and passed by the
"What Color is your Ribbon?" poster on the beige wall

of the waiting room. Pink for breast, orange for leukemia, black for melanoma. And gray for brain. Awareness and support. He shuddered. Brain got very few dollars compared to the others.

What good did awareness and support do without funding for research? He was plenty ticked off at the pitiful amount of money going into research for brain cancer, compared to more publicized kinds like breast, lung and prostate.

The sight of a lively new receptionist with long black hair at the front counter perked him up. As she checked him in, she apologized sweetly about their running late. His excitement wilted when he noticed the colored ribbons she had pinned to her white blouse. None of them gray.

Taking a seat among the crowd of patients, he bemoaned the fact that tax dollars spent on urban developments weren't slotted instead to research cures for cancer, especially the rare kinds like his glioma. Public funds could be better spent on things like that to help ordinary people instead of making the rich get richer by bulldozing old buildings. But demolishing tumors wasn't on their agendas.

He took out his pocket notepad and jotted a jumble of new plot ideas for his novel while he waited, not eager to hear what his doctor had to say.

"Hey, Doc Bierce," the oncologist would always start out, acknowledging Charlie's Ph. D. Then Doc Rivers would stretch out his big hand for a hearty handshake. The man never had any of those support ribbons pinned onto his white coat. There was an old-fashioned look to him that Charlie trusted. "Got some good news and some bad news, which do you want first?"

Ever since Charlie met him last year, he had a mixture of messages. Charlie always said he preferred hearing the bad news first.

Today the doctor nodded. "All right. Even though we got most of the cancerous clumps in the surgery, your glioma is like a hand with 'fingers' that keep creeping into the healthy part of your brain."

Charlie slumped with the weight of the image. Fingers. It sounded a lot like developers who kept creeping into the neighborhood he loved. For him, the two things had become inseparable. How much time did he have left to try and save his town?

"We don't want to destroy the essence of brainy and brilliant you." Doc Rivers nodded in a respectful fashion that Charlie appreciated, even though he knew he was being patronized. "So we can't be any more aggressive than the follow-up chemo series you've already been through."

Charlie kept his mouth clamped shut as he listened.

"But, we are encouraged that even though current therapies don't offer a cure, we do have long-term survivors."

"How long is long term?"

"Well, some for three years," the doctor said, with a nod and a closed-mouth smile.

Charlie left the Cancer Center, blinking at the sunshine that had broken through the clouds, a flicker of hope dancing in his mind. Three years. He could get a lot accomplished. Save Alkali Flat from the crazy growth. His Charlotte might see the error of her ways, respect her marriage vows and come back home. Set a good example for Tiffany on the value of tradition.

It could happen. He vowed to make a difference with his remaining time. Think about some kind of action plan. Maybe step out from living inside the pages of his book.

CHAPTER FIFTEEN

The opposite of bravery is not cowardice but
conformity.

-Robert Anthony

THE DOC'S MEASURE OF HOPE INFUSED CHARLIE WITH NEW
energy. The next day, he set out to visit KD, a small
businessman he knew from when Tiffany was a
teenager. Charlie drove slowly and kept an eye out for
his neighbor's children, darting in and out among cars
parked in front of houses converted into rental flats. He
made his way along sixteenth street and pulled into KD
Kars. Under Veteran's Day Sales banners, Charlie
walked the used car lot and quickly spotted Kevin
Daniels.

"Wish you'd phoned, buddy!" called KD as Charlie
approached. "I'm occupied with these good folks

looking for their Vet's discount deal on an SUV." KD pulled on his red suspenders and nodded emphatically in the direction of a middle aged black couple, surrounded by three tall teenagers bounce-passing a basketball on the lot's blacktop. "What can I do for you, pal?"

"Just wondered what you think of what's happening in our downtown," Charlie said.

KD nodded. "Good timing. I'll come by your place early next week."

MONDAY MORNING, KD WAS AT CHARLIE'S DOOR, THE man hefty as a ranch steer and full of contagious energy. "Happy Vet's Day, buddy!"

Charlie pushed open the screen door. "Come on in. Cup of coffee?"

"Never touch the stuff," KD said. "Plenty wired by God, praise be."

Charlie laughed, relieved. He hadn't wanted coffee himself, ever since the chemo. "A beer?"

"Nah, just came by to see what you're up to. Pay respects, even though you were on the wrong side over the downtown arena project."

Charlie sat and waved KD to the settee. "Never forget the way you pulled the best out of my Tiffany, got her into the ranks of the pros." Charlie waved at a few of his daughter's trophies, set out on the built-in shelves flanking the fireplace. "You still running your youth center in south Sac?"

KD nodded. "It's everything to me, helping out those kids." His face got red and he pulled at his suspenders.

Charlie frowned.

KD wiped his lips. "Wife and I never had none of our own. Vietnam injuries."

"Damn shame," Charlie said. "I never had to go. College. Took years getting ready to teach." Charlie was proud he'd avoided that grinder of a war but didn't want to rub it in to the poor bastards who'd suffered and died. He had never realized KD didn't have any kids, what with him always surrounded by young athletes like Tiffany when she was in high school. "You still on that Ans Botha advisory committee Tiff's husband talked you into?"

"Nah, it hit me they'd be taking young people away from my programs. Kinda selfish but…" KD stood and picked up a trophy topped by a bright pink basketball. "A big operation like that could destroy the one-on-one relationships I've been able to develop with the kids."

Charlie's pulse raced. KD favored keeping things small, the way they used to be.

KD rubbed the pink basketball and set the trophy back on the shelf. "But, that damn Sunny's trying to bring me back on board, part of his outreach to the region. He invited me to the Ans Botha walkthrough last week. It's only a couple months away from opening now. Had to check out my competition. Met that Hillary woman." He clenched his jaw.

Charlie stood. "You know I'm dead set against her

and promoting that place." Charlie tried to keep his voice calm. "It's too late to stop that center, but it's paved the way toward approval of Sunny's high-rise tower." He pounded his fist into his open palm as he enunciated, "Here. On. My. Block!"

KD shook his head. "Isn't there something you can do to stop it?"

Charlie's stomach churned. He couldn't do anything all by himself, no. And what could Justin really accomplish with his environmental maneuvers?

Now KD was interested. And Robert from Tahoe had said he could come by. Charlie exploded with an invitation, "Want to come talk things over with a few other guys who feel nervous about these changes?"

"Sounds good." KD stood up. "Here?"

"Sure. Maybe next Wednesday, one o'clock. Can you make it?"

"Count me in." KD slapped Charlie on the shoulder and turned to go.

"Bring along any *simpaticos* you know, too," called Charlie as KD let himself out.

"Will look for 'em," shouted KD as he started down the wooden stairs. "You need to get these painted, pal. Inspected for structural safety, too."

Charlie's thoughts flew as he turned to fixing himself some white toast. His stomach couldn't take much breakfast ordinarily, but this morning he was hungry with excitement over his compatriots. There were a few guys out at Sac State he needed to get back in touch with, too.

Maybe there was another way, in case Justin's legal maneuvers failed to stop the walls of concrete that seemed to be rising over the block his house was built on.

CHAPTER SIXTEEN

One of the darkest, deepest shames so many of us mothers feel nowadays is our fear that we are bad mothers, that we are failing our children and falling far short of our own ideals.

-Ayelet Waldman

HILLARY PAUSED TO LISTEN FOR THE CLICK OF THE DOUBLE doors closing behind her, then turned to take a last look through the slot windows onto the basketball court. It all seemed safe. At a table set up in the gym foyer Mary and John Kelly were preparing to sell tickets to the game. "I'm ninety-nine percent sure it's safe and secure in there," Hillary said, nodding toward the doors. "I checked under the bleachers, too, for anything out-of-place, and my husband said he'd give it another once-over when he gets here."

The high school athletic director had given Hillary

approval to hand out flyers for the New Year's Day Grand Opening from the other end of the ticket sales table. Mary nodded as she opened a cloth bag, took out a stack of dollar bills and placed them into a section of a metal cash box. "Good. We've never had any of those crazy threats here like you did at Sac Jr. last week." Mary knocked on the surface of the old wood folding table for luck and then crossed herself. "The game tickets are half-priced today, and we're hoping for a big crowd."

Hillary envied Mary Kelly, the perfect "basketball mom," cheerful, collected and successful at getting her daughter, Margie Ann, a full scholarship to UCLA where she'd start next fall. Hillary secretly measured her parenting skills against Mary's and always felt inadequate.

Putting aside her worries, Hillary set up a table-top poster promoting the Center at her end of the table.

This venerable high school was a good place to engage parents in what Sunny's vision could offer. He had helped create something similar for his hometown of Pune, in India, bringing rural youth into the fold where they could achieve their full potential.

Hillary set out a stack of flyers for the New Year's Day Opening Events. She unscrewed the lid on a bottle of soap bubble liquid. On the label was printed: "Fly High and Reach the Sky." She pulled out a wand, fashioned like a tiny basketball hoop, from the bottle and blew a stream of bubbles toward the Kellys, who reached out to pop a few.

The double doors into the gym opened to reveal

Stacy coming out to the table. She laughed as she joined them, swatting at tiny bubbles. "Keisha and Claire are in there helping out." She waved back at the doors into the gym. "Soaking up pointers from the high school players."

"Our girls are honored to get to return balls during warm-ups for this game," Hillary said to Mary.

"It's a good thing the young ones can learn from those ahead of them in the process," said Mary, turning to help John start selling game tickets as a line formed at the table.

Hillary handed out flyers and explained street parking was free on holidays and would let people who parked there appreciate the wide stairway to the glass front and the climbing wall in the entry. She got several parents to sign up for the "Old Dogs, New Tricks" basketball event on opening day at the Center.

Ed strode in from the door to the parking lot. "Hey, Chickadee," he called out as he neared Hillary's end of the table. Mary Kelly turned to flash her a grin. Hillary felt a blush warm her cheeks over his term of affection in public. She introduced him to the Kellys, too busy to do more than smile and nod at Ed. He turned in the direction of the double doors to the basketball court.

Without warning, the door from the parking lot slammed open against the wall.

The staccato pop of automatic gun fire filled the foyer.

Hillary's jaw dropped open.

Mary Kelly slammed against Hillary and fell backwards, her chair toppling to the asphalt tile floor.

"I got the green light now!" screamed a tall bearded man, dark hair slicked back tight against his scalp. He waved a black rifle in the air. "Think I'm not good enough?"

Pop. Pop. Pop.

John Kelly hollered, "Get down!" at the people lined up in front of the table. With horror, Hillary saw a couple of them fall to the floor. She grabbed her phone and punched in 911.

A bullet whizzed past her forehead and grazed John's arm, spinning him around before he crumpled to the ground.

"Here's a history lesson to remember!"

Pop. Pop.

In a crouch, Ed ran past Hillary, his Glock gripped in his hands and firing at the shooter, but to no effect. She was shocked the man didn't crumple. Must have on a bullet-proof vest.

The shooter kept up his barrage of bullets and words. "You bastards keeping up lies, can't wipe me away!"

Pop. Pop.

"Think you can fire the truth tellers? I'll show you fire!"

Pop. Pop. Pop. Pop. Pop.

Hillary's eyes were riveted on Ed, his hands clasped around his gun. The man and the Glock were fused. He leaned in toward the shooter and swung his weapon up in an arc to deflect the man's rifle. At this new angle, the rifle was still discharging. Bullets shattered windows and punctured cars out in the parking lot.

She was horrified to see Ed drop his Glock, against all training and instinct. He grabbed the rifle barrel and forced it straight up. The man kept a death grip on the weapon, his trigger finger firing non-stop, the rifle butt lodged atop his brass belt buckle. Bullets sprayed the ceiling. Chunks of acoustical tile rained down. The rifle arced over to the doors into the gym, bullets shattered the narrow windows.

Pop. Pop. Pop.

The men wrestled for control. Neither gave an inch.

Ed kneed the shooter in the groin. The man screamed, let go the rifle, gripped his crotch and fell face-down to the floor. Ed jammed his knee into the small of the man's back and leaned to pry the shooter's hands out from under him. Clamping his wrists vise-like with one hand, Ed reached for his Glock. But the gun lay a few feet away, just beyond the fallen assault rifle.

Hillary grabbed the Glock and kicked the rifle away.

The man thrashed under Ed's knee. "You're killing me!"

Hillary thrust the Glock to Ed. He shoved his weapon against the shooter's temple. The man yelled, "Go ahead. Kill me!"

"Not today, pal," Ed muttered. "You should be so lucky."

Screaming. Sobbing.

Cursing. Sirens.

Ed kept the assailant pinned.

Over at the table, Hillary could see Mary lying

motionless, her hands covering her face. John was bent over his wife.

From inside the gym, Keisha opened the door a few inches and peeked into the foyer.

"Get back inside," yelled Hillary. "Shooter's down! Keep the girls calm!"

The police dashed in, cuffed the shooter and dragged him outside to a waiting van.

Breathing hard, Ed rushed to Hillary. "You okay?" She nodded, unable to speak. He spotted a few blood spatters on her pant legs and dabbed at the blood with his white handkerchief. "Thank God he never got inside," Ed said, his eyes dark. "Guy looked to me like that teacher the charter school fired."

Hillary nodded.

"Can you talk?"

She nodded.

"Let me hear you."

"I need practice with the Glock," she whispered. "And my karate moves."

Ed grimaced. "Yup. Are you ok, now?"

She nodded.

"I'll go help book him at the jail. You see to things here."

Hillary watched emergency techs work on the barely conscious Mary while John stared, aghast and holding a gauze pad pressed against his arm.

It looked like Mary had been hit in the legs. The EMTs placed her on a stretcher. John walked alongside, holding her hand. "I'm fine." Her voice was barely audible. "Go see...Margie Ann." John kissed her forehead. The techs wheeled her out to a waiting ambulance.

"How are you?" Hillary nodded at John's sleeve, ripped open.

"Bullet barely scratched my skin. Let's see how the girls are."

Hillary led the way to the gym doors. The narrow windows had been shot out. Inside, splinters of glass lay on the hardwood. Students in basketball uniforms walked around in a daze.

Hillary couldn't spot Claire.

John embraced his sobbing daughter.

Other players stood in tight knots, shaking their heads, gesturing with outstretched hands, one wiping blood streaming down her arm as an EMT reached out for her.

Alone on the top row of bleachers sat Claire, her arms crossed over her chest, staring ahead, hugging herself. Hillary climbed up to her. "Princess. Claire. Honey, are you all right?"

Hillary put her arm around her daughter's shoulder and tried to draw her near. Claire sat rigid, her eyes wide open, unblinking.

Hillary stroked Claire's cheek. It was cold to the touch. The girl sat like an ice sculpture. But the blood dripping from her right elbow was warm.

PART II

CHAPTER SEVENTEEN

If you wrong us, shall we not revenge?

-Shakespeare

CHARLIE PULLED INTO THE LOADING ZONE IN FRONT OF THE Senator Hotel, picked up Justin and headed for the Alkali Flat neighborhood meeting, his radio tuned to the Savage Nation. "Even with my Berkeley Ph. D., I could not gain a professorship after applying many times," ranted Michael Savage. Charlie knew this story inside and out and relished its every retelling. He waited for Savage's punchline: "My crime? I was a white male."

On this topic, Charlie aligned himself with right wingers like Savage, another white male denied tenure due to affirmative action. Many times, though, Charlie resonated with the lefties in caring for the homeless, and sometimes like today, he felt himself a libertarian—

keep the fucking government and big business from interfering with urban issues. He was proud to be his own man, in the tradition of his ancestor, the provocateur Ambrose Bierce.

An announcer broke in. "We interrupt this program with breaking news: A shooting at a local high school has resulted in injuries but no fatalities. The assailant has been captured and taken to jail. The situation is under control. Witnesses say he was screaming that it wasn't fair to get fired over teaching American History. Details on the five o'clock news."

"Isn't Tiffany coaching basketball for some high school?" asked Justin.

"Not high school, junior high. She keeps plenty busy shilling for Sunny most of her time."

Michael Savage came back on, now raving against elephant poachers, and Charlie snapped off the radio, his jaw clamped.

Shooter thinks it's not fair. Not fair, huh? And yet he'd found a way to get revenge. Revenge. Charlie had lusted for it ever since that you've-been-fired letter, years ago. That left-wing tenure track committee never hinted at it, but he knew they cut him away because he was a white male caught in the 90s frenzy to hire women and minority academics.

That damned *LA Chronicle* series on professors had put the nail in his coffin, claimed he'd assaulted students. Nearly won a Pulitzer for that piece of trash. Hillary's self-righteous father was part of the team. Charlie's rage still smoldered.

Justin tapped the now-silent radio. "That's what we

don't want. Elephant shooters. School shooters. Violence."

"I can see why the guy would do it though," muttered Charlie. "Felt like that myself when the university cut me off at the knees. Holier than thou with their affirmative action. Affirmative, my ass."

"Now, Charlie," said Justin. "That was a long time ago. Nothing's perfect. You've done all right for yourself, admit it."

"Gave 'em my best years, and they kicked me down into the community colleges. I was the only one to state the truth on their reverse racism. They knew what they were doing, but didn't have the guts to say it."

Justin gave a firm nod. "Let's look at the issue we can do something about, Sunny's hotel proposal, see if we can add to our case with what the association members have to say or do."

Charlie fell silent. This neighborhood meeting couldn't do any harm. It didn't hurt to participate.

But what had they ever really accomplished?

Charlie drove on, his eyesight clouded with hot resentment. He knew the streets of his neighborhood so well he could drive them in his sleep. But he was far from slumbering and beginning to suspect that working out his anger by writing a novel might not be enough.

At the meeting, Charlie laid out the siege his block was facing. Two neighbors offered to write letters to the Planning Commission asking them to stop the wrecking ball from bashing the beautiful old houses.

But another homeowner admitted he was on the verge of accepting Sunny Singh's generous offer for his house. Charlie had a hard time staying for the rest of the meeting and got Justin to leave at the break.

He drove back toward the Senator. "We've got to come up with something more," he said.

"Now, Charlie, patience is a virtue," Justin said.

Charlie squinted his eyes and said nothing.

CHAPTER EIGHTEEN

DIVORCE, n. A bugle blast that separates combatants
and makes them fight at long range.

-Ambrose Bierce, *The Devil's Dictionary*

THE NEXT MORNING, CHARLIE BREWED A POT OF GINGER
tea and set it out on the front porch table to cool. He
needed to take his mind off his troubles. Time to tend
the dark green ferns, at home in the white wrought iron
planter. His mother had started them from her neighbor's cuttings when Charlie was a child. Her secret was
to mix bone meal with fertilizer and feed them every
ten days.

With great care, he sprinkled a scant quarter
teaspoon of her cremains onto the bed of sphagnum
moss the ferns grew in. She'd made him promise to keep
half of her ashes out of the columbarium niche at old St.
Paul's. Charlie frowned. That gray stone church with the

bright red door was eclipsed now, encased on its 16th and J Street corner by the gigantic convention center.

His house would sit isolated like that if more neighbors gave in and sold their homes to make way for Sunny's proposed hotel, under planning commission consideration.

He pulled the edges of his brown cardigan close, sat at his wrought iron table and poured himself a cup of tea, now cooled to drinking temperature on this November morning. He'd already succeeded at keeping down his breakfast, small and bland as it was—one piece of white toast with a dab of butter. The tea was settling and stimulating at the same time.

His mind turned to the problem of Tiffany showing model homes in her husband's housing development, mushrooming in the neighborhood she'd grown up in. She should be helping preserve this block from that damn hotel tower.

Her mother had been a bad influence, running off with that Seattle billionaire last year. How could he bring Tiffany and Charlotte to their senses?

Suddenly a scrawny young stranger barreled up his porch steps two at a time and called out, "Mr. Charles Bierce?"

Before Charlie could think, he nodded.

The young man thrust a large brown envelope at his lap. "Thank you, sir." He turned and ran down the steps, hurried to his Smart car and sped away.

Charlie opened the package and thumbed through a handful of legal papers. Divorce papers from Charlotte.

She couldn't even have the package addressed as Dr. Bierce.

Chicken-liver Charlotte. His blood pounded hot in his temples. She didn't have the decency to warn him, take time from her crowded calendar as "hostess" for the wealthy bastard she'd run off with. She didn't care enough to keep in touch, must not know about his cancer.

He laughed. She might not realize she could be a widow soon and not have to bother with divorce.

A line from Ambrose's *Devil's Dictionary* hit him: "Love. A temporary insanity curable by marriage." He had been crazy in love with the damned woman all through their turbulent marriage. Not sure why he was so taken with her, towering over him at six feet to his five-nine.

Vivid particulars formed in his mind of Charlotte ordering him around. He sat in reverie for a few long moments before he jerked himself back to the present.

He'd failed to change Cheating Charlotte, but at least he could save the town he loved. His strength was returning after the chemo. Doc said it could be a few more years. Time to accomplish some good, leave a legacy.

He chewed at the bare skin where his mustache used to grow.

After losing their lawsuits to stop the Golden 1 arena, the taxpayers group was not doing a thing, cowed into silence by the mounting success of the new ventures. Downtown Commons was swarming with businesses and people, come to check out the supposed excitement.

That Neighborhood Association was so ineffective. Justin had to come up with something that worked quicker and better than environmental ploys that took forever to crawl their way through the bureaucracies.

Charlie buttoned up his brown sweater, went into the house and phoned Justin. "Let me treat you to lunch at Frank Fat's," he said. "I'll make us a reservation for one of the booths."

Sitting in the midst the venerable downtown restaurant where so many political deals had taken place might help them come up with a new strategy.

CHAPTER NINETEEN

LITIGATION, *n.* A machine which you go into as a pig and come out of as a sausage.

-Ambrose Bierce, *The Devil's Dictionary*

CHARLIE PARKED NEAR THE HOTEL AND WALKED WITH Justin in the direction of the restaurant, passing by empty storefronts. Charlie nodded at a nest of sleeping bags puddled in an alcove fronting an out-of-business shop. "Can't tell if some poor fool is asleep or dead in there," he whispered.

Justin thrust his leather-gloved hands deep in his overcoat pockets, his jaw clenched.

They passed the abandoned Greyhound bus station, its glass front coated with whitewash. "Another hollow shell thanks to developers." Charlie gestured at the skeletal building.

Justin nodded. "Did you know this was where the

Unabomber came in and out to deliver his packages back in the 90s? Have you seen the new series out on him? He was a Harvard student in the early 60s, warped by a three-year experiment on the effects of humiliation."

Charlie shook his head. "No, but I read part of his manifesto. The guy was right about some things," he said. "He was against mass entertainment and the harm from spectator sports. He claimed they rob people of human dignity and freedom."

Justin frowned. "But his kind of violence is never right."

It hit Charlie that the Unabomber and the *Black Sunday* bomber shared understandable motives, but Charlie kept his thoughts to himself. Still, he knew beyond doubt that the defiance of the powerless against the tyranny of the powerful is the same in life as in fiction.

INSIDE THE RESTAURANT, THE HOST LED THEM PAST THE elegant black-and-silver bar to the back. Charlie slid into a dimly lit, mahogany-paneled booth and offered Justin one of his rare smiles. "I like to support the old-time businesses." He ordered water from the attentive waiter, took off his cap and set it on the leather seat beside him.

Justin ordered a Jack Daniels rocks and set the menu aside. "A damn shame so many little guys are going belly up. Justice is blind in the wrong ways lately."

"Go ahead, order that steak you love." Charlie

looked over the menu for something that would go easy on his stomach. "You're still strong and healthy enough to plan for the future." Charlie nodded at his cousin. "Me and my condition," he rubbed his hairless scalp, avoiding his incision, which was still not fully healed, "my time might be short. Got to be part of a legacy to save our town."

Justin ordered the restaurant's special New York steak. Charlie asked that a slice of banana cream pie be brought at the same time as a bowl of won ton soup. The waiter nodded and left them in the privacy of the booth.

"What kind of legacy are you thinking of?" Justin took a swallow of his whisky.

"Something to stand out, stand up and shout my intention." Charlie banged his fist on the polished wooden table top.

"Well, those Taxpayers Opposed to Pork didn't do the trick trying to put the arena to the voters, deny public funding," said Justin. "Court knocked down our lawsuits, and now we've got the mishmash of Downtown Commons. Trying to be a great American city, along the lines of New York's SoHo and San Francisco's SoMa. Marketing it with the place name of DOCO."

With his fingertip, Charlie traced invisible circles on the tabletop. "It's like they're clear cutting forests," he flicked a few specks off the table, "buying up old businesses and houses to put up way more than a parking lot." He watched Justin for his reactions. "Might have to send a louder message, maybe tear down the abominations they put up."

Their food arrived. Justin sliced off a bite of his steaming steak, cut on the diagonal and smothered with grilled onions in Frank Fat's special oyster sauce. "We're better than that," he said. "Like I showed you, I'm taking the environmental hazards route to allow no more projects until the whole impact is investigated."

Charlie blew on his hot soup, swallowed a sip and his eyes widened. "No more projects! That's it!" he shouted. "No more development. Stop growing down-town! Enough is enough!" He set his spoon down. "NOMO! Let's call it NOMO. For no more DOCO."

Justin's fork was half-way to his mouth. "NOMO!" He waved a bite of special steak around in the air. "I like it. Gives us a name to go by."

"Combat gentrification, leave a legacy." Charlie pounded the table a few times, setting up ripples in his broth. "How about we start by picketing that new Ans Botha Center before it opens?"

"Not bad, cousin," said Justin. "Nonviolent protest. Turn public opinion into a force for good. Not that different from what our Ambrose carried on. A war using words as weapons."

Charlie's head felt clear and his mind sharp as when he was a young professor. He nodded. "I can call the son of a student from my old days, Victor Ramirez. He's teaching history out at Sac State, kind of an activist. I bet he can get some students on board." Charlie set down his soup spoon and forked into his banana cream pie.

His stomach felt a helluva lot better than it had this morning. NOMO protesting could be effective. But he would still get his guys together, set up a meeting to kick things around with Robert and KD in case words couldn't excise the malignant building craze.

Call a meeting for next week, maybe the day after Thanksgiving. Black Friday. The similarity to *Black Sunday* hit him. But he certainly was not going to be bombing a Super Bowl in Sacramento.

CHAPTER TWENTY

People cry, not because they're weak. It's because
they've been strong for too long.

-Johnny Depp

HILLARY WENT IN TO CHECK ON HER SLEEPING DAUGHTER.
Claire lay in bed, one arm curled over her forehead as if
warding off blows, crying out a string of sounds.
"Suh…suh…" What was she trying to say? Shooting,
shooting?

The yellow labs, Daisy and Darius, lay in their
shared bed, mother and son growing old together. They
gazed at Hillary, their blond eyebrows raised quizzi-
cally over their brown eyes, as if picking up on how
distraught she was. She knelt and fondled their ears.
"Shhhh. It's okay," she whispered. "Our Claire is going
to get through this." She had to believe they
both would.

• • •

HILLARY THOUGHT BACK TO THE NIGHT OF THE SHOOTING. Without a glance or word to Hillary, Claire had climbed down from the top row of bleachers. She huddled next to another student who'd been grazed by slivers of glass from the windows shattered from the struggle to control the rifle. The EMT finished working on that student and turned to Claire. He cleaned the wound on her right arm just above the elbow. "You are mighty lucky, little lady," he said as he applied a gauze dressing. "It's just superficial."

Lucky. Maybe so, maybe not, thought Hillary. It was Claire's shooting arm.

Keisha was unhurt and stood watching the procedure. After Claire got bandaged up, she stayed right by Keisha's side, wide-eyed and frowning as they walked around the gym checking on their friends.

Hillary shot a worried look at Stacy, who said, "Let's calm down, go back to my house for macaroni and cheese."

Claire was quiet all evening, curled up in the corner of Stacy's corduroy sofa, watching *Clueless* and *The Sisterhood of the Traveling Pants*. Wrapped in an old Monarchs fleece throw, she fell into a deep sleep.

It was time to go home. Hillary gently shook Claire's shoulder. No response.

"Let your girl be," said Stacy. "You know she's safe here."

"I can't. I have to watch her, make sure she's okay."

"I'm up all night anyway, with all that goes on here in the hood. Don't you fret."

Hillary shook Claire's shoulder again and whispered her name. She stroked Claire's cheek, warm to her touch. But no response. It was as if her daughter had moved out of her body.

"She'll be better come morning," Stacy whispered.

Hillary drove home alone, her heart heavy.

Now nothing seemed to make sense. Claire had let Hillary change her dressings and the wound looked as if it was healing quickly. Still Claire hadn't spoken more than a few words at home since the shooting. Hillary was glad to let Keisha stay over at their place for the weekend. The girls binge watched *Stranger Things* when they weren't out hooping it up in the driveway with one-on-one variations of H-O-R-S-E, each calling out a shot for the other to try and match. Hillary couldn't tell if they were having fun or in a grim contest to reach for perfection.

The counselor at Sac Jr. High had phoned today. He said he was on a team with the high school counselors concerned over the students who'd been injured in the shooting. He had been keeping an eye on Claire, who had refused to come in for a private session. "It's good that your daughter has kept up regular attendance. We know students gain security from having a predictable routine."

"She hardly says a word here at home." Hillary felt anxious revealing what she'd noticed but the man sounded like he focused on the positive. "Does she talk at school?" Hillary asked.

"Her teachers and coaches tell me she is responding as normal in class and at practice. What might be troubling her at home?"

Troubling at home. The question felt like a gut punch. "We are trying to figure that out," Hillary said, thanked the counselor and ended the call. Claire was keeping up with basketball practice. And eating. She would nod, too, or shake her head in response at home. Hillary had to believe they could help Claire work through this shock. But how?

HILLARY PACED THE LIVING ROOM FLOOR. IT WAS PAST midnight. Ed should be home soon from a task force meeting on gangs in the region. The house felt cold and barren. She made herself a brandy and soda and sat down with pad and pencil to brainstorm. They had to come up with something to help Claire heal more than the wound to her arm. But what?

Nothing came to mind as she stared into space, the notepad blank when she heard Ed's key in the front door.

He bent to kiss Hillary, lift her drink and take a swallow. "Where's mine?" He collapsed into the recliner next to the fireplace. "Just kidding. I'll go get it, Chickadee. But first, I'll rest my eyes a second. We've got triple the work since discovering the high school shooter's in a mixed race gang."

"Mixed race?"

"An off-shoot of the Proud Boys—Black, Latino and Asians who marched with white supremacists in Portland last year." He dropped his chin onto his chest and closed his eyes.

Hillary padded out to the kitchen and made Ed a drink. Just as she was setting it down next to the recliner, a wild shriek came from the hallway.

Claire raced into the living room, eyes squeezed shut, waving her arms in the air. "Gran! Where? Where? Where?"

The dogs followed her, whining softly.

Ed jumped up. "It's all right, Princess. It's all right." He reached out. "It's just a dream." He lifted her and held her against his chest. "Just a bad dream." He brushed her hair off her sweaty face, looked at Hillary and nodded toward the hallway.

Hillary ran to Claire's room. Her pillowcase and sheets were damp with sweat. Hillary took out fresh linen from the hall closet and changed the bed. Heart hammering, she returned to find Ed in the recliner, his sleeping daughter peacefully draped across him.

Hillary mouthed, "Her bed's ready."

Ed nodded and struggled up to a sitting position, cradling Claire, who lay limp across his lap. Suddenly she stiffened out straight, as long as her petite frame would take her. "Gran," she whispered. "Where are you?" She opened her eyes and glared at Hillary. "Where is Grannie Sarah?"

Hillary stood rooted to the floor. Sarah. That's what Claire's moaning "Suh...suh..." must have meant.

"You let her die!" Claire jumped up and ran down

the hall. "You couldn't protect her. Like you couldn't protect me!" She grabbed her arm where the glass shard cut was still healing and darted into her room, kicking her bedroom door shut.

Hillary followed and found the door locked.

Ed came up beside her. "Princess, let us in."

Silence.

"Honey, let's talk about this," said Hillary.

Nothing. The dogs, locked out of the bedroom as well, whimpered nearby.

Strains of Linkin Park's music drifted out into the hallway. The door flew open and Claire reached out for the dogs. Once they were in the bedroom, her words burst in a volley from her lips. "What if a shooter gets you, Mom? Huh? Did you ever think about that? Do you see how Maggie's mother is in a wheelchair? What it's done to Maggie?" She slammed her door shut and turned her music up.

Hillary stood immobile, stunned at the force of her daughter's anger.

"Jesus." Ed paced the living room floor. "What the hell are we going to do?" He downed half his drink in a couple swallows. "It looks like she's blaming you."

Hillary sat bent over, elbows on knees, fingertips pressed to her forehead.

"Claire is really suffering." He finished his drink. "She has what happened to Sarah mixed up with the school shooting and Margie Ann's mother getting hurt so bad."

Hillary's stomach tightened. She raised her head to look straight into Ed's eyes. "It wasn't my fault. I was asleep when it happened to Sarah."

"I know, honey, but Claire was only six back then. She probably expected you to ward off all bad things in life. It's magical thinking, but it shows she understands how strong you are."

Ed smiled at her. She slumped forward and sighed, as he continued, "Now at twelve, it looks like she thought you should have protected her from the bullet that shattered the gym window."

Hillary crossed her arms over her chest. "You don't need to remind me. I feel guilty over those things."

"She might need to see someone professional, not just the school counselor. You have to face it. She is seriously traumatized, and we don't want it building to anything worse."

Hillary threw her shoulders back. Seeing someone. That would mean laying bare the story of being abandoned by her mother.

"It wouldn't hurt to…" Ed began.

"What?"

"Like I said, contact one of those therapists, you know, on that list the school gave out."

"Those people want to involve the whole family, Ed. Don't you know we would get dragged in, too? Claire's reactions lately are probably exaggerated by her hormones and the stress of trying to get to the top of her game."

"Well, pride goeth before a fall. Who said that?"

"It's from the Bible somewhere—but pride's a good thing."

"Look, if you don't want to get involved with therapy, maybe you could, you know..." He paused for a beat and watched for her reaction. "...try to find your mother. Maybe having her in Claire's life would help. Look what a comfort Stacy is to Claire. You said you would try and find your mother a few years ago when you got home from Ireland. What happened to that?"

"That woman can't even be called a mother. It hasn't looked like finding her would be any kind of blessing. We've gotten along fine without her." Hillary frowned and finished her brandy and soda.

"Until now," Ed said.

She had to get him off this. "Want a fresh drink?"

He narrowed his eyes into dark slits. "You can't keep running from it. I've had Walt on it. He's got short wave radio contacts all over the world. He's good at this private eye stuff, Chickadee."

"Don't Chickadee me! What if that woman is dead! Or worse, some kind of homeless drug addict now?" She took a big swig of her drink.

"You'll never know unless you open up and hear what Walt has discovered." Ed walked around behind the recliner and massaged her shoulders. "I've been saving a packet of information."

"I'm not ready for it," she said, pulling away from his hands. "You've got to let that subject drop!" She went to the kitchen and started to set up the coffee for the morning. Ed came up behind her and stroked her arms. "Our girl is in pain, really hurting. Why not see what Walt's found?"

She shook her head.

Gently, he turned her to face him. "For Claire's sake? Maybe this is the wake-up call you need. You know you want to find her, in your heart of hearts."

She was going to jump right out of her skin if he wouldn't shut up. "You talk about my heart. But my heart means nothing to someone like her, leaving when I was so young. Never reaching out for me again. I am always there for Claire."

Ed kissed her on the tip of her nose, on each cheek and then on her lips. "Think about it," he murmured.

She kissed him back with fervor. She would think about her mother tomorrow.

CHAPTER TWENTY-ONE

I don't need therapy. All I need is the gym.

-GymQuotes.co

She bent to the hardwood and slipped her fingers under a massive sheet of cardboard, lifting an edge off the floor and pushing it up. It swayed as it rose. She stretched her arms wide, and managed to stand it up vertically. Where was the doorway? There was only flat cardboard against her palms. High windows cut in. On her tiptoes, she could see her daughter on the other side, shouting and chasing a ticking orange ball. She had to get to her. But there was no doorway.

HILLARY LAY WITH HER EYES CLOSED, SHUTTING OUT THE morning light. She peeked at the clock. Six thirty. Ed had performed his disappearing act again, slipped out soundlessly for downtown.

She listened for the ponk ponk of Claire's basketball in the driveway.

Silence.

No Claire out getting her half hour of shooting practice before breakfast. She must have slept in, exhausted from her stormy night.

Out in the kitchen, Hillary sipped French Roast left over from Ed's pot of coffee, but it burned in her stomach and she switched to water. She waited until seven o'clock, and then, worried Claire would be late for school, she tapped on her bedroom door.

Nothing.

She knocked.

Silence. She tried the knob. Locked.

"Claire, Claire!"

Nothing. "Claire!" She waggled the doorknob again. The lock held.

She texted Ed:

see Claire this morning?

no

she's not up

sick?

room locked

use emergency key

Where was that tiny key? Hillary rummaged through the kitchen junk drawer, pawing around pencils, small spiral notebooks and random loose keys before she spotted the thin shank of metal curved at the top like a miniature cane.

She'd never had to use it before. It was tricky to get it to stick in the right spot. She waggled it around in the tiny hole in the doorknob but couldn't keep a grip on the metal. The shank slipped all the way into the hole with only a quarter inch sticking out. Heart pounding, she got tweezers from her bathroom and pulled the tiny key out again. Praying under her breath, she pushed the key in and tipped the lock mechanism.

She opened the door.

Claire's bed was empty, sheets and blankets lay on the floor in a jumble, the dogs' bed empty. The room was freezing cold. The curtains were pulled aside, and the window was open. Hillary leaned out and spotted the window screen lying on the lawn. She shuffled papers on Claire's desk, looking for a note, but nothing.

Her belly cramping and her fingers numb, she texted Ed:

she's gone and so are the dogs

Jesus call Stacy

Before she could call, her phone rang. The words tumbled out of Stacy. "Hilly, I'm sorry not to call before. Your girl is safe. Scared us awful showing up at three in the morning, but people up all hours here. Your girl was in a state."

"Why…" Hillary could barely speak. "Why didn't you call me?"

"Forgive me. She was begging me not to, didn't want you to think she was crazy."

"What? Crazy?"

"Come on over, honey. We'll make it right."

Her fingers quivering, Hillary texted Ed and let him know Claire was safe. She drove down Second Avenue toward Oak Park, her fingers chill against the steering wheel. The street ran under the freeway where a couple of homeless men slept, bundled in sleeping bags, backs against the concrete, sitting up leaning against each other.

Thank God Claire had taken the dogs with her. It wasn't safe out here.

Stacy met Hillary in a wide embrace, whispering, "Your young one's wore out."

Hillary sagged into the older woman's arms. "I'm so glad she's safe. I can't even be mad at you for not calling last night."

Stacy poured a cup of chicory-laced coffee for Hillary. "Good for the nerves, drink up." She nodded toward a closed door and said, "Got her in my bed." She thumbed toward the rear of the small house. "Dogs in the back. Keisha went on and caught the bus for school."

Hillary shook her head. "I know she's suffering from the shock of the shooting. But it must be more than that? Don't know what's got into her."

Stacy nodded. "It's what's got out of her, honey. Her starch is wilted. Them gunshots punched her, drained the gumption out of her. Her game isn't the same."

Hillary sipped at the coffee and rolled it around in her mouth. It was soothing, mellow. Claire was safe.

Stacy sat with a faraway look on her face. "Reminds me of the time my gumption was kicked out. I ever tell you about it?"

Hillary shook her head.

Stacy stared out the window into her back yard. "That's a story for another, day." She turned back to Hillary. "But you can believe, took me years to get it back. Now I've passed it on to Kee Kee, and she shares it with your little gal. Sometimes your girl calls me Sarah, you ever notice that?"

Hillary rubbed her arms as goose pimples rose. "No," she whispered.

"Names sound alike." Stacy cocked her head, her lip thrust out. "I can hear her stirring." Stacy stood and wiped her hands on her apron. "You take her home. Let her know you will protect her."

Claire opened the door. "Maa! Is Dad okay?"

Hillary's heart leapt at the sight of her. "Of course, why wouldn't he be?"

"You were right!" Claire darted over and gave Stacy a hug. "I'm not crazy. They're okay!" Then she tucked herself into Hillary's open arms. "I had an awful dream. You and Dad were shot full of holes, lying in the graveyard. No one was home in our house."

She started laughing wildly, then shut her mouth and turned to Stacy. "Thank you, for taking me in last night."

Stacy walked to the front door. "Time for you to get back where you belong, young lady. Your warrior mama got your chariot waiting, and I'm gonna let those dogs out for y'all." She marched to the side gate and let the yellow labs free. They ran to the Rav4, tails wagging furiously.

"Let's go home, Maa." Claire rubbed her eyes and

stretched. "I can still make most classes and practice." She ran out to the car.

Practice. Troubled by her child's erratic emotions and behavior, Hillary was grateful for Claire's devotion to the sport. Basketball and Stacy seemed to be saving the girl. Or was it the other way around?

Maybe Claire could use a grandmother, kind of a backup mother figure. But Hillary's own mother wouldn't play the role of wise and loving elder. If she could ever be found, that is. Better to let the past go, keep to the present, get the Center opened, a place where everyone could prepare for the fresh start of a new year.

CHAPTER TWENTY-TWO

MIND, n. A mysterious form of matter secreted by the brain. Its chief activity consists in the endeavor to ascertain its own nature, the futility of the attempt being due to the fact that it has nothing but itself to know itself with.

-Ambrose Bierce, *The Devil's Dictionary*

AFTER A LUNCH OF WHITE RICE AND BOILED CHICKEN, Charlie went out to his detached one-car garage. He fired up his red convertible and put the top down. The car had been his only concession to midlife crisis. Best purchase ever with help from his pal KD. Kept him feeling like a young man, loaded with testosterone and ready to take on the world.

Until the last few years.

He drove down the alley bare headed, to catch the warmth of the November sun on his bald head. He was on his way out to Sac State, check out the lay of the land. It was only a few miles to the college, so no worries about skin cancer on his bare scalp.

He laughed. Skin cancer. He should be so lucky.

CHARLIE PICKED UP HIS MAIL IN THE ENGLISH DEPARTMENT office, grudgingly grateful to be in their part-time faculty pool and assigned a freshman English class every few semesters when they were desperate. The pay was lousy but the ego boost made up for it, still getting to teach at the four-year school. But no one here or even at a community college had offered him a class this fall.

He liked to stay in touch, tease the department secretary Linda, grown old and gray and near retirement. He still joked around and made her blush, all in good fun. People needed to keep a sense of humor in these tense times. Those MeToo women were just a bunch of man haters.

The place had changed so much since he taught full time back in the 90s. But ads selling the latest textbooks were still the same. He tossed the flyers into a waste bin and walked over to Tahoe Hall. Might as well see if he'd caught Victor during an office hour. No such luck. He'd phone him later, see when would be a good day and time for him to come by the house.

It was different with Don in the Chemistry Department, his buddy from the old days when they served together on the curriculum committee. He practically lived in his lab.

After a few exchanges about the weather, Charlie turned to the topic of teaching at the community college level. "The way I keep sane after reading the incomprehensible essays I get from those students is to write fantasy fiction. It's in my genes, you know."

Don stopped wiping the long black lab counter and stared at Charlie. "Your genes?"

"Ambrose Bierce. Ever hear of Owl Creek Bridge?"

"Can't say I have. Course I don't read much of what you literary types like." He snorted derisively. "But I've thought of that from time to time, maybe try writing science fiction or medical thrillers when I retire. You ever read those?"

Charlie pulled out a tall stool and sat down, making sure to keep his hands off the clean surface. "A different genre attracts me lately, political thrillers. My favorite is *Black Sunday*, by Thomas Harris. The book centers on bombing a Super Bowl game." Charlie stretched out his arms. "From a blimp into a huge stadium open to the air. Outlandish, right?"

Don nodded and went back to wiping the counter as Charlie continued. "There was a rumor that Harris was an English professor before he got rich and famous with his Hannibal Lecter books."

"Ah, the lure of the big stage for so many of us lowly academics." Don shook his head. "Rich and famous, what a concept."

Charlie nodded and cleared his throat. "I'm toying with an edgy plot..." he studied Don to check for reaction. Seeing none, Charlie continued "...to bomb

Staples Center, but as it says in *Black Sunday*, the hardest thing is to find the explosives."

Don stopped wiping and frowned at Charlie. Heart rate elevated, Charlie continued. "You have any ideas? Bombing a covered basketball arena would be harder than a stadium open to the air, right?"

"You know," muttered Don, "that sort of thing is not only illegal but deadly as hell."

Charlie pulled at his chin, wishing his goatee would start to grow back. He nodded. "Of course. That's why I need your expertise, buddy."

Don frowned. "I have to keep a sharp eye on my students, more so in these times than back when you and I were new. I get the FBI out here nosing around on a regular basis. Taking some of my students off campus to grill them." Don gritted his teeth, tossed his rag into a hamper and straightened a couple glass tubes standing in racks on the long black slab of a counter.

"And?" Charlie stood, rocking on his heels, his heart racing. "Any of them turn out to be dangerous?"

"One on a student visa was deported last spring, yeah." Don shook his head. "Fellow from the Ukraine, actually."

Charlie nodded, hesitant to come right out and ask for details. Don turned away, sorted through a cubby and pulled out another white rag. He walked the length of the long black counter dragging the rag along. After he folded up the rag and tossed it into the hamper, he turned back to Charlie. "So, what's the situation in your novel, pal?" asked Don. "What kind of explosives? Let's go grab a pub lunch and you can set out your story for me. Have you read that new book on the aftereffects of terrorist bombs?"

Charlie nodded. "Yeah, gruesome. Great young author out of India. Lots of breakthrough writing is coming from there. Vikram Chandra and so on. Got inspired by Rushdie, no doubt." Charlie relaxed. He was on safe ground now, discussing his field—literature. He'd be able to string Don along with a plot tracing the activities of fictional white supremacists who wanted to frame some Muslims by bombing Staples Center in L. A.

Get Don's advice on an explosive of just the right type. As backup. After all, it was possible no more would be needed to save his block of Victorians. The City Council could reverse anything the planning commission might be shortsighted enough to go along with. Or even if the council approved plans for Sunny's tower, a restrained strike against the Ans Botha Center at a time no one would get hurt might still save his neighborhood. Like getting rid of the tumor might have already saved his life.

Feeling young and frisky for a change, Charlie sang out, "My treat, today, old pal."

As Don slipped out of his white lab coat, he said, "You know, bomb building is not as difficult as you might imagine."

Charlie's heart skipped a beat. "Tell me more," he said and led the way over to the university dining commons.

It was good to have a friend like Don.

CHAPTER TWENTY-THREE

The pen is mightier than the sword.

-Edward Bulwer-Lytton

HILLARY LED THE WAY OUT OF THE ATHLETICS BUILDING. "Looks like they've beefed up security. Got to guard against crazy shooters." She clenched her teeth and frowned. "It's so different from back in the 90s."

Stacy hooted. "Calling the basketball courts 'The Nest.'"

Hillary shook her head. "They want to play like they just flew out of a hornets' nest. That name boosts the Hornets' PR buzz. Everyone's got to build their brand." Hillary headed across the quad. "I'm grateful they agreed to have the basketball teams play exhibition games at the Center."

"Keisha's got a poster of the women's team taped over her desk. Our youngsters get to learn from the college players, they get people seeing how good they are, fans come out to the games here, close by as the crows fly." Stacy chuckled.

"It's a win-win. Have a coffee on me." Hillary nodded in the direction of the dining commons. As they passed a student newspaper vending box, Hillary read the headline out loud: "Sac State economics professor caught in viral video using racial slur."

Stacy nodded, her lips in a tight, straight line.

"The truth's out in the open now." Hillary sighed. "Back in the '90s we kept most faculty dirt hushed up."

As they neared the dining commons, she slowed and whispered, "Am I seeing things?" She jerked her head in the direction of a plate-glass window.

At a counter inside, facing the quad, sat Charlie Bierce, head-to-head with some man. Suddenly, as if Bierce knew she was near, he raised his head and stared directly at Hillary. He smirked and jabbed his finger at her.

She eyeballed Stacy, nodded in his direction and then pivoted away and picked up her pace, her heart beating double time. When she neared the library, she ducked into a Starbucks and ordered two cups of French Roast, the closest they would have to her friend's chicory-laced brew.

While they waited for the drinks, Hillary said, "Did you see him?"

Stacy nodded. "Bierce looked like he was up to something with that other guy."

"And then he looked right at me and shook his finger." Hillary set the two coffees on a pub table. She fanned her hot drink. "That Bierce. On the first day of Intro to Great Lit he blared out that good students would have already acquainted themselves with the required readings. His list included *Paradise Lost* and a book by some ancestor of his, *The Devil's Dictionary*."

Hillary couldn't help herself. She wrote out the word on a paper napkin. "Devil." She crossed out the D. "It has the word 'evil' in it." She stared at Stacy. "That nastiness must run in his family."

Stacy nodded. "He's a mean one all right."

Hillary downed half of her coffee. "I'll never forget it." She slammed down her cup, coffee sloshing over onto the plastic table top.

While she mopped at the liquid, words flew from her lips. "In the first week, an overweight kid wearing coke-bottle glasses raised his hand and struggled out of his desk to ask about the impact of blindness on authors like John Milton. Professor Bierce shook that *Devil's Dictionary* in the air and shouted 'ABDOMEN, noun. The temple of the god Stomach, in whose worship all true men engage, and you have the audacity to ask about Milton's eyes.' Bierce set the Devil book on his podium, jabbed his finger at the kid and yelled, '*Sit* if you can *fit* into your *desk*!'" She took a deep breath.

Stacy leaned forward, her paper cup gripped into an oval.

Hillary nodded. "Humiliation scorched us all. But no one said a word. And then, he shot us down for our silence. 'You've nothing to say? You are dumb in both the literal and figurative senses?'"

Stacy sipped at her coffee.

"He'd scrawl nasty comments all over our essays. 'You don't belong in college,' he would mutter as he strode the aisles handing back papers covered with so much red ink they looked like horror movie props. After class, some students would slam their papers into the trash can outside the building, cursing Professor Poison."

Stacy licked her lips. "Been there."

"I kept my papers and ran them by my father, for his advice on writing. I had a hard time showing my midterm blue book to him, though. It had red scrawls over every inch of the margins. On the last page, Bierce had written: 'You'll never make it as a journalist, my dear, the genes of your famous sire haven't passed on to you.'"

"My father was furious and got his *Chronicle* editor to okay a series on bad professors. Today, Bierce's pattern of attacks would be called 'verbal abuse,' and he'd be taken to court, at the least."

Stacy looked around the small coffee shop. "Some teachers are soul killers," she said. "One out at the JC flunked me for not using perfect SWE in Freshman English class."

"SWE?"

"Standard Written English. White folks' talk. I dropped out of college."

Hillary sighed. "More than a few students in Bierce's classes stopped showing up as the weeks wore on."

Stacy raised her cup in a toast. "It's a different story today for my Keisha. She's got wonderful teachers."

Hillary finished her French Roast. There was something mysterious about the connection she felt with Stacy. They were different in so many ways, yet alike, too, in their devotion to their girls and their future.

She had to put a stop to any more trouble Professor Poison might be dreaming up against their Center.

AFTER SHE DROPPED STACY OFF, HILLARY DROVE HOME, trying to picture where she'd stored her father's notebooks. She remembered seeing them when she went through his things after he died. After taking care of the funeral arrangements, she had to get the little house in Carmichael ready to put on the market. His article clips and notebooks were methodically filed by date in a couple of cabinets in the garage. She had glanced through them, saving a dozen or so, including three or four related to the professors series. She remembered her father had been unable to verify some of the students charges, so those notes weren't part of *The Chron*'s series. If they'd been, she suspected the paper would have won the Public Service Pulitzer.

OUT IN THE DETACHED DOUBLE GARAGE, SHE RUMMAGED around in cardboard storage boxes, but no luck. Then she went inside to search. They'd moved here a few years ago after Ed retired as a deputy in Stockton. The house was a roomy single-story Mediterranean with four bedrooms on the ground floor and a half basement they used as a den. She looked in the guest bedroom, but there was nothing but a twin bed and an empty dresser. She was grateful to have one of the bedrooms for a home office and not have to always be stuck downtown in Sunny's suite of offices.

At her computer, she opened the *Chronicle's* archives to the series of articles on the professors. She read her father's story about Charlie Bierce out loud, her voice taking on the bold cadence of her father's tones as she went over the patterns of Bierce's verbal abuse. She could almost hear her father talking to her from the grave. The clanking from the old furnace in the basement provided a counterpoint rhythm.

The basement.

She ran to the basement door and down the steps. In the wood-paneled room, she spotted an old chest of drawers. Yanking open the bottom drawer, she saw the long narrow notebooks, clustered together.

Clutching the dozen notebooks in both hands, she carried them upstairs and set them on the dining room table where the light was better. As she flipped through them, the damp notebooks reeked faintly of mildew, but her father's block printing looked as fresh and authoritative as ever.

And there it was. Tuesday, November 12, 1991. An interview with Bea Samuelson that never made it into the paper.

Hillary read the words aloud in the empty house.

My twin, always picked on. Mother thought it was sweet to name us Bea and Birdie. She was called bird brain. Bullied in high school. Tried running the car in the closed garage.

Did better in college. Until Bierce. Wouldn't speak for hours after his class. Didn't leave a note but it was him. Mother had a nervous breakdown, I dropped out of school to care for Mother. We can't prove anything. I'll deny everything. Get that devil professor gone.

Hillary closed her eyes. An image of the twins that sat near the classroom door came to her, one girl the petite shadow of the other, Professor Poison handing back a paper to the thin pale twin, repeating her name, "Birdie, Birdie, Birdie," as he scowled down at her.

The girls vanished half way through the term.

Hillary leafed through the rest of the notebooks. The twin looked to be the only lethal case. A weight pressed on Hillary's heart. Thank god the newspaper article series worked. It was the final unacceptable mark on Professor Charles Bierce's record and got him dropped from the tenure track at Sacramento State University.

Her father had pointed to the old saying that hung on his *Chronicle* workstation wall. "The pen is mightier than the sword," he said, and added, "Sometimes."

"He can't hurt students anymore," Hillary said with relief.

"That kind of man, he'll want revenge," her father warned. "No matter how long it takes. Keep an eye out."

Her father's published words had saved so many students back then. It was up to her to stop Bierce's word war against the Center and the students of today.

CHAPTER TWENTY-FOUR

Thanksgiving has wings and goes where it must go.
Your prayer knows much more about it than you do.

-Victor Hugo

HILLARY POURED COFFEE INTO ED'S MUG AND CARRIED IT
to the breakfast nook table. "I've got mixed feelings
about this so-called Meal of Thanksgiving today. Not
sure what I'm grateful for anymore."

"The win streak my Irish ballers are on is a start for
me." Ed lifted his mug in a salute and sipped at the hot
black brew. "Also, I'm thankful Claire wasn't hurt more
seriously at the high school. Did you call that counselor
back?"

She sighed and shook her head.

"Be a good idea for you to reach out. You might
even run into him over at the school today."

She grimaced. "Those counselors, always want to

dig into the family dynamics. It might work for some, but I just can't go there, you know that."

He leaned forward and kissed her. "Well, I'm grateful for you, in any case, my Chickadee. Plus, eating over at the high school saves you from having to cook." He smiled. "Just pick up that pumpkin pie you ordered at the bakery, and we're all set. Get a pecan, too, if they have some. My favorite from when Grandma Kiffin made it from freshly shelled nuts."

Claire walked in, rubbing her eyes, and sat down. "I want yams, Mom, with marshmallows melted on them like you always make."

"You've got 'em." Hillary warmed with pleasure at Claire's request, grateful she had the ingredients on hand in the pantry. Her daughter was back to being her old self this morning.

OUTSIDE THE BAKERY, HILLARY STEPPED ASIDE FOR MARY Kelly, just leaving in a wheelchair, a boxed pie and a bag of soft rolls on her lap. Her daughter Margie Ann was intent on navigating the wheelchair out the double doors. They both looked up and smiled, but their eyes told a different story.

"How are you doing?" Hillary felt both chilled and warmed at the sight of them, even closer now than before.

Mary said, "We're lucky my mother Rosa is coming to live with us soon." She looked up at her daughter. "Give some relief to Margie Ann. Let her get back to her studies and her game."

Hillary nodded. "Something to be thankful for. See you at the school, yes?"

Mary gave a thumbs up.

IN THE BIG MULTIPURPOSE ROOM, ED CARRIED THE PIES AND Hillary's yam dish over to the buffet tables. The room smelled of roast turkey and dressing and the sweetness of pumpkin spices. Claire and Keisha and a few other Devils tossed imaginary basketballs up toward the folded backboards. Hillary found Stacy and sat down across from her, saving a seat for Ed.

On the stage, the principal addressed the gathering. "Welcome to this day of gratitude and healing. All of us, administrators, teachers and counselors alike, are thankful no one was killed in the awful tragedy. The gym foyer is being repaired, the windows replaced, bullet holes patched and the walls scrubbed, primed and painted. The gym will be renamed the Providential Palace in gratitude for our good luck."

Hillary shuddered. Seemed a bad idea to use a name like that. Could jinx the gym. The vulnerability of their new Center crossed her mind.

The principal continued, "Please get into the buffet line when your table number is called. Our staff have chosen to seat themselves among you at your tables. Please take this opportunity and get to know each other better."

Hillary turned and offered her hand to a young woman taking an empty seat next to her.

"I'm one of the school counselors." She patted her name tag. "Dr. Bolden but call me Sherie."

Hillary's jaw dropped. Did this woman know Hillary'd been contacted by that other counselor? It wouldn't help anything to probe into what Hillary worked so hard to forget all these years.

INTRODUCTIONS PROCEEDED AROUND THE TABLE, AMIDST exclamations of how good everything smelled. Claire and Keisha gobbled the food they'd piled high on their plates, laughing and miming red waddles hanging at their throats. Hillary absently touched own neck as the girls ran off to chat with their friends.

Hillary was grateful Sherie's attention had been monopolized throughout the meal by the man sitting on her other side. Hillary could overhear him ranting about how poorly so many kids were being raised nowadays and bragging on what a wonderful father he was. The woman seemed to be a good listener and reminded Hillary of herself back in her reporter days.

At last, Sherie turned to Hillary. "This pecan pie is delicious. Who made it?"

"I think it's one of ours, but it's just from the bakery down the street."

Hillary swallowed her last bite of pumpkin pie as Sherie continued. "It's nice to get together," she said, "informally like this. We're feeling good about the progress we see."

Hillary sensed the woman was about to give her one of those "but..." messages.

"We love how parents are coming to school and chatting with us," Sherie poked the last bite of sticky pecan pie onto her fork and waved it in Hillary's direction, "building emotional support structures under their traumatized students." She popped the pie into her mouth and began chewing.

Hillary put her utensils on her empty paper plate. "Our daughter is doing all right."

"It's a rocky road for many of them. Some have turned to dangerous practices to relieve their anxieties. We are here to help all of you, parents too."

Holy Mary. Mother of God. Dangerous practices? "We're grateful for Claire's basketball. It seems a sort of therapy in its own right," she said.

Sherie nodded. "It's not clear why some develop PTSD while others don't. It can happen immediately or weeks or months later, even years, sometimes. That's why we are taking appointments for over the Christmas break."

Hillary rubbed her Mary and Ganesh medals and nodded at Sherie. "Her father and I are here for Claire." It had to be enough.

CHAPTER TWENTY-FIVE

Growth for the sake of growth is the ideology of the
cancer cell.

-Edward Abbey

OUT ON THE STREET AN ENGINE RUMBLED, VIBRATING
Charlie's parlor windows, and today the clamor seemed
fitting. His heart pounded at the thought of what Justin
would say if he knew about this meeting.

Charlie walked out onto the porch and looked down
while KD parked his '69 Chevelle and took the stairs
two at a time up to the top. Charlie reached to pump
KD's hand and said, "Appreciate how you value classic
cars...and neighborhoods."

KD grinned. "Got this ride outfitted with a 396 big
block. Everyone knows when I'm coming. Lucked out
and got one of your solid gold parking spots."

"The city is charging big bucks," grumbled Charlie.

"They have to cover their sweetheart deal paying for the arena. Glad you could get away." He opened the front door.

Inside, KD took off his bomber jacket, hung it on the coat tree in the entry and stood pulling at his suspenders. "Can't stay too long. Car buyers will be all over the lot, but Black Friday is more of a kickoff for the whole holiday season."

Seconds later, the doorbell clanged. It was Robert, announcing he hadn't had to hunt for a parking place. "My wife dropped me off. She's Christmas shopping at Macy's across from the arena. We don't have any big stores up at Tahoe, so Black Friday doesn't mean much there."

"The almighty dollar." Charlie scowled. "Making it or saving it is all that counts for some people. Nothing against your wife, pal."

"The truth is the truth," Robert nodded glumly.

A few minutes later, Victor showed up. "I was glad to get your invitation last week, Professor, and curious to learn what you've got on your mind."

Charlie introduced them and the three got settled on his red velvet furniture. "There is a fire inside me." Charlie slapped his chest. "Deep down inside, you hear me?"

The three men nodded. It warmed Charlie's heart the way they resonated with him. He looked at Robert. "You've been away, but a couple years back, we tried everything legal to stop this foolishness." He waved in the direction of downtown. "Damn judges threw out our lawsuits. Voters were never told the truth. City saw to it we got shot down and the arena got put up."

Victor nodded. "History shows you can forget democracy when it comes to the power brokers."

KD punched his fist in the air. "I thought the arena was great at first but it led to projects like this damn Center. Big shot Sunny Singh wants to lure my athletes up from South Sac. Damn foreigner comes in and tries to ruin what I've had going all these years."

Charlie's scowl relaxed into a smile. "My Tiffany credits your program for getting her that scholarship to play at Duke."

Robert stood and moved aside the lace curtain at one of the windows flanking the narrow marble fireplace. "I still care about this neighborhood even though I sold my house." He hooked the curtain tieback over a fastener on the wall and pointed at a yellow Victorian house next door, visible through the window. "But I found out the buyer was a front for Sunny."

Charlie made a fist, knocked at his chest and coughed before he spoke. "We've got to show them, show everyone what a mistake it is, that arena sparking these other projects. Got to stop the gentrification from spreading."

Victor stood, locked his hands behind his neck and stepped into a hamstring stretch, buckling the thin living room carpet. "What brings you to call us together?" He nodded at Robert and KD still sitting on the sofa.

Charlie placed his open hand against his heart as if pledging allegiance. "This block, where my house you're in right now sits. Sunny Singh wants to tear down the whole block and put up a high-rise tower." He looked each of his friends in the eye. "The planning commission is going to vote on it soon. They might try and take my house by eminent domain, call it blighted."

Victor ran his palms over his black hair. "The government can't do that for a private project. I covered that last year in Public Affairs 101."

Charlie scowled. "I wouldn't put it past them to try. Got to stop this."

"How?" Robert asked. "Can't take protest signs to the capitol steps the way those buffoons did a few summers back. Crazy anarchists citing history and freedom."

"Those neophytes!" Victor smacked the top of the fireplace mantel, causing a few porcelain figurines to tremble.

"Watch yourself," Charlie said. "Mother's china."

"Sorry, Professor." Victor stepped away from the fireplace. "Those freshmen were greenhorns facing off against a motley bunch of counter-punchers. Fighting with knives. Now, my graduate assistant Kaz, there's a real anarchist, intelligent, dedicated."

Charlie sneered. "Need more than a few knives. Want to stop Singh before he snowballs community enthusiasm for this new project of his, so soon after his houses and that Ans Botha Center. Sunny and his promoter Hillary Kiffin, both." He couldn't bring himself to admit his daughter was part of that greedy gang.

He went behind the red velvet sofa and pulled out a

manila folder. "Here's what my cousin Justin and I came up with to educate the public, get them on our side." He opened the folder to reveal printing in block letters across the top margin: NOMO.

Responding to the puzzled faces of the men, he said, "Yes. NOMO. Stands for No Mo. Get it? No. More. No more downtown development."

Victor let out a whoop of laughter. "Good one! NOMO. Echoes DOCO. No more downtown commons. Very clever."

KD frowned. "What will you do with it?" he asked.

Charlie circled the room, waving the folder. "The day before the planning commission meets to take up Sunny's tower proposal, we picket that Ans Botha Center, which Sunny plans to open by the end of the year. Great time to protest yet another project by him."

"Ah," Victor said, "I'll get together with Gabriel in the Art Department. We've been looking for worthwhile extra credit assignments, get students to make signs. Part of American history, protesting."

Charlie smiled. "Justin and I will come out to campus and go over our ideas with you. We need all the help we can get." He closed the folder and set it down. "And we want to make a show of it, get the press to cover it, spotlight the power of the planning commission."

Robert scowled. "Don't see how a few picket signs can stop a boulder from rolling down the hill."

Charlie folded his arms across his chest and stood in front of the fireplace. He put on the grim face he wore to intimidate students. "It. Is. Possible." He started off a word at a time before he built up his pace. "NOMO might not work. I don't want legal beagle Justin to get wind of it, but we might need a Plan B to stop them from ripping up the past and replacing it with outsized concrete boxes no humans need. Keeping things small," Charlie lectured on, "keeping the town the way it should be—might be impossible. Unless," he shouted, flinging out his arms and puffing up his chest, "unless you are willing to join me and blaze a new path."

He was gratified to see the three of them silent, spellbound by his rhetoric, like his students used to be.

Charlie gulped in a big bite of air and held it. His face turned red and took on a sheen of fine sweat that crowned his bald head as well. The scar from his surgery pulsed along his naked scalp. On a controlled exhale, he spoke: "We. Own this town. Not those greedy bastards. Us. Not them. We have to show who's in control."

His friends nodded in time with the rhythm of his words.

Charlie had them now. "It's true, the picketing is a long shot to stop Sunny from tearing down my block. I'll never sell, but others are saying they might. My house will stand alone as an island of sanity in a sea of ruin." Ambrose would have liked that line.

He took a deep breath. "I don't have any definite designs for a Plan B. I need some good minds to help work it out. It could require stepping outside the law."

Victor sat forward and said, "My assistant Kaz might want to join in, Professor."

KD frowned. "I've got a neighbor. Retired military. Been at loose ends lately."

Charlie stood, his heart racing. "This is our town," he said. "They can't take it over. We'll give them plenty to think about before we let them grow more monstrosities."

AFTER HIS PALS WERE GONE, CHARLIE GRATED GINGER root onto a piece of waxed paper, shook it into his flowered teapot and poured in hot water from his kettle. He inhaled the fragrant steam, glad for its warmth on his face. Despite what the doc told him, this might be the winter of his life—his last winter.

He and Justin would go out to the college next week and fine-tune the plans for NOMO picketing. Maybe Victor and Gabriel's students were more clever than the ones Charlie had had to put up with. And picketing might do the trick, dissuade the planning commission from granting Sunny permission to tear down his block. But if it didn't work, now he had something more than fiction to work on. And friends to help him.

CHAPTER TWENTY-SIX

In matters of truth and justice, there is no difference
between large and small problems, for issues
concerning the treatment of people are all the same.

-Albert Einstein

PAYING SCANT ATTENTION TO THE CAR RADIO, CHARLIE
glanced over at Justin, who was leafing through a book
titled *Picketing and Protest*.

"This guy," Justin slapped the front cover of the
book, "collected supreme court decisions on picketing
and demonstrating. Useful for meeting with your guys
out at the college."

Charlie veered onto a side street. He parked in front
of an East Sac mansion in the Fabulous Forties. Where
the rich lived. Too good for his Alkali Flat neighborhood, these folks. Likely the Sac State President lived
here, considering his big salary.

"Getting a damn migraine aura," Charlie said, closing his eyes.

"You get migraines?"

"Weird because it's not the kind of headache that usually comes with brain cancer. I don't get the headache though, just this shimmering black and white pattern in my line of sight."

"Want me to drive?"

"Nah. I'll just sit here. Takes about fifteen minutes for the crazy thing to move past my field of vision. We've got time. Don't have to meet Victor and his guys until four."

Justin nodded. He opened his book back up. "Good suggestions here for how to keep the picketing from spiraling out of control."

Charlie considered marching around the block the Center was on as peaceful enough. He rested with his eyes closed for twenty minutes before he drove out to the college.

"WELCOME, GOOD TO SEE YOU." VICTOR MET THEM IN THE hallway and led them into his walled off portion of a larger space. "Used to be the Department Chair's office before they remodeled," he said. He gestured to the seats across from his desk.

Charlie studied the wall hangings. "Got some nice Royal Chicano art here."

"I remember these guys," Justin said. "We grew up with them. Sorry the movement faded and La Raza Galería Posada store moved down to Old Sac."

"We are simmering, 'on the back burner' as gringos say." Victor flashed his brilliant smile and sat behind his desk. "Got to get the credentials first, then we'll rise again." He laughed. "This is my last semester teaching as a graduate student before I start on my doctorate at University of Toronto. That place is known for turning out a fair percentage of noteworthy anarchists. Our numbers are rising in today's political climate."

He flashed a proud grin and continued. "Got my students on board to help with your project, Professor. Good experience in First Amendment freedom of speech tactics. NOMO you calling it, right?"

Charlie nodded. "That's it. Catchy, yes? Counteract the smart asses with their DOCO."

"Keep it non-violent," said Justin. "Zero in on urban development paid for by the public against the people's wishes. Send a message."

Charlie watched the interplay between the two. It was important to keep the NOMO plan separate from Plan B. Justin would never go along with anything outside the law. Victor was in on both plans. Charlie could trust him to keep them separate.

"Just what Cesar Chavez would have ordered," sang out Victor as he stood to open the door to a man wearing a paint-spattered white shirt. "Meet Gabriel, from the Art Department."

The slim middle-aged man said, "My students have been busy. They have painted signs for some to carry." He nodded at a young woman holding an iPad with a photo of a NOMO sign. "Others will create mini-murals on canvas at the same time they march along. We will let the bright colors of justice inform the hearts of the people."

Charlie's pulse raced. "You talk in the tradition of our cousin Ambrose. Instead of artwork and images, he used his reporter's pen."

Victor nodded. "Last month, I covered the railroad scandals in class. Those nineteenth century railroad barons lorded over the economy. Bierce's articles in the *San Francisco Examiner* stopped the deal that would have let them forget about repaying the taxpayers."

Charlie bobbed his head. "That's us. All of us taxpayers. If we work together, we can make a difference here and now. In Sacramento. Stop the next rip-off, the city helping to pay for the hotel Sunny Singh wants to build right on the block my father grew up on."

Gabriel swiped through dozens of photos on the iPad as the young woman held the tablet steady, her gaze steady as she said, "Take a look. We'll put on a show. Engage the town. March from the Center to City Hall."

Charlie's eyes could barely keep up with the flashing colors of the artwork on the iPad. "Yes! March from the Center past my block and on to City Hall. Get the politicians' attention."

Justin was nodding, a big grin on his face.

This NOMO picketing might make Plan B unnecessary, Charlie hoped.

CHAPTER TWENTY-SEVEN

There may be times when we are powerless to prevent injustice, but there must never be a time when we fail to protest.

-Elie Wiesel

CHARLIE GAZED UP AT THE ROOFTOP OF THE NEARLY completed Ans Botha Center. He had to admit, except for the four-story glass front featuring that slab of climbing wall, there were no frills here—a functional edifice. Still, it stood as one more malignant growth that was killing life as it ought to be.

He scouted the area. Local TV vans were setting up shop. Students gathered on sidewalks, arguing over who got to carry which signs. What could be more educational than practicing freedom of speech? Gabriel's art students showed the extra lengths they'd gone to. Who would have thought of painting king-sized helium balloons for picketing signs? Looked like a moving mural the way the young protestors had arranged mini-posters painted in the La Raza style to play on words and images interactively as they marched down the sidewalk.

NOMO MOWING DOWN
NEIGHBORHOODS

WILL YOUR BLOCK
BE KNOCKED OFF NEXT?

STOP CITY THEFT
OF OUR HISTORY

PEOPLE DROVE BY HONKING THEIR HORNS WITH THUMBS up. Charlie stayed in the background. Until time for his press conference at City Hall, he wanted Justin to be the main NOMO representative, with his distinguished square-jawed and non-threatening appearance. Justin and the students themselves, let them be the voices.

Charlie walked over to where KRAN's Janine Ramsey was interviewing Victor about the role of higher education in urban settings. "Would you say you offer an objective American history class or more of an idealistic view molding the next generation's leaders?"

the reporter asked, holding the microphone toward his face.

"I take a balanced approach. It's a fact, ma'am, that a whole block where La Raza artists worked while their kids played baseball in the fresh air," Victor waved in the direction of Charlie's block, "will be destroyed, excavated as a pit and then caged over by a steel and concrete structure. We want to show that enough is enough. With public support, this Center we are picketing can stand as the last gentrification project."

Charlie smiled. This young man knew how to handle the press. TV monitors showed photos of the Alkali Flat neighborhood in its heyday, even back as far as the 1860s when Charlie's house was built.

"We plead with developers to carry out their wealth-building in places that do not trample the past, nor obliterate the history of the city," Victor said.

Charlie nodded and kept his smile in place in case the cameras were on him. He wanted to be seen as one of the good guys. He *was* one of the good guys.

By lunchtime, civil service workers, members of the press and onlookers had massed near the front of City Hall where Charlie held a press conference. "We need people joining us at the planning commission meeting tomorrow evening," he said, looking somberly into the TV cameras. "Mr. Sunny Singh wants a green light to tear down another block, this time the one my own house sits on. His newcomer money is swamping our old-time values. I tried but could never get my house on the preservation list as a proposed city landmark even though it's older than most and has the Ambrose Bierce history. We need community support so we don't get crushed by big-business bulldozers."

By the end of the afternoon, Charlie went home exhausted but hopeful. The march was all over TV. This picketing might really work, get the message across, halt the massive mowing down of tradition.

CHAPTER TWENTY-EIGHT

EXHORT, *v.* ...to put the conscience of another upon the spit and roast it to a nut-brown discomfort.

-Ambrose Bierce, *The Devil's Dictionary*

CHARLIE STUDIED THE COMMISSIONERS ON THE PLATFORM behind the circular counter in the city council chamber, perched high like divine figures, judging who would go to heaven and who to hell. The ways they got onto the commission in the first place were suspect. In the past, Charlie himself had applied, citing his background in California literature and work with his neighborhood association, but he was not selected.

Sitting close to the podium were members of the local media, keeping track of it all. On the far wall of the chamber sat that damn Hillary Kiffin. She looked so smug in her navy blazer, with her auburn hair pulled back in a bun. So professional. She wouldn't even have to say a word. Charlie knew that staffers had already worked with Sunny's people and laid out their arguments.

The picketing had aroused support for his cause though, and two more people had signed up to give public comments. He just hoped it had changed the public sense of how these endless projects harmed the city. He hoped the resistance to more of the same would have got through to enough of the commissioners.

"On Agenda item number three," intoned Chairman Weatherford after the first two items had taken nearly an hour to process, "do we have the staff report ready?" The staffers always got the first pitch, a chance to set up the conversation the way the big shots wanted it to go. The city staffers were on Singh's side. They were so predictable. Blah blah blah.

A bright-eyed young planner launched into her presentation: "The applicant's mixed-use tower project will bring a fresh face to this blighted block, now filthy with leavings from the homeless, from paraphernalia of drug users, and threatened by aging structures about to crumble and collapse."

Charlie was outraged. Lies, lies, lies. Any problems on the block were due to owners deliberately letting their properties go, thinking they would soon be profiting from Sunny's purchase of their houses.

The young planner continued, "The Preservation Director has reviewed the buildings on this block for historic significance and determined that none of them meet the requirements for listing on the Register of Historic and Cultural Resources."

Charlie nearly choked with anger—how little they understood history.

The staffer clicked through a series of architectural drawings on the overhead projector screens, focused on various elevations of Singh's proposed twenty-story tower. Standing tall, the young woman concluded, "Two months ago, the Subdivision Review Committee voted unanimously to recommend approval of the proposed tower, allowing it to move forward on the condition it be built around any parcels declining to sell."

Charlie's head was throbbing. He nodded to Justin. Finally it was time for their public input.

Justin stepped to the podium and flashed a confident smile. "Thank you for the opportunity to address this issue," he said.

He turned to wave at their half dozen supporters in the audience. "We oppose this project, clearly designed solely to maximize the applicant's profit. It is horrific to consider tearing down this historic block, one of the first in Sacramento after the early flooding taught the lesson of building above basements to ensure safety when the waters rose. The house I grew up in, myself," Justin patted his chest, "along with my cousin Charles," he turned and gestured at Charlie, "that house should be on the preservation list, not on a block to be demolished. It was built by our great grandfather, with his own hands." Justin raised his hands and waggled them back and forth. "This is a block of heritage homes. They need to be restored and reevaluated for preservation. There is plenty of land elsewhere that can be used for high density infill and more hotel rooms to attract event dollars and satisfy the city's updated general plan."

As Justin thanked them and sat down, members of the commission maintained neutral expressions except for Commissioner Tim Kovar, who was nodding with a half-smile on his face. Charlie felt they could count on his support. Kovar was known for his position a few years back against Sunny's housing project, claiming that knocking down old residences to build high density, expensive housing could result in more homeless out on the streets. The man was right.

A young woman Charlie had known since she was a child stepped up to the podium facing the commissioners. She looked up at them with a serious face but said nothing. Charlie admired her self-control as many seconds of her allotted two minutes passed by in silence.

Failing to hide his impatience, Chairman Weatherford cleared his throat loudly. "Did you want to address the commission?"

"I wanted you to hear the sound of silence, first," she said. "I am Josephina, granddaughter of Ernesto Villa, and representing him and many others who are silent today, gone from the earth now. My grandfather never built a house on this block we now find under threat of obliteration. He couldn't afford that, no. But he raised his family in a modest rental there, raised up my father, sent him to school, raised him in the American dream of seeing to it that your children have it better than you did. I am proof of that now, an attorney in private practice in San Francisco. I want that little house he rented, and in which he lived out the dream, to be preserved, not torn down and turned into dust."

Charlie felt warm all over. If only his own daughter had this spirit. He took his turn at the podium. How would he be able to compress his plea into the allotted two minutes?

"Commissioners...My mother told me that the desk in my little bedroom was where our ancestor Ambrose Bierce wrote his last short story in 1914. Over a hundred years ago."

His heart was racing like one of the nail guns hammering up walls of Sunny's condos. He studied the impassive faces of the commissioners before he went on.

"Should the house that this famed writer worked in be torn down before the facts are searched out? He was known to have disappeared in Mexico in 1913. Could he have returned to the California of his long association writing for the *San Francisco Examiner*? Perhaps have hidden away in Sacramento's Alkali Flat? Please vote "No" on this proposal to wipe out a literary mystery. If that's not reason enough to establish my house as an historical landmark, then...then I'm in the wrong world." Charlie's legs were shaking as he walked back to his seat.

A man in a mariachi suit strode to the podium, silver buttons flashing along the sides of his pant legs, a broad-brimmed black and white hat in his hands. "We musicians and artists," he waved his hat towards the others in his group, "we carry in our hearts the suffering and the joy of our culture. This block you want to rip apart and build an anonymous tower on, that piece of land needs instead to be restored, to have its traditions respected, its past recognized and the joy of our culture preserved. No working families would be able to afford the high cost of condos in this tower. You will push more people out onto the streets. Please deny this application."

Those in his group stood and sang the first few lines of "Cielito Lindo." A couple of the commissioners laughed and clapped while others held their faces as if set in stone.

The chairman called for a vote. Long seconds passed.

One at a time, 12 of the 13 commissioners spoke the dreaded word, "Aye."

Charlie couldn't look Justin in the eyes. They had not been able to convince anyone except Kovar. Now Charlie would have to appeal the commissioners' recommendation, bring back the picketing, put pressure on City Hall to back off on Sunny's project.

Still, Charlie had hope his neighborhood might be saved without going to Plan B. It was a thin slice of hope, the same size of hope he held that his brain tumor would shrink.

CHAPTER TWENTY-NINE

Do not be like the cat who wanted a fish but was afraid
to get his paws wet.

-William Shakespeare

VICTOR AND HIS GRADUATE ASSISTANT KAZ ARRIVED AT
Charlie's house first. KD brought along his neighbor
and introduced him as Henrik Bloom, a recent immi-
grant from Sweden after a tour of duty in Afghanistan.
"Guy loves a challenge."

Grim faced, Charlie said, "Let's face it. We got shot
down on the planning commission. Our last chance is
coming up in less than two weeks. There's just a very
slim possibility for the city council to override the plan-
ners. Most all of them are cut from the same cloth. Let's
see what you've come up with." Charlie waved them
into his dining room.

Victor passed around a copy of a blueprint. "Ok, not

sure what you need, Professor, if the second round of picketing doesn't pan out. But I thought it could be useful to cover some basics. I picked the brain of my cousin Louie, owns Linchpin Engineers, up in Truckee. This cousin," Victor said, "he's a little on the edge, knows backchannels for getting the job done, if you know what I mean."

Stone-faced, KD nodded as Victor continued. "I sat with Louie at his computer and went over time-lapse video of construction stages for commercial buildings. He showed me the order of placement in the foundation for the uprights." Victor reached out and picked up the blueprint from the table. "To reverse the process, you place something there," he pointed to a place near the middle, "and half the building falls to the basement."

Charlie stared bug-eyed at Victor over the audacity of the idea. "You're kidding? How could it be that easy?"

"It's the forces coming together at that one exact spot, Louie said, makes it implode." Victor ran his palms over his dark hair and exhaled loudly. "He told me they only do implosions when they can't take a chance on ruining nearby structures. It's all about strategic placement of the explosives—they use dynamite. But he said it could be other explosives." Victor tapped the blueprint. "That's where your buddy over in Chemistry could come in handy, I'm thinking. But maybe for a starter, go with something milder." He looked at Kaz who stared back with a scowl. "Not so dramatic. Set it up when no one's around. Nobody gets hurt. Message delivered."

Kaz stood and pulled his backpack off and pulled out three books. "I say collapse the fucker." He passed around the books. "*The Failure of Greed* and *Capitalism's End* show why. *The Anarchist Cookbook* tells how."

"That might be going too far, too fast," Charlie said.

"Just picking up where Ted Kaczynski left off," Kaz said. "Create Armageddon, start over fresh." He fingered a yellow silk scarf knotted at his throat. "Took my name in his honor."

The others stared at Kaz a moment then looked at each other. Charlie sensed they were surprised to be in a conversation with a man whose hero was the Unabomber.

But KD's neighbor Henrik stood up. "How about a lightweight pressure-cooker type bomb? Fill it with messages instead of blowing up the building? Kind of a warning bomb, so to speak?"

KD nodded. "We can engrave blank dog tags. I've bought 'em for kids in my sports camp." He looked at each man at the table. "We can get stainless steel tags made with chromium, for hardness, withstand a blast."

Charlie leaned forward, excited but unsure if this was a legitimate pathway forward. "Even if Don can help us with the right kind of explosive, it's got to be hard to get into the building and find that key spot, the weak spot, in case we want to do more than messages."

"Got to find someone who worked on the foundation of the Center," said Victor. "How about checking in with the union to see if any guys were laid off, maybe disgruntled?"

"Brilliant. Which union?"

"Don't you have a computer, for Christ's sake?"

"Don't believe in 'em. Do all my writing on paper." Charlie reached back and pulled out a legal pad from the top drawer in the built-in sideboard. "Not that any of my academic articles ever get accepted. But typing them up supplies the department secretary with an extra income—keeps her stimulated, too, and ready to fill me in on the faculty gossip." He started writing on the pad.

KD scratched the stubble on his chin. "I've got a lead on a construction union over in West Sac," he said. "I'll get in touch with him. Guy owes me."

"Let me work on it, too," said Victor. "How the Center was built could be a perfect research project for my Urban Studies students."

Charlie smiled. His skull felt like it could hold the pressure without exploding today. No headache threatened. He invited the men into his kitchen for a beer from his favorite local brewery—it was time to celebrate this kind of progress. And drink to their success—if it all worked as planned. And nobody got hurt. He certainly was not another Ted Kaczynski.

But he did have to make sure Justin didn't catch on.

CHAPTER THIRTY

My first dunk ever was in middle school. We were
playing, me and my church friends, and I dunked it,
and I swear I could not sleep that night.

-Jeremy Lin

IN THE ELDORADO HOTEL BREAKFAST ROOM, WAITING FOR
the waffle maker's beep, Stacy elbowed Keisha and
whispered, "Got your dunk ready?"

Hillary watched as Keisha crouched low, then
sprang high and whipped her arm up, nearly touching
the ceiling before she slammed it down, jamming an
invisible ball into an invisible hoop. "Watch me get back
at Jeremy and Mac."

Claire scowled and dragged her short blond hair
straight back behind her ears. "Stupid boys. Hanging
with 'lotta bunk, girls can't dunk' even after you
showed 'em."

"No video, no proof." Keisha shrugged and picked up a plastic fork to pop a hot waffle off the non-stick surface of the appliance. "Today'll be different." She set the steaming waffle on Stacy's plate and poured more batter onto the hot grids.

Stacy took her plate over to the butter and syrup station. Hillary prayed Keisha could show those arrogant young boys how wrong they were. But dunk attempts often misfired, the ball careening off the hoop instead of going through, leaving a player feeling weak and foolish.

THE BOYS WERE AHEAD BY ONE POINT AS SECONDS counted down at the end of the fourth quarter, most of their bench standing ready to cheer at their victory. The media team was videotaping the game for community services purposes. But zigging and zagging, Claire threaded her way through the boys' defense and flung the ball in to Keisha, who'd slid over under the rim. Max and Jerry double teamed her but she pivoted to the other side, leapt up and slammed the ball into the net a half second before the time clock expired. Coach Tiffany was hoarse from shouting directions but screaming, "Yes, yes, yes!"

A couple of the boys had to be coaxed by their coach before they would give obligatory good sportsmanship handshakes. But Max and Jerry buddied up right away with Keisha and Claire and seemed to be aware that having them on their mixed team would be an advantage.

Hillary considered this as added validation that their girls were truly special. She was proud of the way her daughter made other players better. In the girls locker room, everyone was laughing and crying at the same time. After Tiffany high fived each one of the Devils, she stepped back to address the group. "Due to this win, you will all be placed on teams of mixed boys and girls, scheduled to play against college teams tomorrow," she said. "Best of all, day after that, you will play against rookies from NBA and WNBA teams who are coming for an exhibition game at the Reno Sports Center." The girls strutted around the room, mimicking passing and heaving up basketballs, looking serious and silly at the same time.

HILLARY WAS CONCERNED THE GIRLS NEEDED TO TAKE IT easy, but they were too excited to hang out and wait for dinner and instead wolfed down a few protein bars. Wearing BLACK LIVES MATTER tee shirts, they ignored the frigid temperature to run down the street in the direction of a school basketball court, yelling back that the coach there had invited them to scrimmage with local kids who'd seen the game and were excited at the chance to learn from the Devils.

So young, and the girls were role models already. Hillary must be doing something right as a mother, wasn't she?

CHAPTER THIRTY-ONE

What's in a name?

-Shakespeare

HILLARY AND STACY GOT TO THE HOTEL LOUNGE IN TIME for Happy Hour. Tiffany, already seated at a cocktail table, said, "Our girls are out celebrating the win by helping younger kids with their game."

Hillary laughed. "Claire's really into sharing that Mamba motivation Kobe's been talking up."

Tiffany fanned her face with the bar menu. "I'd have a Sprite if our Devils were here," she said. "Role model you know. Or, if the test showed a line."

Stacy raised her eyebrows. "A line?"

"You know, pregnant. But no bun in the oven and a big win today. Time for red wine." She looked at Hillary. "Good for the heart, yes?"

Hillary nodded. "We're still in the wine grape business." She ordered a bottle of Lodi Zinfandel to share with Tiffany, a light beer for Stacy and sweet potato fries for appetizers.

When the drinks arrived, Hillary toasted, "Here's to our devilishly good Coach!"

Tiffany took a sip and set down her glass. "The girls need to keep up these stellar performances, if they're going to impress old Foggy Bottom."

"Who?" Hillary and Stacy asked at the same time.

"That's what I call him. He's the veteran AAU coach we are stuck with in Sacramento. Among the worst, I'm sorry to say."

"Worst in what way?" asked Hillary.

"The guy cares more about getting his ego stroked than developing players. Can't see potential. He selects big girls for his team, those ready to win tournaments, hardly holds any practice games and forget about teaching them fundamentals."

Hillary pulled her hair back and twisted it into a loose knot. "It will kill those girls if they don't make the team."

Tiffany drained half her drink. "Main problem is anyone can start an AAU team and appoint themselves head coach—old Foggy Bottom did ten years ago, and now he rules our town's team."

Hillary ordered another round of drinks and changed the subject. "Speaking of men in our town, I'm concerned about your father. He's been so public against the Center. It seems like a crusade he's on."

Tiffany picked up a steaming sweet potato fry and waved it around to cool. "He put his heart and soul into stopping the arena, and losing those lawsuits back then built up his outrage for any developments."

Hillary's eyes flashed. "Can't you get him to lay off?"

"He won't listen to me."

"If he keeps up his rantings, I might have to discredit him, remind everyone what happened back at the college. It was before your time, but his nasty disposition got him kicked off Sac State's tenure track."

Tiffany sat up straighter. "He was…" her voice cracked, "always wonderful to me. I'm torn, having him so dead set against what Sunny wants to do. He believes downtown improvements are destroying Sacramento."

"But they're not. The Center alone boosts the whole region." Hillary's voice rose to a higher pitch. "A couple star players from the Sac State Women's team have agreed to celebrate the Center's opening with us. You as a coach know how exciting that is. We don't need your father poisoning the well."

"He wants to leave a legacy, but I'm afraid he's getting weaker and going out of his mind."

Hillary finished the last of her wine and set her glass down with a thump. "If he keeps up his campaign against us, I may be forced to reveal some shocking charges against him."

"What do you mean?"

"My father's unpublished notes show your father drove at least one girl to …" Hillary stood and towered over the seated Tiffany.

"To what?" Tiffany got off her pub chair and looked down on Hillary.

Hillary stood on tip toes, eye to eye with Tiffany. "Her twin said she killed herself."

"That was probably an accusation from a student who couldn't pass his class," Tiffany said, her eyes blazing. "You wouldn't stoop so low!"

Hillary nodded. "I've tried to reach the source of the story, but she's nowhere to be found. Still it fit with what some of us suspected back then. Let your father know it would be best for him to leave the Center alone."

"You're making too much of this." Tiffany regained her friendly manner and she gave Hillary the look of a player on the same team. "I don't think you've got anything to worry about from my poor old sick father. He can't really do anything to hurt the center now."

"The ball's in your court, Tiffany," Hillary said. "Don't lose the game for us."

CHAPTER THIRTY-TWO

GUILT, n. The condition of one who is known to have committed an indiscretion, as distinguished from the state of him who has covered his tracks.

-Ambrose Bierce, *The Devil's Dictionary*

CHARLIE NODDED TO THE SECURITY GUARDS INSIDE THE marble foyer of the library. The two burly men looked casual and friendly but why were they even here? Did someone think the scruffy homeless would barge in and steal books off the shelves? Maybe use them for insulation against the cold wet ground they slept on in Cesar Chavez park across the street?

He was grateful Tiffany had phoned last night and again asked him to curtail his efforts against the Center. When he mounted a vigorous defense, she interrupted and said she had to warn him. Hillary had threatened to release some unpublished interview notes from his students way back when. Now he was more incensed than ever. He certainly never did anything wrong—worked his tail off for those ungrateful students. What all did that blasted Hillary know, anyway? Got those nosy-body genes from her father. But he hadn't been able to eat a bite of breakfast.

He smiled at the guards. Always best to be on good terms with the law. His gut was rumbling and his palms sweaty as he waited near the elevators for Justin.

JUSTIN ARRIVED ON THE DOT OF ELEVEN. "OK, BUDDY, what are we doing here?"

"Support the library, show it's still needed and wanted. A good deal for the taxpayers. Need your expertise, teach me how to use the search engines, use that legal beagle nose, help me track down some kind of dirty linen on holier-than-thou Hillary Broome Kiffin."

"May I ask why we're so hot on her trail?" Justin wore his habitual half-smile of inquiry. "She's just the mouthpiece of Sunny Singh, right?"

"Didn't you watch Sactown Saturday? Hillary's the woman whose father wrote that piece about me back in the 90s. Prissy little English major back then, one of my students, thought she was so smart with her daddy dean of the Capitol Press Corps. Hinted at his article on the TV show."

"So what's the harm?"

"I don't trust her, she could rattle some cages, show me in a bad light. Her father's story led to my being denied tenure at Sac State. I went home and looked for my copy of his story but can't find it. Think it had a lot of quotes from students and staff. Not flattering. Tiffany said she hinted at lies from other students too, that never got published."

"Really?" Justin unbuttoned his coat and smoothed his pin-striped vest over his ample torso. "But that was, what, well over twenty years ago."

"I don't want that woman threatening me with what she might imagine." Charlie scowled. "Got to preserve my sliver of legacy."

"Legacy?"

"You know, I have to get Sunny's tower denied by city council. Get my house on the preservation list. Think of the future."

"So what does Hillary have on you? What all did you do back then? You realize your lawyer has to know the truth."

Charlie rubbed his fingertips over the skin where his eyebrows used to be. Damn things itched now that the follicles might be coming back to life. "It wasn't that big a deal, even though the tenure committee objected, but now..." He coughed.

"Now?"

"You know all this *Me Too* business. Women believe they can file charges retroactively. Throw their accusations at any man they think they can get money or revenge out of."

With squinted eyes, Justin stared at Charlie. "You don't have any secrets in your closet, cousin? Nothing to tell your lawyer?"

"Just the honest truth I wrote on some of their

papers, might not sound politically correct in today's world."

"That's all?"

"I might have said a few things in my office, but they were just the facts."

Justin frowned. "Okay, what's your plan for today?"

"Got to find some dirt on Hillary. Something to bring her to her senses. Turn the tables. For example, why she doesn't use that god damn Broome last name she used to be so proud of?"

"Let's do it," said Justin, hitting the elevator button.

On the second floor, they sat at adjacent computers. Justin showed Charlie how to run background checks of several kinds. Charlie focused on both Hillary Broome and Hillary Kiffin, looking through character references. He kept at it for an hour but came up with nothing.

After he used the bathroom, he walked the stacks, observing several homeless men sleeping in corners of the library. Damn nice of the librarians not to blow the whistle, let the guys grab a few winks. This is what tax money should go for, caring for these who've lost their way, not more damn foolish buildings to make the rich richer.

He returned to where Justin was looking through county, state, and federal records for arrests, convictions of felonies and misdemeanors, court records, warrants and even sex offenses. "Nothing. I'll try scouting educational references," Justin said. "Don't give up yet."

At his computer, Charlie hunted for another twenty minutes with no luck. He began to doze off.

Justin elbowed Charlie awake and pointed to his computer screen. "Think I've got something on her. Columbia University student newspaper. Take a look."

Charlie leaned over and there it was in headlines: PLAGIARISM AT COLUMBIA.

"Hot damn," whispered Charlie as he read. The article was mostly about a faculty member who'd been caught using the work of another professor as his own, but it included academic dishonesty charges against three graduate students, as well. Hillary Broome was named. She'd been found guilty of plagiarizing in her final project for her Master's in Journalism.

Charlie pointed to the story and whispered, "There's just one line about her in this story. They considered revoking her degree but decided against it due to the brevity of her offense."

"Still, this is damaging information she won't want made public." Justin said and gave a rare grin. "Get her to back down on the benefits of that Center, admit how it might damage the ambience of the neighborhood, agree with you that Sunny's proposed tower could be even worse for Alkali Flat."

Justin printed out a couple copies of the article and emailed it to himself, too.

"Now, I've mastered the computer search function, let me run a check on myself, while I'm at it," Charlie said. He found a few stories in *The Sacramento Bee* on his role with STOP, Sacramento Taxpayers Opposed to Pork, and their lawsuits to stop the robbery of the public treasury. Also some articles in the *Suttertown News* on his presentations before the Preservation Commission and the Planning Commission.

Then there was that piece in the *LA Chronicle* series about bad professors. Nothing else about his career as a professor at Sac State or the community colleges in the region. His cheeks burned with shame that he'd been reduced to driving from one campus to another to barely make ends meet, financially.

Freeway flyers they were called, the part-time adjunct faculty, the peons laboring for dimes on the dollars in the factories of the mind. What a far piece he'd fallen, like the dying soldier in cousin Ambrose's Owl Creek story.

Still, today he'd dug up a way to combat and maybe shut down that witchy woman promoter working to spread destruction.

Charlie stiffened his spine, clear headed and ready for the long game.

CHAPTER THIRTY-THREE

If at first you don't succeed, try, try again.

-Thomas H. Palmer

HILLARY FOUND CLAIRE UP BEFORE DAWN, SEATED AT THE dining room table, scrawling numbers onto a sheet of white paper with a red marker. Ed was out of town on emergency security meetings. It was up to her to support Claire on this long-awaited day, time to try out for an elite Amateur Athletic Union team. Getting selected on the River City Wonders would let Claire leapfrog ahead of school and recreation teams, get a chance to be placed on the watch list of Notre Dame scouts.

Hillary leaned against the dining room doorframe and spoke in a low voice. "You might want to try some yoga. It's a good way to calm yourself, get over the jitters."

Claire ignored her, finished writing and held up the paper. "I always win if the score is more than 40 for our side." She looked straight at her mother. "I just visualized it being 45 to 28."

Hillary stretched tall, her feet at shoulder width, her arms down at her sides, palms facing forward. "It's not hard. You let the energy flow through your body, activate your hands so they feel dynamic." She wiggled her fingers. "Consider their relationship to the ball." She raised her eyebrows and smiled.

Claire crumpled the paper into a ball. "It's no use." She darted past Hillary and ran into the kitchen. "Tryout is drills anyway, not really a game." She tossed the paper ball into the trash bin and got a box of Wheaties out of the cupboard. "Dad's gone and coaches are not allowed to come." She slammed the cereal box onto the kitchen counter and got out a bowl and spoon. "You know I hate that crazy yoga you do."

Hillary closed her eyes and stood in the pose for a long minute. Too nervous to eat, she sipped at her coffee as Claire downed cereal, topped with raisins and walnuts. At least she was starting out well with the most important meal of the day.

Hillary put energy bars into Claire's gym bag and filled her water bottle before they got on the road to pick up Stacy and Keisha for the ride to City College.

Inside the gym, the odor of mingled sweat and rubber assaulted Hillary's nostrils. She spotted a man down at the far end who must be the one Tiffany called Old Foggy Bottom. A short, heavyset man with dark eyes, he was dressed in gray sweat pants and a bright blue River City Wonders sweatshirt. A commanding presence, he stood erect, clipboard in hand, gesturing to a couple of assistants, young men who looked like college players. Hillary felt a surge of apprehension—chunky and solid as a bear standing upright, the man looked like he hadn't a soft spot anywhere. Like he had no clue what these youngsters were going through.

Claire and Keisha set their gym bags on a bench and joined the dozens of other girls on the floor. Hillary had seen most of them before, from school games and recreation leagues, wearing the various colors of their teams. They were moving their bodies through warm-up stretches, Claire and Kee Kee doing the ones Tiffany had taught the Devils.

Old Foggy Bottom, as Hillary'd begun thinking of him, walked out to the middle of the court, a whistle clamped between his teeth, his plump lips alternately pursing and retracting around the stainless steel whistle. The girls clustered around him and came to attention as he blew his whistle a few more short blasts. "Call me Coach Robeson," he boomed.

Hillary wondered where he was from, making three syllables out of his name, Robe-ah-son, delivered with a slight Southern accent.

He continued, "I'm the man giving you a chance to cut in line, head for the big time. We've developed half a dozen players who've gone on to full scholarship rides at the best colleges and two of them are now playing in the WNBA."

He paced back and forth, knocking his knuckles against his clipboard for emphasis. "Get yourself ready for drills where you can show off your talent. Bottom line is your dribbling and shooting." He mimicked the actions with his free hand. "After that, passing and cutting for layups."

He clutched the clipboard with both hands again and held it at arms' length. "Due to limited resources, we cannot offer a spot to every player. I'll be keeping track of each move you make today." He slapped the front side of the clipboard. "Got your records right here. Girls not making it will be on 'standby' and get referred to camps and clinics to prepare for next year. We will push our selected players to be champions, not just wannabes. Our season runs from January through July, and consists of 25 games. We want girls who are ready to win. Our team will compete in 'Jam on it Nationals' in Las Vegas, 'Coca Cola Nationals' in Anaheim, and the 'Nike Hoop Summit' in Portland. That's where the college scouts will find you. The younger the better, from their angle."

He nodded to his assistants who grabbed basketballs from racks at the side of the court and threw them out onto the floor. "Bottom line," he growled, "the ten girls showing most promise will scrimmage near the end of the day. Except for rebounds, don't worry about defense—get a good offense going and that takes care of the 'D.'"

It sure was like Tiffany had said—bottom line this, bottom line that. Hillary was glad to hear him discount defense since that was not Claire's strength.

"If you don't make it on the scrimmage, watch and learn." He wiped his sweaty brow with the back of his hand. "Parents you gotta leave now. You can pick up your girls at 4:00 pm sharp. Those who've made the team will be wearing their new RCW jerseys."

A white-haired woman raised her hand to ask a question, but the coach ignored her. Hillary and Stacy left the gym. Hillary was as worried as the others looked, as if their girls' lives were at stake.

AT 3:50, HILLARY PULLED INTO THE CITY COLLEGE parking lot.

The inside door to the gym was locked. She and Stacy paced the foyer along with the other parents and grandparents.

Hillary wished Ed was in town, she felt the need of his upbeat presence. She turned to Stacy, who was listening to a white-haired woman standing next to her. It was the same woman who'd wanted to ask a question that morning. "I can't take this pressure at my age," whispered the woman, tears pooling and ready to run down her cheeks. "How do you do it?"

Stacy gritted her teeth before she said, "This ain't such a much."

The woman drew back. "How can you say that? My granddaughter Megan said she was ready to jump from Golden Gate Bridge if she wasn't selected."

"Girl doesn't mean it. Got to take it in stride," said Stacy. "Not much to this when you've seen way worse, honey." The woman pulled a tissue from her handbag and blotted at the tears running down her cheeks.

A man nearby patted her on the shoulder said,

"There's more to life than basketball. Kid's self-esteem should not depend on a game."

Hillary envied his serenity. She tried to melt the icy lump in her belly over what rejection might do to her Claire, but the fear wouldn't let go.

AT 4:04 THE DOORS WERE FLUNG OPEN TO REVEAL A cluster of laughing girls wearing bright blue RCW jerseys.

A few behind them were somber-faced and still wearing their school and recreation club jerseys. With slumped shoulders they made their way to retrieve their bags from the side of the gym.

Hillary spotted Keisha wearing a blue RCW jersey and, right next to her, there was Claire still in the red Devil's uniform she'd worn that morning. Hillary's heart sank while at the same time she found herself grinning at Keisha.

Claire stood near, smiling and clutching a white bib with blue ties flying from the corners. "Coach let me and Megan," she pointed to a tall redhead standing next to the woman with the white hair, "be the two reserves. If anyone has to drop out of the Wonders, whichever reserve does best in the final school game gets to be on the Wonders. Isn't that great, Mom! I know I can take our team to a win."

Hillary felt awash in emotion—a new hope in her heart, a new fear in her belly.

Could this be the daughter she knew? Calling the outcome great?

CHAPTER THIRTY-FOUR

The good old days, when each idea had an owner, are gone forever.

-Paulo Coelho

IN THE RAV4, CLAIRE WAS CHATTERING ABOUT GETTING TO go after school to the music department along with Keisha. The new teacher was letting students come in and try out the different drums, see if they wanted to take any up in the spring semester. He was letting them take home drumsticks and brushes to practice on their own. Hillary was relieved at how happy her daughter sounded.

Back at home, Hillary stared out the window at the bare grape vines, dormant now in December. Al Perkins over at Speedy Soles had called, concerned about the demonstrators gathering this morning at the Center. He asked her to put his sponsorship on hold.

She drove downtown. There were double the number of demonstrators. It looked like artists from the La Raza Center had swollen the ranks of student and NOMO volunteers. The stark red and black United Farm Worker flags added to the drama of the signs and murals.

Her ring tone belted out its rendition of "We are the Champions." Hillary glanced at her phone. The screen showed it was Paul at Veganese North restaurant. He'd been threatening to back out of his contract. She couldn't afford to lose more sponsors. She let the call go to message, parked a block away from the Center and sat in her Rav4 observing the colorful spectacle.

There was Charlie, dressed in a fleece-lined jacket and a black cap with ear flaps, leading a line of students clutching strings anchoring blue and white helium balloons flying wild above their heads. They headed down the block and toward the corner.

Behind them, a stocky man in a mariachi suit walked backwards, waving his arms directing a half dozen muralists who danced along, brushing paint on a swath of canvas strung between two poles.

At first, it looked like they were painting random graffiti until Hillary made out the letters *N O* and *M O* taking shape in fancy fonts.

On another sheet of canvas, artists were painting *Dia de Los Muertos* skeleton figures fighting men in business suits using dollar signs as swords. It reminded Hillary of battle scenes from ancient cultures. Gorgeous as art. Deadly as public relations.

She got out of her car and approached Charlie as he

returned from circling the block. "This Center is a project you should support, Charlie," she shouted. "It'll give girls opportunities your daughter Tiffany had to fight for."

He ignored her.

She tried a different tack. "You should be picketing the block your house sits on, the block you're trying to save, not this one."

That got his attention. "That is my legacy, don't want people tramping all over it," he yelled.

"What kind of legacy is this? Undermining a project that will lift up our young people?"

"We'll take our cause," he waved his arms in a circle indicating the picketers, "into city council chambers tomorrow, see if they have the spine to stand up to the greedy guts." He shook his finger at her. "And to their flunkies like you."

She went back to the car and phoned Sunny. "What are we going to do?"

"Anything you can offer to lure him off the case?"

"It's a legacy thing with him to save his run-down neighborhood. He's taking it out on our Center, wants to stop your tower going up on his block. Thinks he's got a chance to hold back the ocean. Guy looks like he's orchestrating a funeral procession. I wonder…" Her voice faded away.

"What?"

"Let me run this by Roger, my boss when I was ghostwriting. He runs his publishing company from San Francisco. See if he can offer Charlie a book deal on the history of Alkali Flat, tempt him with a better legacy than ruining our Center."

On the phone, Roger questioned the practical aspects. "The guy is sick? Cancer? How could he take on a book project?"

"He knows his neighborhood inside and out and worships his ancestor, the famous Ambrose Bierce. I bet Charlie could come up with a draft you could get one of your ghostwriters to whip into shape." The more she thought about it, the more appealing the bribe sounded.

Roger laughed. "You want to write it?"

"Too busy with the Center."

"I'll ask Jennifer. She just finished our biography on The Donald. It's selling like crazy. Go ahead and offer your guy a deal."

Working from her downtown Singh Properties office, she located Charlie's home address in their data system and then wrote up a contract outlining an agreement. Charlie would halt the picketing in exchange for a book deal with Roger's company, complete with a professional ghostwriter to edit and polish the manuscript.

She drove the blocks towards Charlie's house. When she passed the Center, he and his supporters were still marching along as home-bound commuter traffic began to back up in the downtown. Drivers honked their horns, some with thumbs up and others down. This picketing was sure to be hurting the Center's approval rating. It had to stop.

At Charlie's, she walked up the wooden steps, paint peeling off the bannister railings and the screen door frame. She slid the envelope into a slot between the door jamb and the wooden screen door.

This had to do the trick.

THAT EVENING HILLARY'S CELL RANG WHILE SHE AND ED were listening to Claire demonstrate how the drum brushes she'd borrowed from the new music teacher worked, using the glass-topped coffee table in the living room.

It was Charlie. "What the fuck do you think I'm made of, lady?"

Hillary felt like she'd been punched in the face. She took her phone into her office and shut the door. "I thought you'd like a chance to leave a real legacy, something positive, not ripping apart what we're doing to build the future."

"That Center Sunny built has already demolished a part our history, the block my friends and I played on, where artists and music makers gathered, now leveled to the ground and replaced."

"If you don't take the book offer, I'll have no choice but to show you for who you are, make public my father's interview notes about what kind of professor you were. And I mean a story the editors left out of the article, of a girl named Birdie, who killed herself over your verbal assaults. Do you remember 'Birdie, Birdie, Birdie'?"

Silence.

Then sounds like Charlie was choking. Hillary waited.

He spat out, "You wouldn't dare."

"Try me."

"You're such a goodie two shoes, lady. What would people think if they knew about your plagiarism?"

Her breath caught in her throat. How did he know about that?

"Yes, ma'am, inquiring minds have found out. Now, here's my counterproposal. You join us in our NOMO campaign. At the city council meeting tomorrow. You speak up against Sunny's proposal to crush my block with his tower."

She couldn't think of what to say.

"Pretty little fix you're in now, eh?"

She got a mental image of him grinning, looking like some kind of evil imp. "I'll...I'll..."

"You'll what?"

"I'll think of something, you can be sure of that, Professor Poison." She disconnected. Long-suppressed guilt and shame over her own 'P' problem flooded her face with a hot flush.

Maybe now was the time to come out and confess publicly. She should have done this long ago, instead of hiding her byline as a ghost writer and now a public relations consultant, using Ed's last name.

It would be hard, humiliating even. But she could write a mea culpa for the Columbia newspaper, include the timeline. Her blunder had happened the day her father died. It was more complicated than that, of course, but students needed help threading their way around emotional topics, getting over panic attacks at assignments, understanding the concept and value of intellectual property. She could start a program for high school and college students, call it P. P. P. for Plagiarism Prevention Program. That would take the sting out of Charlie's threat. Go a long way to pay for her sins.

She laughed. Even Claire had been in better spirits today, tapping out rhythms with that drum brush she'd brought home from school. Maybe it wasn't so urgent that Hillary find her long-lost mother right away. She could let it go until after the Center was safely opened.

CHAPTER THIRTY-FIVE

ALLIANCE, n. In…politics, the union of two thieves
who have their hands so deeply inserted in each other's
pocket that they cannot separately plunder a third.

-Ambrose Bierce, *The Devil's Dictionary*

CHARLIE, JUSTIN AND VICTOR WALKED FROM CHARLIE'S
house to City Hall for the six o'clock start of the meeting. Charlie's planning commission appeal was listed
near the middle of the city council agenda. Neither
Hillary nor anyone else from Singh Properties was
present. Charlie clenched his jaw. They must feel
they've got this in the bag.

THE MAYOR WAS FLANKED BY FOUR COUNCIL MEMBERS ON
each side, the nine of them seated on that same raised
semi-circular platform the planning commissioners

used, as if to lord it over members of the public seated below.

The meeting dragged on in its snail's pace. Justin scanned through his printout of the agenda. He elbowed Charlie, pointed to a consent calendar item and whispered, "A couple hundred thousand for artwork by the Royal Chicano Air Force, to hang in Golden 1." He brought up the item on his iPad, clicked into the details and whispered, "…consistent with the City's goals of enhancing livability in the community."

"Ha," grumbled Charlie. "What community? Instead of preserving the living sites of the muralists, just hang their work up on an arena wall. Make it seem like those activists support urban destruction."

A council member frowned at the noise of their conversation. Justin muttered, "Funding for the artwork will be from cigarette and hotel tax."

Charlie looked over at Justin's iPad screen. "At least their legacy gets honored, unlike for the Ambrose Bierce House."

AFTER THE STAFF SET OUT THE PLANNING COMMISSION recommendation in favor of Sunny's tower project, complete with architectural drawings shown on the flat screens, Charlie's appeal came up for public comments. He was surprised to see a matronly, olive-skinned woman step ahead of him to the lectern. He recalled her showing up a few times at the neighborhood association meetings. But she'd never said a word.

Now she spoke. "I am Shua. My name means truth

and justice." She looked up at the half-circle of decision makers. "Justice. Two days ago, we were thrown out of our flat by our landlord," she said in a low voice. "We had nowhere to go, nowhere. I just came from visiting my four children in the receiving home because they are not allowed at the adult shelter out on Bannon Street. Don't let this happen," her voice trembled. "...to other families. Please." She turned and wiped her cheeks with a wad of tissue before she walked slowly up the aisle and out of the council chambers.

Anger rose to heat Charlie's face. How was she managing? How had she been able to get herself to this meeting? He stepped up to the lectern and looked at each face in the semi-circle of powerful people above him. Then he waved his arm back in the direction of the doors the woman had left through. "That mother is just one of hundreds of poor people thrown out on the streets by greedy slumlords, eager to cash in on selling their property to make way for projects like Sunny's. You can put a stop to this cruel growth. Bring some justice to our corner of the town."

Charlie hurried on, so as to not run out of his two-minute time allotment. "Mr. Singh's twenty-story tower will further dwarf the neighborhood. We already had to deal with the 25-story tower the state put up for the Environmental Protection Agency, which cuts off our sunlight with its long shadow. The mixed-use tower near the arena only got approval for 16 stories. How much justice is there in allowing Singh's twenty stories to surround a historic house like mine on a small corner of what's left in a residential neighborhood? I urge you to vote 'yes' on my appeal."

He sat down, his head pounding, barely able to hear Justin take his turn at the lectern, warning if the appeal was turned down and Sunny's proposal went forward, it would damage the value of Charlie's property despite not actually taking it. In that case, Justin said, he would file a Government Abuse of Property lawsuit and argue its relevance to this situation.

Victor addressed the council next. "I'm Victor Ramirez. I grew up in this neighborhood, flourished here among the diversity. Now I'm proud to be teaching history out at Sacramento State University. My book on the damage gentrification is wreaking all over America, and specifically on the landscape of Sacramento, is scheduled for release in the spring. Urban renewal is fine in its place, but it's time for a return to the basics, to the human scale before the little people got swamped and swallowed up under the politicians and billionaires reaching for the sky. I urge you to consider the assault this tower would have on Alkali Flat and approve Mr. Bierce's appeal against it."

The council woman representing downtown spoke first. "It could be prudent to table this item and request further study by staff for the impact on housing in Alkali Flat."

Another member agreed with her and noted Charlie and Justin's comments had got through to him. "I'm not in favor of turning Sacramento into Los Angeles North in terms of more homeless on the streets and numbers of high rise buildings."

An energetic young member argued the council should support the planning commission's recommendation and deny the appeal. She held her microphone close to her lips and said, "Let's get real. This proposal will allow Mr. Bierce to keep his corner home while the proposed tower borders the side and back of it, similar to how the convention center cradles old St. Paul's church and contextualizes the past inside the sweep of the future. Mr. Singh's tower is even better designed to fit unobtrusively into the neighborhood due to its staircase design leading gradually to the taller sections of the building. Plus, it's so environmentally sound." Other members nodded in agreement.

The vote was 7-2 against Charlie's appeal. Sunny now could move forward with his tower, surround Mother's house. Grim-faced, Charlie and his friends left City Hall. It was bitter cold outside, but Charlie could feel a hot rock lodged at the base of his skull.

Justin buttoned up his gray topcoat. "I'll get that Government Abuse of Property lawsuit filed," said Justin. "It's been an intriguing challenge to write up, keep the character of the neighborhood intact. This thing isn't over." Square-jawed and bareheaded, he strode away toward his office.

Victor walked with Charlie back to his house. "Justin's legal maneuvers take forever and don't even work," Charlie said. "I can't let my block be destroyed without Hillary's damn Center sharing the pain." Charlie kept to himself other reasons for his ire. Shut that frigging Hillary down, and what she thinks she knows about me way back when.

Victor kicked brittle sycamore leaves off the sidewalk. "Call KD. Let's fine tune Plan B. I know Kaz is waiting in the wings, impatient with your jumping through these government hoops. He's hot to trot." He turned to look at Charlie. "May be too hot to handle."

"I can control rebelling students." Charlie had to believe he still could.

CHAPTER THIRTY-SIX

Technological progress has merely provided us with more efficient means for going backwards.

-Aldous Huxley

CHARLIE ADDRESSED THE MEN SITTING AROUND HIS DINING room table. "Now that city hall has failed us, I want to deliver a communication on New Year's Day at the Center. Present a perfect vision for 2020 laid out before the guests at the Grand Opening."

Kaz was emphatic about the need to collapse the Center. "Forget about a vision. Send an unmistakable message. Three c4 packages in the right place will bring it down. You set it to go off when the building is empty, say an hour before the doors open, you show it's your ideals that count and not killings." He pounded the table with his fist. "Or, for even more impact, an hour after it opens."

KD shook his head. "There's no need to go that far. We can pack one c4 block with dog tags. Buy them blank, the chemical resistant aluminum kind. They'll deliver our messages. Use a Dremel, print 'em with 'NOMO in 2020' and like that."

Kaz pulled at corners of a yellow scarf tied around his neck and scowled as KD kept up his spiel. "A few tags might get twisted but most of them get scattered like New Year's Eve confetti in the Center's entry, just got to have the timing and the placement perfect."

"Perfect, yes." Charlie stared at KD.

Kaz took off his yellow scarf and placed it on the table. "Let me tell you about perfect. The secret to using any explosive is location, location, location. You have to place it in the correct location in order to get what you want out of it. I've studied buildings. Three blocks of c4 can shatter the strategic main pillar. If you can't do that, you're not going to get much other than," he whipped his scarf off the table and whirled it in the air, "smoke."

KD scowled. "Taking down the building is overkill, man. We can make custom embossed tags. Could even use lightweight pressed board, pine or spruce or like that. Dremel can engrave wood or aluminum. Easy. Safe. No one gets hurt, everyone is impacted."

Charlie nodded. "I prefer a word war rather than exploding the building itself. My family tradition is to use words as weapons. How can we sneak in on New Year's Eve and place it to go off at the noontime Grand Opening? Shower the messages onto the crowd as they come in. A new kind of Happy New Year!" Charlie laughed, then frowned. "What if we get caught sneaking in with the package?"

Victor stood. "I've been learning to fly drones, preparing for the social justice doctoral program in Canada. You can slip inside the building, Charlie, take along a detonator made of a watch. In case outside security stops you, you won't have any explosives on you. When you're inside, text me, and I'll fly the drone over and release the package onto the roof for you."

"A watch?"

"There's a simple Casio that works perfect for this. Trust me, Charlie. We'll have it all ready to go for you. But where would be the best place to put the package?"

Charlie rubbed his forehead. "There is a climbing wall inside the lobby. Could we put it on top of the wall? Let the tags shower down like confetti?"

Victor pursed his lips. "I've got a lead on a worker that was fired from that Ans Botha. Going to talk to him about union injustice tomorrow. He might help out on placement. Want to come along, Professor?"

Charlie agreed to go with Victor the next day.

KD adjusted his suspenders over his plaid wool shirt and put on his bomber jacket. "Good plan."

As Kaz hauled his backpack onto his shoulder, he shook his head. "Those tags won't be strong enough communication to stop the greedy developers, I warn you." He tied his yellow scarf back around his neck. "But, I'll go along, Charlie, keep a lookout, be your grunt labor after you figure out where to place the package."

Charlie nodded. He wasn't certain how far he could trust Kaz but sure didn't want to be out at midnight all alone hiding some kind of newfangled device made out of a watch under his coat.

CHAPTER THIRTY-SEVEN

Knowledge is power.

-Francis Bacon

CHARLIE AND VICTOR DROVE OUT IN VICTOR'S BEATER Chevy to call on Tim Wheeler. Victor took the narrow "I" street bridge across the Sacramento River into Broderick. Much farther and they'd have been in the vast rice fields of Yolo County.

As he drove, Victor explained to Charlie how he found Tim. "I've been researching an article for the *Labor Studies Journal*. Got as far as interviewing a building trades president on the benefits of membership but couldn't get him to open up on their problems. On my way out," Victor said, "I presented a made-up case of union injustice to the hottie at the counter, hoping she'd share something she knew. She commiserated and told me about a worker named Tim, who claimed he'd been taken off a project unfairly. It wasn't that hard to get his name from her." Victor laughed. "After I asked for her number."

"You devil," said Charlie.

"All's fair, etc. She gave me the guy's phone number, too."

"Wish I still was in the running," said Charlie. "That cheating Charlotte wasted my best years."

"Tim's an ironworker," said Victor. "I called him and he complained he damn sure hadn't celebrated Labor Day after getting booted off the job, and here's the best part, it was the Ans Botha Center he'd been working on. He's been out of work since September. Said he'd have plenty to say."

Victor threaded his car through a mixed zone section of small businesses, hay and grain brokers and modest homes. He parked in front of a faded-blue house of a nondescript style and they walked up a cracked side-walk. Charlie pushed on the doorbell but didn't hear any buzzing or chimes, so he knuckled a rat-a-tat-tat on a section of the front door where the paint wasn't peeling.

Nothing.

The unmistakable sound of a televised basketball game blasted from inside the house. He walked across the dead grass to a front window, partly covered with flower-print drapes drawn nearly closed. He rapped on the glass.

The front door shot open and there stood a red-bearded giant of a man, clutching a bomber-sized bottle of Red King Ale. "Come on in, y'all," he boomed. "I'm Tim."

Charlie and Victor squeezed their way past Tim and entered the living room. "Have a seat," Tim gestured with his ale bottle toward a black sofa with a few creases and cracks in the leather.

"Knicks and Bulls," he said waving the bottle toward the big screen TV before plunking himself down in a black recliner. "Been following sports real close this year," he said, scowling. "Lots of free time since I got blackballed by that damn Sunny Singh." He polished off the last of his beer and hollered out, "Annabelle!" He turned to Charlie and Victor. "She got the day off."

A petite and very pregnant brunette appeared at the door to what Charlie assumed was the kitchen. She stood at attention and said nothing.

"Baby, another Red King for me and drinks for my friends, here." He nodded in Charlie and Victor's direction. "Been busy with more than just TV sports." He turned to stare at Annabelle's belly. "That's my boy in there."

"Let me help," said Charlie, and he followed Annabelle into the kitchen. "We'll just have anything."

Without a word, she reached up into a cupboard, took out three matching plastic tumblers and placed them on a flimsy bamboo tray. She grabbed a pitcher of iced tea from the white refrigerator and handed it to Charlie. "We used to rent a nice house in Bridgeway Lakes, over in West Sac," she murmured. "But since Big Dog got the boot..." She gave a weak smile. "We're making the best of it." She pulled out a bottle of Red King.

As they returned to the living room, Charlie noticed Tim had turned the TV sound down and was waving his arms in the air. He reached out to grab the bottle Annabelle was handing him.

"We started," he bellowed, "by placing that first vertical and shaping the steel skeleton." He threw his head back and poured beer down his throat, the muscles working to handle a couple of great gulps. He wiped his mouth with the back of his hand.

Victor nodded, a frown on his face. "First one. How many are there in total?"

"Dozens, maybe, never counted 'em, just manhandled 'em in and got 'em all welded. Some of 'em though are key uprights. Someone wants to take down that place, only have to locate those main buggers."

Charlie frowned at Victor and wondered if he'd brought up this topic? Charlie turned to Tim. "We don't want to collapse it," said Charlie. "We just want to place a package of messages to shower down on the crowd in the main entry when it opens on New Year's Day. Need to know where to place that kind of package."

His mouth shut, Tim stared at Charlie.

Victor cleared his throat and nodded toward Charlie, "As I said, my friend here, he's writing a novel where terrorists take down Staples Center. We had just wondered how that could be accomplished for a smaller place like Ans Botha."

Tim raised his bushy red eyebrows and showed a gap-toothed smile. He took a swig from his bottle.

"Now there's a solid idea!" he roared. "Those buildings for sports are mostly empty space. You situate your explosives in the right places, produce a turning moment of the right force, huff and puff and blow their house down." He laughed so hard he began choking.

Charlie and Victor sat silent, waiting for him to continue.

"We done a bang-up job, round the clock, working our tails off. Big fucking deal Sunny and his supervisors made of it. Got on tv and like that. Bragged on the best times were coming."

He yelled for another beer and Annabelle followed his orders. After he'd taken a few swallows, he sat quiet for a few seconds, shaking his head. "Big shots from city hall and the company came to treat us workers to lunch, was what they said. Food trucks it was, not bad sandwiches, really."

He stood and stretched his arms up nearly touching the ceiling. "It was the building's 'brain' the big shots were all fired up about. The computers, fancy electronics. Said the Center was going to monitor the young players, learn when they had concussions—building's going to know who people are, what they like."

Tim punched one fist into the other as he carried on, growing louder by the word. "The big shot Sunny, he rubbed me the wrong way. I didn't make a secret of it, sonofabitch, damn foreigner. He musta heard me 'cause the next week, random testing called me in, found me positive. But I had nothing for months, maybe weeks anyway."

He polished off his ale. "Got me kicked out of the

union. Saw me as a loser. Me!" Tim tossed his empty bottle toward the wall. Charlie was glad to see it miss the window by a foot and settle onto the carpet, a few ale bubbles settling into the dingy fibers.

"Yes, sir." Tim switched his TV to YouTube. "Better yet though, you key in the security code, place your packages at strategic columns in the basement level and your building will come down on itself. Did you see them twin towers in Vegas couple years back? Here, look at this." He played a video showing implosions of two outdated Riviera Hotel towers. As the buildings collapsed, Tim punched his fist in the air and bellowed a laugh.

Charlie coughed. "On the other hand, how would someone know where to put a package so it would rain down dog tags in the front lobby?"

Tim spoke slowly, looking right at Charlie. "You wanna be chickenshit." Tim shook his head. "Use the rock-climbing wall, backs up that damn tall entry, pulley system hauls stuff to the top. Now you haul your package of tags up to the top of that climbing wall in the lobby, use them pulleys they got rigged up for the climbers safety." He swatted the ceiling, causing loose flakes of dingy white paint to snow down. He looked at Annabelle. "Woman, bring me a beer."

As Annabelle tiptoed over and bent to pick up the bottle on the rug, her hair fell forward. Charlie could see the bruise at the side of her neck. Charlie shuddered. In his mind, the use of physical force should be reserved as a last resort only and never toward a woman.

Tim turned the TV back to his NBA game. Charlie gathered up courage and asked, "Any clue on the key code numbers they use to get into the building?"

"Honchos always use their own birthdates," he growled. "That Sunny's a Scorpio, just like me. Got big stingers." Tim frowned at the sight of Annabelle with a rag in her hand, squatted down and scrubbing at the carpet. "Where's that beer?" He turned the volume up high.

Charlie and Victor let themselves out. Plan B was shaping up the way Charlie hoped it would.

PART III

CHAPTER THIRTY-EIGHT

A safe fairyland is untrue to all worlds.

-J. R. R. Tolkien

CLAIRE CRUNCHED AWAY ON HER WHEATIES.

Hillary was thrilled—it looked like her levelheaded Claire was back to stay.

"Honey girl." Hillary poured herself some cereal and stood to get a few strawberries to slice on top. "I did some research to set your mind at ease, you know, after Margie Ann's mom suffered that horrible injury from the shooting?"

Claire stared at her and kept chewing.

"Well, the chances of losing both parents while a person is under 18 are just one in a million. Your dad and I are here for you, so you don't need to worry about a backup granny on standby." Hillary sliced a fat berry in half and watched the two parts fall onto her cereal.

Claire jumped up. "I want one. I miss Grannie Sarah. I never got close to Dad's mom. Keek has Stacy. Don't you understand!" She slammed her half-full bowl of cereal down into the sink, a fountain of milk splashing up onto the counter at the same time the ceramic bowl split in two. "I want one! Is your mother dead, too?"

Claire ran out of the room, leaving Hillary standing at the kitchen counter, her arms leaden. Holy Mary, deliver me from this, I pray. Bring my girl back to her true self.

HILLARY WAS ASTONISHED. IN TIME FOR THIS PIVOTAL game, her prayer had been answered. Was this going to be the new normal, like watching a living ping pong game? Claire had bounced back to her upbeat self. Her moodiness could be a sign of a serious problem, but Hillary felt sure this was not the time to address the issue. Jumpy inside as a steel ball in a pinball machine, she held herself steady and prepared her new camcorder.

It was weird the way Foggy Bottom had set it up. The outcome of today's basketball game would decide which of the two girls he'd named as reserves would get onto the AAU Wonders team—the tall redhead Megan or her own petite Claire.

Hillary shot footage of the girls getting ready for the game, happy with the results she'd had with her new JVC video cam with 1080 high-def. It was plenty good enough for YouTube.

The girl's bathroom was crammed with young women of all sizes and colors. There was not enough room at this school for a separate space for each team. Claire's pals on the Devils were decked out in their red uniforms and had added matching red headbands and wrist bands, for good luck. They were hyped and talking trash in earshot of the Cheetahs even though they'd been warned not to by Coach Tiffany. "Trash talkers are benched talkers" was her mantra. "Let your play be your voice, on the court."

Keisha nodded, her hair styled in six-inch sunburst spirals to intimidate opponents by lifting her towering stature even higher. She glared in the direction of the Cheetahs. The winning team's best players would go on to compete in the tryouts for Northern California's high school programs. But more important to Hillary, either Claire or Megan would be selected as a full member of the AAU Wonders team, and the other girl would no longer even be a reserve. Megan had never taken the game as seriously as Claire. Hillary felt confident her daughter would be the winner.

Keisha was yelling at the captain of the Cheetahs: "We're a lock—get ready to crumble." She gave a one-arm hug to Stacy who had squeezed into the crowded bathroom and edged her way over to plant a kiss on Keisha's cheek. "Me and my Bibi here, we believe in our Wonder Woman, Claire the killer point guard!" she screamed and reached out to high five Claire.

"You can't guard me," yelled Megan, the red-headed Cheetahs center, a full six inches shorter than Keisha but towering over Claire. "Believe you're Kobe Bryant's Gianna?" Megan shouted into Claire's face.

"Who you think you are?" Keisha shot back. "Why you talking? How you get this far?" Keisha punched Claire lightly on the shoulder. "Come on, sister, let's get this party started."

Hillary got it on video. Sunny wanted coverage of games in other places before the Center opened, use the before and after film for marketing the ambitious programs he envisioned for the Center. Hillary would edit it down later to the most tension-filled two minutes for a YouTube basketball trailer. It was good to be doing something other than sitting and watching helplessly as her daughter played this critical game.

OUT IN THE GYM, HILLARY SPOTTED ED HOLDING A PLACE for her on the top row of bleachers. She climbed up and high-fived him and the other excited Devils' parents. When the gym doors opened and Margie Ann's mother was rolled in, Hillary felt a stab of sorrow. She heard that Mary had nearly recovered from gunshot wounds to her arm and leg, but lately suffered a severe setback, a mysterious infection. She was being pushed into the gym by Margie Ann's grandmother, Rosa. They stopped a few feet inside the doors. Stacy had saved a place for them near the end, where there was room for the wheelchair.

Hillary's eyes locked on Claire who stood at center court, holding the basketball and gazing steadily at

Rosa and the wheelchair. What was her daughter thinking?

The familiar rhythm as Claire turned to dribble the ball on the court, along with squeaks from shoes darting across the hardwood, reassured Hillary This would be the good future for Claire. It had to be. What might come after today?

Hillary let herself daydream: high school, college—maybe not Notre Dame but some good basketball college—then a career for Claire. A women's team might be born again in Sacramento. That would be big time. If it ever happened. Some diehard Monarchs fans had suggested picketing the Golden 1 Center if the owners kept ignoring the promise they made when keeping the Kings in town. Was it really a promise or only an alluring fantasy?

AT HALFTIME, THE DEVILS HELD A COMFORTABLE 25-18 lead. Not huge but good enough to think a win could be in their pocket. If they won, Claire would get onto the AAU Wonders, if not then Megan would be chosen.

The Cheetahs came back hard in the second half and produced four lead changes before the last minute, when the Devils led by a single point.

With twenty seconds left, Keisha shouted to her grandmother "This one's for you, Bibi," as she leaped up to block what looked to be a Cheetahs' game winning basket. Keisha heaved the ball in a half-court pass to Claire for the crucial last possession.

Hillary filmed her daughter catching the ball. But

rather than run with it, Claire walked it up, staring at Rosa sitting next to Mary in her wheelchair.

Hillary's blood froze. Claire was moving like her feet were stuck in a tub of honey. When she got the ball to the other end, she lost her handle on it and turned it over to Megan, the Cheetahs' red-headed center. Megan picked it up and dashed back to the other end, scoring at the last milli-second and winning the game.

"Oh my God!" Ed stood with his mouth hanging open in disbelief. Hillary couldn't say a word. She leaned against Ed to keep herself from collapsing, the camcorder lens pointed at the floor, still rolling.

IN SHOCK ALONG WITH OTHER DEVILS' FANS, HILLARY forced herself to go to the girls bathroom, maybe get footage of the way they were handling the loss if it wasn't too horrible. Her daughter stood in the middle of other Devils gathered around her, Keisha ramrod tall behind them, looking like a warrior on the Serengeti plains. Serious. Ready for another hunt on another day. But Claire with her gray eyes looked pale in the extreme.

Claire was talking to her teammates. "This is a sisterhood, a family. I let you down," she said, tears welling at the corners of her eyes. "It's my fault we won't get to the high school tryouts." Her lower lip quivered, and she hung her head. Margie Ann and another girl started crying. Keisha remained grim-faced, staring with narrowed eyes into the Devils' unknown future. Stacy wore an expression of sorrow, her hands raised at each side acknowledging the present circumstance.

Hillary slid the camera strap over her shoulder and held out her arms toward Claire. But her daughter ran to Stacy, who gathered her in a long embrace. Hillary stood stock still before she remembered the video cam still rolling and pointed at the floor. She turned it off then went to find Ed. Claire would go with them, as long as they were both there. The two of them would take her home and comfort her.

WHEN THEY GOT HOME, CLAIRE ROUGH-HOUSED WITH THE bouncing Daisy and Darius for a good five minutes before she went to her bedroom without saying goodnight.

In the living room, Ed paced the floor. "I'm worried sick over her meltdown. She seemed like in a trance at seeing Rosa pushing that wheelchair."

Hillary stared blankly at the photos on the mantle. "She seemed so ready. I thought this game would bring a reward for so many things she's invested her body and soul into."

Ed shook his head. "We've got to give her some time."

Hillary waited for a half hour before she went down the hall and knocked on Claire's bedroom door.

"Honey?"

Silence except for a rustle of some kind.

"Princess?"

Silence.

Ed walked up behind Hillary. He tapped on the door. "Claire?"

The bedroom lock turned and Claire opened her door.

"I'm sorry," Claire said, holding her arms up and clutching at her red Devils' wristband. "I thought it would make me feel better, but…"

For a couple seconds, they all stared at a thin red line running wet diagonally along the inside of Claire's arm toward her elbow. Down on the carpet, lay a wire drum brush.

She started sobbing and fell into Ed's open arms. Hillary reached to form a clumsy group hug around the two of them.

CHAPTER THIRTY-NINE

To be great we need to win games we aren't supposed to win.

-Julius Erving II, Dr. J.

THEY WALKED AS AN AWKWARD THREESOME INTO THE bathroom. Claire was half sobbing and half laughing hysterically. Ed seated her at the vanity bench. Hillary forced herself to inspect Claire's wrist. There were scratches across the inner surface of her wrist, but only one was bleeding. Hillary held her daughter's arm under a slow stream of water for a minute and washed the scratches with soap. "They don't look deep."

She wound soft gauze around Claire's wrist and taped it in place as Ed said in a calm tone, "We're here to listen."

Claire hiccupped. "Yup. I'm sorry, I really am." She

shook her head. "I'm going to have to go see one of those counselors, aren't I." She frowned.

"Couldn't hurt. Might help. Let's try some hot chocolate for now," said Hillary.

They got Claire to bed with gentle hugs and kisses, and her agreement to go see Dr. Bolden next week.

HILLARY STOOD IN THE KITCHEN RINSING OUT THE HOT chocolate cups and putting them into the dishwasher, her stomach burning. Ed went out to the garage for a minute and came back in to stand behind her. He slipped his hands around her waist. She turned to face him.

He had a thick manila envelope clutched under his arm, pressed against his side. "It's going to take more than a counselor, you know that. Here's the bundle Walt put together," he said in a husky tone. With his free hand, he reached to smooth loose strands of hair, dark auburn now from sweat, off her face.

"How about a drink?" She put on a bright smile, reached for the Irish whiskey bottle and waved it up in a salute. "It's a Jameson night." He nodded. She mixed him a whiskey and water and one of her own.

In the living room, she lifted one of the drapes off its tieback and let it fall to the floor, shutting out the dark winter, then did the other side, buying time, weighted with worry. There was no way out.

She sat on the old velvet sofa, in her favorite place at the end near the Tiffany lamp. She was shaking, her hands trembling, the ice cubes tinkling in her glass. The manila packet still clutched under his arm, Ed sat in the corduroy club chair at right angles to the sofa and took a slug of his drink. He closed his eyes for several seconds then leaned forward, pulled the packet from under his arm and set it on the coffee table.

This was the man she loved and could trust, who had her best interests at heart. She stared at his long lean face as she took a few swallows. This was going to be it. She sat straight and rigid, feeling like a tower of glass, about to be shattered.

He tapped the top of the packet. "Looks like she pretty much definitely goes by the name Paisley."

Hillary started laughing and choking simultaneously. "Pretty much definitely. From a flowerchild bride named Joanne to a full-fledged artistic soul Paisley." Hillary couldn't stop a string of quiet sobs. Ed sighed, his lips pursed, nodding and waiting. She stood and walked in circles in front of the fireplace, suddenly silent. She grabbed a poker and thrust it into the charred remnants of last week's fire. "Paisley. Like that awful cloth she made." She jabbed the half-burnt log and stabbed at its cold blackness until it broke in two. "Go on."

"Well, she's still an artist, so that made it easier for Walt, but…"

Hillary held her breath.

"But she's not in Tahiti anymore. You know, where that post card came from, right?"

Hillary nodded and waited, but he did, too. "So where is she?"

He cleared his throat. "Well, she was in Mumbai for

a long time."

Hillary's eyes widened. "India?" She gulped down half her drink. Maybe the woman would be too far away for a chance at finding her. Never have to really take her on. Hillary could feel the whiskey uncoiling her nerves, and lengthening the fibers of her muscles from the tight hold she kept on them.

"Yeah," Ed carried on. "Seems she moved around for years with some man, an artist named Bill Williams, used to teach at Sac State. Ever hear of him?"

Hillary shook her head, feeling drained. "Might, can't remember the name."

Ed stood, took her glass and walked out of the room. She could hear him in the kitchen refreshing their drinks. What was the name of that man Daddy used to shout out from down the hallway back in Carmichael, waking her in the night from her teen aged nightmares?

Ed returned. "Hard to believe, but it looks like now…" He handed her a fresh whiskey and water. "She might be in San Francisco."

A cold flash knifed through the veins of Hillary's arms and settled in her chest. She took a deep breath and held her glass to her hot cheek. "Tell me she's not that close," she whispered.

"That's what I'm least sure of."

"Why?"

"She's moved around a lot in recent years. There are five addresses for her. Some in California but others…" He patted the packet. "Walt's got the details here. Did a helluva job. Don't know if she's homeless or what." He closed his fingers into a fist and bounced it against his lips.

Hillary sagged forward and rested her chin on the edge of her glass tumbler. She closed her eyes and sat in silence a few moments, picturing the blood trickling down Claire's arm. She set her glass on the coffee table, straightened and threw her shoulders back, exhaling loudly as from an invisible cigarette. "It's time."

Ed nodded. "I can't get away now and Walt's tied up, as well, so you may need to do some sleuthing, yourself, Chickadee. I can find someone to work with you."

She took a deep breath and let it out slowly. "I can do this," she said, frowning and looking Ed straight in the eye.

"Do you really want to go it alone? Maybe wait 'til I can get away—do it together?"

"I'm ready." She raised her glass in a toast. "Here's to climbing the mountain. Get a grandma for our girl." She drained the last of her drink. "How bad can it be?"

She picked up Walt's packet and slid out a photo.

It was a picture of a woman with curly hair as white as a spring cloud and dressed in an orange print sari. The woman was setting a banana on a tray in front of a golden statue of a four-armed elephant with a broken tusk. "Ganesh, I've seen him before." She smiled.

This was what the dreams had been about. She waved the photo around as if it were wet and she needed to air dry it. "Paisley, always with the colorful, the offbeat, the broken. Always outside the lines." She pressed her lips together and began to weep.

Ed sat next to her on the velvet sofa and slid his hand behind her back, turning her to face him. "It's late now. Save the rest of the packet for tomorrow morning." He handed her his big white handkerchief.

CHAPTER FORTY

Life is about timing.

-Carl Lewis

Ed slid the manila envelope across the dining room table to Hillary as if they were playing air hockey. He went back to the stove where he was cooking, one of the ways he tried to relax on the weekends from the stress of his work.

She opened the large envelope, fanning the contents out into a wide arc across the table. On top were maps of Hawaii and India, and then a few scattered photos that appeared to summarize the forty years since she'd last seen her mother. A black and white snapshot as Hillary most clearly remembered her, young and slim with flowing blond hair, looking like she did in the sewing basket photo. Another with a patterned fabric wrapped around her waist, a white, five-petaled flower tucked behind her left ear. Then a plumper version of her mother with salt and pepper hair, wearing an orchid lei and standing in front of a painting of Ganesh. Ganesh! What was he there for? Hillary's stomach did flip flops as she set that photo aside. And last, a woman with stark white hair, long and flowing over her shoulders. Had she grown thin again?

"Walt's been working on this for some time, hasn't he?" She kept her tone light to mask her mixed feelings —partly annoyed and feeling betrayed Ed had worked on this without telling her, yet now grateful to sort through these clues.

"Kept him occupied since he retired." Ed slid a spatula under the edge of an omelet. He tilted the pan until the uncooked egg mixture seeped underneath for its turn on the sizzling skillet.

She patted the maps and set them aside. "Well, I'm sure not going to Hawaii, and forget about India." She turned to thumbing through Walt's stapled reports and pulled one out. She set it down with a thump, her eyes wide. "California is plenty to deal with. These photos in here look like she could be close by, in midtown right here." Her heart beat in uneven rhythms and she tried to breathe with her belly to steady herself. "Could she have come back to Sacramento?"

"I don't think so, Chickadee. I stopped by a couple of those places and talked to some of the gallery folks. Showed 'em her picture, an image Walt created in Photoshop, with a tool that shows what people look like as they age." He flipped half of the omelet over a ham and green pepper filling and tapped it lightly with the spatula. "Nobody's seen anyone who looks like her."

Hillary cleared space on the table for their breakfast and shifted her attention to the meal. She poured coffee and set mugs next to their plates, now filled with Ed's Denver omelets and buttered rye toast. "I'm so lucky to have you!" She embraced her husband. "Detective to the max and now a chef!" The Farm to Fork theme she'd help create for the campaign to market downtown commons had inspired Ed to learn to cook.

Later while he did the dishes, she went back to Walt's reports. The pages on top gave the name Hillary remembered her mother by—Joanna Helen Broome, born in Sacramento's Sutter Memorial Hospital, December 21, 1952. Walt had clipped a Zodiac sign to the page and a description of Sagittarius: November 22 – December 21, independent and flighty, bold and truthful, will say what is on their mind, even if it crushes your very soul. Scatter-brained, spontaneous and impulsive, adventurous and fascinating, can't settle down and stick to monotony and routine, not happy unless pursuing the next daydream."

Hillary felt bowled over by the description. It sounded so right on. Her mother was just eighteen when Hillary was born, after a whirlwind courtship by the insistent young journalist, Jake Broome.

Joanna Helen Broome. Sagittarius. Also clipped to Walt's report were more photos. Joanna in a protest demonstration, an anti-war hippy, make love not war with flowers in her hair. Then another, shot with her standing in the doorway of her little studio in the back yard of the Carmichael house. Her mother wore a gauzy top with a daisy chain loosely binding her long straight hair. Hillary loved it the few times her mother sat with her on the back lawn and wove wreaths out of flowers for her, too. Once or twice.

In another photo, her mother held an artist's palette to one side like a waiter at a fancy restaurant, offering blobs of color to eat. Her mother's other hand held a brush in the air like a conductor's baton, ready to come down on a large white canvas propped on an easel. Hillary had been afraid to go inside that tiny cottage in the yard, her mother's studio, splattered with paint and fabrics, every inch taken up with something or other. It was worse when her mother started letting sparrows fly in and out and nest in the corners of the ceiling.

"How did Walt get these pictures?"

Ed was scrubbing the omelet pan and pretending not to hear her.

"Ed, I'm asking you a question. How does Walt happen to have these photos?"

"The man has lots of friends in lots of places. Sometimes, it's better not to know, in this private eye business." He held up the dripping pan. "Let's just say I trust him. And you should too." He shook the pan in her direction...

Hillary turned back to the reports. The next two gave her mother a different name: Paisley Joan. That was it. Just two first names, no last name. Paisley. Then it was true. Such a frilly and scalloped image, random dots all over the place. Unsteady, ungrounded. Hillary felt heavier than ever. The images, now all in color, showed her mother moving her home a lot and with a different man by her side in each place. A few in Tahiti, then in a Mumbai art gallery, and in three places in Hawaii. One photo showed her in front of a shop in Kona pointing at "Paisley Joan" lettered in gold on the storefront window.

About halfway through the stack of reports was the address of a warehouse in Oakland, cubicles of spaces inhabited by garishly dressed off-beat looking characters. Walt had paper clipped a newspaper story on a similar place that had burned to the ground a few years before. He'd scrawled "This is not where she was said to have been living."

Near the bottom of the reports was an address of a condo in the old Hills Brothers Coffee building and a note that she might have been seen selling fabrics in a street fair in San Francisco, on Embarcadero across from the Ferry Building, near the foot of the Bay Bridge.

Ed finished the dishes and stood behind her, rubbing her shoulders as she sat slumped over the mound of papers and pictures. "You might be better off looking in Oakland, but none of the artist quarters are all that safe. I'd want to go with you there. Why not try San Francisco Art Market today? Near the Hyatt Regency across from the Ferry Building."

"She was so picky about the art shows she would enter, only those her art teacher approved of." Hillary felt herself grow hot with anger and shame. That teacher was the man her mother had run off with. She could picture him hovering around her mother at gallery openings, a bearded man wearing a shiny vest, congratulating her father for marrying such a talented artist. Hillary felt the fire of betrayal scorch her again. She leaned back against Ed's cool fingers. "It's hard to believe she could have sunk so low and ended up in a tourist trap selling her work."

Ed kept kneading. "Sometimes you find excellent photographers and jewelers offering their works there. It's not just cheap trinkets for sale."

San Francisco by the bay, wild and crazy. Home of creative chaos. It gave Hillary the jitters during the few times she'd been there. Could her mother be there? "Ok, I'll drive to the City, you take care of Claire." She frowned up at Ed who leaned to kiss her. "Got it covered. Text me as you go along, Chickadee."

On Google, she found reasonably priced parking a few blocks from the Ferry Building. Light traffic for a Friday mid-morning got her there in an hour and a half, feeling queasy the whole time and listening to meditation music to stay calm. She parked and walked toward the landmark clock tower of the Ferry Building, grateful for this bracing sunny and cold day. Barely noticing pigeons pecking at crumbs, she made her way along the brick sidewalk edging the Hyatt Regency, studying the face of each vendor lining the curb. Just before getting to Embarcadero, she came upon the cluster of tents freelancers had set up for the day. Cries of seagulls vying for leftovers from food stalls punctuated the steady traffic noise.

Her head was spinning as she made her way

through the Justin Herman Plaza. Swaths of water poured from the immense and boxy Vaillancourt Fountain and made her think of giant concrete worms, morphed into squared off tubes and bleeding clear fluids. She wound her way through the narrow aisles between the tents. Feeling lightheaded and sick, she checked out the face of each vendor, even the men, afraid to miss any chance to find her mother. At a booth strung with tee shirt tops and dresses, tote bags of canvas in neutral and black, she stopped to admire images of zoo animals—lions, giraffes and elephants—some tees and totes decorated with black and white faces wreathed in dreadlocks. But there was no face anywhere like the one she was looking for.

The next booth was loaded with yarn bracelets for tourists, each with a different name woven into it, neat and tedious. This would certainly not be her mother's work. Those block-lettered bracelets were opposite of what she remembered her mother creating. She moved on to a booth with tie dyed wall hangings. But in it, the woman dunking a hunk of fabric into a pan of dye was not even as old as Hillary. Disappointed, she moved on.

Popup tents and scrawny winter tree branches cast jagged shadows on the plaza ground. She looked for signs in fanciful scripts or artistic logos announcing the artist's name, but most booths had none except for a "MY TIE DYE HAND MADE" tent run by an Asian couple.

One artist had a unicycle chained to a lamppost. An older and very heavy woman sat on a folding chair, wrapped in a hooded jacket, facing a flimsy portable easel that looked like a giant three-legged spider. She was intent on painting, her lips pressed together in concentration, ignoring potential customers as they passed. Hillary crouched down and got pretty close before she made sure this was not her mother, and the woman didn't even glance away from her work. Would her mother ignore her, too?

Hillary spotted a series of tote bags hanging from the top edge of a booth, decorated in tear-drops and dots outlined with tiny scalloped edges. A charge of recognition hit her over this paisley design. But two young men behind the counter gazed at one another with smiling eyes before they turned to her. Their designs were just coincidence.

Hillary shivered. The day was growing cold and foggy. The brick pathway had changed to speckled squares of granite. She shuddered. It would be good to finish up here and get a latte inside the Ferry Building before going home.

A failure. No mother today. That was all right. She would come back to San Francisco and try that condo address another day. Now she could make it home in time for dinner with Claire. Find out what happened with Dr. Sherie Bolden at school today.

CHAPTER FORTY-ONE

The beginning of knowledge is the discovery of
something we do not understand.

-Frank Herbert

INSIDE THE FERRY BUILDING, HILLARY SAT AND SAVORED A
cup of hot chocolate at a small-batch chocolatier. She
bought a can of their special blend to take home for
Claire.

On her way back to the parking lot feeling revived,
she searched again for a Paisley Joan sign. Or even a
petite white-haired woman. As she was about to give
up, she spotted a popup canopy at the end of a row, its
top edge flying swaths of fabrics in bright colors, its
side open. At the front corner on a round platform
stood an elephant sculpture a couple feet tall. Hillary
gasped. Ganesh. Looked like it was made of bronze.
Why would the Hindu idol be here? God of gateways,

she recalled Sunny's description. Gateways for luck with new enterprises. Maybe her luck was turning.

Behind the front counter stood a petite woman with silvery hair streaked with blue and pinned with gold hair clips. She was fussing with a bulky printed scarf draped around a display stick figure. The woman raised her glasses and bent to peer under the scarf to inspect something.

Hillary stared. The scarf looked so much like the black and red paisley cloth her mother designed and made into clothing for her wear in the second grade. Hillary had come to hate it, even as a child sensing it didn't go with her copper hair and generous scattering of freckles. But her mother had to have it her way. Artistic temperament, Daddy had called it. After she ran off, he added some adjectives in front of the word "artistic." Selfish. Egotistical. Insane.

It must be her.

Was it her?

Hillary studied the woman's hands. Her blue veins showed how the years may have changed her, but her fingers had a distinctive look. Each telltale baby finger reached to half the length of the ring finger. It must be her.

Now that she might have found her mother, what would she say? She squared her shoulders, sucked in a breath of cold air and stepped to the counter, senses alert. The space reminded her of an exotic Seven Eleven, the countertop stacked with folded fabrics and hanging on a back wall, paintings of women and flowers in the style of Gauguin.

Tourists with cell phones chattered in foreign languages as they snapped selfies in the colorful market place. Hillary studied the woman. Except for her glasses, white hair streaked with blue and hollows in her pale cheeks, the woman looked like Claire. How had Hillary not seen the resemblance before?

The woman adjusted the silky gold sari she wore and waved at Hillary. "Hi, there," she said. "I'm Paisley." She flashed a smile, so much like Claire's that it took Hillary's breath away. "Please feel free to look around. I carry art and fabrics from all over Polynesia and the Far East. Some already sewn into these free-flowing caftans." She shook out a square of material and held out to the side. "Are you looking for anything in particular, dear?"

Looking for anything. Dear. Hillary's throat constricted. She sucked in a deep breath. "Just looking."

"How about a sari like this one?" The woman smoothed her hand across her chest along the orange disk borders of the gold sari. "They're not that hard to wrap. A complimentary handout goes with it." Her face looked open and inviting, as if Hillary were a welcome new customer. "Or, I could show you how to make the pleats in front, if you have the time."

Hillary's heart clattered in her throat. Time. If I have the time. What about all the time that's passed us by? If you really are her.

Losing her nerve, Hillary pivoted on the hard surface of the bricks toward the parking lot. Yet as her other foot hit the ground, she could almost feel Ganesh seem to stretch out his trunk toward her. She felt paralyzed, and on impulse, she turned and looked back.

The woman stood staring at her from under the shade of her canvas tent at the open side of the canopy. Hillary looked down at the brick where Ganesh sat on a short platform. A sign in front of him read A NEW BEGINNING FOR YOUR GARDEN?

Her elephant nightmare flashed into Hillary's mind. His trunk had been pointed toward her, and his hand with its palm facing forward.

A tall man walking by stopped to nod down at the statue. "Willst du das für deinen Garten?" The blond woman alongside him sang out, "Überhaupt nicht!" and aimed her camera at him. Other tourists pointed and laughed.

Hillary's blood drained from her face. Unsteady, she stood nearer the elephant. "Are you Joanna Broome?" she whispered.

"Broome?" The woman stepped toward her, swayed and reached to hold onto the frame of a painting. "Broome?" She cast a vacant look at Hillary. "Who's asking?" She stepped out from under the canopy.

Hillary clamped her jaws shut in disbelief. Paisley didn't know her own daughter.

The hours, weeks and years of caged hurt and anger, of grinding her teeth in her sleep, ignited inside Hillary's clenched jaws. Searing heat shot down her throat into her chest and raced along her arms. She threw her hands in the air and screamed in a voice she didn't hear as her own, "You don't know who I am?"

The petite woman lifted her glasses and peered at

Hillary. She narrowed her eyes, poked her head out like a turtle's and suddenly rushed forward. As she came closer, she stumbled and pitched forward.

Hillary crouched to catch her. Time slowed.

The woman fell.

Hillary was too late.

The woman hit the side of her head on Ganesh, rolled over and lay inert on the bricks.

A thread of red coursed through her silvery hair at the temple.

Her eyes riveted on the woman, Hillary screamed, "Call 911, call a doctor!"

CHAPTER FORTY-TWO

Blood is thicker than water.

-Ancient English Proverb

HILLARY'S MIND REELED FROM THE SHOCK OF THE accident. Tourists gathered near the fallen woman, still bleeding from her head. No one moved to touch her. They wanted to know what happened. "Was ist passiert?" asked the German man. Hillary shook her head, glumly. He and his wife frowned and tsk-tsked over the elephant, but the sculpture looked just as before, his bronze surfaces glowing with an exotic yet innocent radiance. Hillary stood dazed and irrational, suspecting Ganesh had been somehow involved in the incident.

Sirens blared help was on the way. Emergency technicians parted the crowd and bent to work on the unresponsive woman. Hillary felt horrible, guilty as sin. Could her outburst have led to the woman's fall?

One of the EMTs asked what happened. Hillary told him the woman had been walking toward her and had seemed to stumble and fall and hit her head on the elephant sculpture. Hillary left off the part that she'd been screaming at the woman.

The techs worked on the woman for some minutes, stopped the flow of blood, but were not able to bring the woman around. They transported her unconscious to the waiting ambulance.

Hillary, not sure if she wanted to or not, asked if she could ride along. The driver said their company allowed only family in their emergency vehicles. He said they were taking the woman to San Francisco General and got the name Paisley Joan from Hillary, but she didn't say she was her daughter.

Hillary was relieved not to have to give any other information nor take responsibility for the canopy full of merchandise. She assumed someone would take care of it. This was not the time to worry about details like that she told herself.

In her foggy state of mind, she had a hard time recalling the direction where she'd parked her car a few hours ago. After a couple wrong turns, she made her way back to the right parking lot. Some minutes passed before she recovered herself enough to text Ed.

may have found paisley
bad accident
on way to hospital

She plugged her phone into her car charger and with its GPS assistance, she managed to thread her way through the city to San Francisco General. Parking was another story, and it took three tries before she got found a spot in the right lot. Following the path from the lot to the ER felt like walking a labyrinth, knowing you would end up in the right place but not knowing how.

Finally, she got to the waiting room front desk. She waited behind a line painted on the asphalt floor, second in line after an old man in a wheelchair. When it was her turn, she stepped up to the window. "I'm here about an older woman—well not all that old but—she came by ambulance, bleeding and unconscious. She had blue hair. Well, not blue but kind of silvery blue. Blood in her hair. Where is she?"

"And who are you?" The man behind the thick window was in scrubs but Hillary couldn't read his name tag, her anxiety clouding her perception.

"I'm her daughter." The man poked at several keys on his keyboard, frowning. It was taking too long— where was her mother? At last he stopped, and said, "Good, we need information to get her admitted. First your information." Hillary found herself able to think and speak clearly.

"Now, your mother's name and address?" The clerk held his hands over his keyboard, waiting.

"Her name?" Hillary stammered out, "P-p-paisley. Paisley Joan." She held her breath. Was that the right name? The clerk punched in a few seconds, then asked, "Last name?"

"Joan," she laughed. "She's got a first name as her

last name." Sounded crazy but then others had done that, too. Some had just one name like Prince. She stood feeling numb as if time had stopped but the man was typing fast.

"Birthdate?"

Hillary spat out, "It's today. December 21, 1952." Shocked that it was at the tip of her tongue after all these years. Nearly forty years apart. She had to hold the counter to stop herself from swaying, fainting.

"Address?"

"I, well, I..." What was she going to say? "We haven't been in touch lately, so I've not got her address, actually." Her heart pounded and she felt faint. "Not got it memorized, I mean. Not sure...where she lives now."

"No current address? What's the last known?"

"Um..." What could she say? She held up Walt's packet and jiggled it near his face. "I've got it in here if you could wait a minute."

"Take a seat," he pointed at the standing room only waiting room, "and come back when you're ready." He waved her away and nodded at the young man in a wheelchair behind her.

Hillary took the only empty seat in the crowded room, forced to sit next to a child of about four or five who was coughing and crying.

She slid the papers out of the packet.

It had been almost an hour since the petite woman had fallen. What was happening in there? That was a lot of blood. But head wounds bleed a lot she recalled hearing. What if she...

Hillary shook her head and tried to stop worrying but thoughts kept creeping in. Paisley Joan couldn't die before...Before what? Before Hillary got a chance to rip her up and down for running out on her and never contacting her all these years? For slicing off that part of her soul? Before begging her to live and be the grandmother Claire seemed obsessed with having? Hillary's throat tightened with guilt and remorse .

Walt had been so thorough—how had he learned all this? But there were two San Francisco addresses. Which one was the real thing? Ok, name, Paisley, and no longer Joanna Helen Broome. Nor even Paisley Broome. She must go only by Paisley Joan now, but her tent hadn't any name sign.

What had come over her to scream at her mother that way? Cause her to fall? Maybe die?

If it was her mother.

Hillary thumbed one of the addresses into her phone. Showed just a few blocks from the Ferry Building. Could her mother live so close by? The other address was way south, practically to the airport.

Surely the hospital wouldn't run an address check, would they? How could Paisley afford to live in the upmarket blocks around the Embarcadero?

She returned to the clerk's desk and gave the address south of the city, the one near the airport.

"We'll call you back up soon," said the clerk, but suddenly changed his directions to her. "Hit the button by the door and go on back."

Hillary kept her eyes straight ahead as she walked

past curtained off alcoves of patients toward what looked like a nursing station.

"I'm here with Paisley," she addressed a woman with a lanyard decorated with a huge RN on her chest. The nurse looked at her with a vacant stare. "Paisley. Joan is her last name," Hillary said, her nerves alert and tingling all over her body like goose pimples gone wild. "An old woman with blue hair, came in an hour ago, bleeding." The nurse at the counter, iPad in hand, waved Hillary down to the far end. "We need her medical history. Now. Date of birth?"

"Well," Hillary said, trying to remember what she knew about her mother. If this woman was her mother. "She had me when she was 18 years old. Today is her birthday, December 21, 1952." The nurse typed in the information fast and looked up. "And...? Allergies? Surgeries?"

Wasn't there that time with appendicitis they used to talk about? Or was that her father? "Maybe an appendectomy."

"What else?"

Hillary frowned. "I can't think of anything else now. How is she?"

"She's in surgery. Have a seat in there," she said and pointed to a door marked FAMILY WAITING ROOM. "We'll update you when we can."

Hillary texted Ed.

think I found her she fell
now in hospital surgery
What the?
how is Claire

watching WNBA reruns.
ok text you later

HILLARY POURED HERSELF A CUP OF COFFEE FROM A plastic urn, the coffee watery but welcome.

What if this woman wasn't her mother?

The TV was playing a rerun of All in the Family with closed captions. Her eyes drifted over to a low table, meant for children. A plastic carton crammed with crayons stood at spiky attention next to a stack of coloring books.

Hillary watched a child of three or so scribbling outside the lines of an elephant in a jungle color book, her father ignoring her in favor of All in the Family.

A doctor in scrubs came in and told him he could go see his wife, and they left Hillary alone in the waiting room.

As if drawn by some elusive force, she knelt and thumbed through the jungle book, then looked at the others. One was on Star Wars, another on Beauty and the Beast and one was an adult coloring book of abstract designs. She opened it to a black and white line drawing of a mandala.

She found her fingers selecting a red crayon and scraping it fast on the page, forming blood red streaks outside the lines. Her head spun. She felt hooked on the enterprise of slashing the crayon on the diagonal, back and forth on the paper, aching to obliterate the neat black and white mandala, her mind gone, her subconscious in control.

A woman and a girl of five or six burst into the room.

"Hannah," said the woman, "look." She nodded at the table and the girl pulled out a short chair next to Hillary, still kneeling in front of the coloring book, hand frozen over the midpoint of the page she'd been sawing through.

Calmly, the girl took hold of the Beauty and the Beast color book and opened it to a page near the end. With her slender fingers, nails painted lavender with white polka dots scattered on them, she selected a blue crayon and began coloring Beauty's gown, staying inside the lines with care.

Hillary sat mesmerized a few seconds. Then she returned her red crayon to the plastic container, shut her adult color book and stood up from her kneeling position, feeling lightheaded. The girl remained intent on her project of filling in the line drawing of Beauty's blue gown.

A man in scrubs opened the door. "Paisley Joan's family?"

"Yes," Hillary said, and sat down next to the chair that was holding her purse and coat.

"You're her daughter, Hillary Kiffin, right?" He looked at a chart on a clipboard. "We've had to stop transfusing her. It's some kind of incompatibility reaction and she's having trouble breathing. We'd like a sample of your blood to cross match."

Hillary felt faint. "Of course," she said and followed his directions to the ER Lab.

• • •

MINUTES FELT LIKE HOURS, BUT SOON ENOUGH THE SAME man in scrubs returned and introduced himself. "I'm Dr. Pevik. Vascular Center."

She nodded. What was he going to tell her?

"Did you realize you have one of the rarest blood types on the planet?"

Vaguely she recalled hearing about that when Claire was born and then again when she miscarried a few years ago. But it never seemed significant.

"Yes, but—"

"It's your mother's too. She came in with a traumatic brain injury but also severely anemic. We had to open her skull and drain blood from the injury, but we're having trouble ensuring cerebral oxygenation. She's on oxygen and fluids now to keep her IV line open but her reaction earlier could bring on a stroke."

Hillary sank to the chair.

Dr. Pevik was rubbing his hands together as if to scrub them of bacteria. "So, if you would please, get back to the lab, now. They're waiting for you."

Wait, wait, she screamed silently. I'm not sure I want to do this. But she sped down the corridor to the lab. Was it time to reconnect with her mother who'd run off so long ago? Her blood relative. Not the way Hillary'd ever imagined. So intimate with this woman she hardly knew.

An hour later, Dr. Pevik opened the door of the waiting room and stood in front of Hillary. "We're giving her your blood," Dr. Pevik said. "We don't know how she'll respond, and no one will be allowed in until she is stable. You might want to go home and get some rest."

Hillary's arms and legs felt drained by more than the blood she'd donated for...for her mother? How could she safely drive back to Sacramento in this condition? She sat staring at TV reruns until her eyes glazed over and she fell into a restless sleep. A couple hours later, at the sound of Dr. Pevik's voice, she jerked awake.

CHAPTER FORTY-THREE

I've never looked through a keyhole without finding
someone was looking back.

-Judy Garland

DR. PEVIK STOOD GESTURING AND TALKING TO HILLARY.
"You can see her now."

She rose, aching all over. "Thank you, Doctor." He
nodded and disappeared through the doorway.

She called Ed. "You won't believe what has
happened. I had to give blood to save her life. Now
she's awake. I have to go see her, see if…" she paused to
catch her breath, "…we are really kin."

"Take your time, Claire and I are glued to watching
Kobe and the Lakers in rerun highlights." Hillary could
barely say goodbye, she was so overwhelmed with
conflicting emotions.

She proceeded down the hall to the ICU, her feet

barely lifting off the floor with each step. At the doorway, she stared at the figure in the bed. The woman looked small and pale against the white-sheeted hospital bed, her blue-white hair vanished under a swath of white gauze. She held a pink plastic tumbler. She wore fuchsia lipstick and was sucking from a yellow plastic straw. Hillary had the impression of a bright flower. She approached the bed and stood at the railing. What should she say?

The woman set down the tumbler and chirped, "My dear." She held out her hands, palms up and reaching for Hillary. "The doctor tells me you saved my life."

Hillary nodded, wide-eyed.

"And you claim to be my daughter—is that right?"

"Well..." Hillary began.

"If so, that is a fantasy I find hard to believe. Tell me about yourself."

"I'm..." Hillary felt tongue tied for the first time in her life. Well, not the first time—there was that time when her mother tore up the coloring book. And those other times, too. When she had to hide all that junk food in her room, food she craved to swallow the anxiety, making her fatter than ever and bringing on her mother's lectures about beautiful bodies, slim, light and lithe, not like chunky and plodding Hillary. No wonder she'd taken up yoga and karate as an adult.

A series of images flashed through her mind. About herself. About her motherless self, all those years pretending it wasn't real, that she wasn't so different from her friends. Pretending it was normal to be raised by a doting father. Pretending her mother was dead.

"Yes," the woman sang out, sitting up in the bed. "Tell me."

"My mother was an artist," Hillary began. "She painted and made fabrics out in a cottage in the back yard. I was her only child." Her mouth went dry as she watched the shifting expression on the woman's face. "She would weave me circlets of daisies from the back yard for my hair."

The woman gasped and fell back onto the pillows.

CHAPTER FORTY-FOUR

They say that abandonment is a wound that never heals. I say only that an abandoned child never forgets.

-Mario Balotelli

THE WOMAN LAY FLAT ON HER BACK, BREATHING FAST, then dug into the sheets with her elbows and moved forward on the bed. She sat up and leaned toward Hillary, her arms outstretched. "Yes! You are my Hillary girl. I've dreamed of this day." She gasped and waved her hands in the air. "Why didn't you ever write back?"

Write back. Hillary flushed with anger the full length of her body. "There…" She took a deep breath and started over. "There was no address on that…" She sank onto the bedside chair then straightened. "No address on that post card we got from you."

"That post card? What about the birthday cards I painted and sent you each March?" Her mother's hands formed into fists, and she shook them near Hillary's face, then opened her fingers out flat and used her hands like knives chopping at the air. "It was so hard for me to sneak to write to you. He…"

She inhaled in a series of jerks. "He said he'd leave me if I kept in touch. I had to sneak to paint your cards."

Her jaw agape, Hillary stared at this woman. This fiery woman, charged with righteous energy. All these years and Hillary still felt attacked by the sound of her mother's voice. Hillary's cheeks burned. "Never. Never got any. Cards."

"No? None?"

"Nothing. Just that post card from Tahiti with the bright yellow hibiscus." Tears pooled in her eyes. "Remember that one day we sat outside your studio and you picked those little white daisies with yellow centers?"

Paisley stared with a half smile on her bright fuchsia lips.

"You chained them into wreaths and put one on both of us. That postcard reminded me of the daisies. All you wrote on the back of the card was to take care of each other. I sat it on the mantle, but Daddy took it off, ripped it half and threw it into the fireplace. 'Let's face facts, honey girl,' he said. 'She's gone. Think of her as passed on.' He took me everywhere with him and never talked about you anymore."

"Never?"

"It was like you had floated off the earth and been sucked up by the stars. He put a padlock on your studio out back and threw away all his pictures of you." Hillary choked out the next words while she watched her mother clamp her lips inside her mouth. "Daddy and I, we acted like we had the best life ever—father and daughter, so much alike. He turned me into a mirror of him, an objective reporter."

Hillary felt her heart beat double time. She was a secret plagiarist her father would have disinherited if he knew the truth. "He told me to tell people we met that you were dead."

Paisley fell back onto the pillows. She shut her eyes. "He was like that—arrogant, didn't give me a chance— took all the fame for himself. I couldn't help but turn to Bill."

She sat back up, her eyes turned to marbles of gray ice. "Your father wanted me home celebrating his every byline, a mirror for his happiness."

Hillary squinted at her mother. She could recognize her father in these words. It had been her job, too. Praising him and his prize-winning writing, even though her life with him had been rich and full. But not normal, no. She sat and listened as the woman carried on.

"And even when I went crawling to him and asking for his mercy and protection, he looked down his award-winning nose and ordered me out of his life." Her eyes turned glossy as if the ice were melting. "He ordered me to leave, run off with Bill who was retiring to Tahiti. Your father wouldn't support me any longer." Tears rolled down both cheeks and into the folds of skin bracketing her fuchsia lips.

Hillary sat in silence before she noticed a square box near the plastic tumbler on the bedside table. She pulled out a couple tissues and handed them to her mother, who lay back on her pillows, but didn't bother wiping her tears.

After a few seconds of stark silence, Hillary asked, "Why would he order you to leave?"

Paisley sighed. "He never told you?" she whispered.

Hillary shook her head, inhaled and held her breath.

Paisley raised her white eyebrows into steep arches then closed her eyes. Hillary watched as silence took up every space in the room not occupied by beeps from the machines. Her mother's jaw dropped and soft snores puffed out from between her still-bright-fuchsia lips.

HILLARY LEFT THE ROOM AND STOOD IN THE HALL IN A daze. A nurse came by and asked if she was all right. "How long will she—my mother—have to be here in the hospital?" Hillary nodded toward Paisley's room.

"We're not sure yet," the nurse said. She frowned and tapped into a computer stationed outside the room. She scrolled down the page, then turned to Hillary. "But it would help if you could bring some clothes to have on hand when she gets released."

Clothes. Where did Paisley live? Hillary sat in the waiting room and pulled Walt's reports out from the envelope, looking for that condo address. It was way closer than the one in south San Francisco. She would go check it out, see about getting her clothes.

After finding the address, she phoned Ed to see how Claire was doing.

He sounded dead tired. "She's a trouper. I let her know what was happening with you, and she said she was curious about how it would turn out. She seems pretty calm. But, a man was spotted on the rooftop of a parking garage a couple blocks from the Golden 1 Center. Near your Center actually."

Hillary's heart hammered in her throat. "What was he doing?"

"Said he was practicing getting his drone to film old Sac for his history students. Seems legit, a Sac State teacher. We've got a dozen undercovers roaming at random all the time. Some go by to check the high school and college gyms, too. It's not all fun and games downtown, but don't want that news to get out, spook the public."

"So where's this guy now?"

"At the station for questioning but they can't hold him long. At first, he was joking and said he's a bird watcher." Ed snorted a derisive laugh. "Not to worry, Chickadee. We've got security super tight for game nights at the arena. And for the whole downtown." He sighed. "Thin coverage for schools and colleges but working on it. I don't think this parking garage incident is serious."

Hillary could tell he was trying to make light of dangers that came along with the sophisticated arena and the thriving capital city. "There wouldn't be any bird-watchers finding their way to our Center?" She heard her own hollow tone of worry.

"We've got our ears to the ground and our eyes to the skies, Chickadee. You just relax."

Hillary hung up, folded her arms across her chest and rubbed at the goose bumps rising on her arms.

Ed had not even mentioned her mother. So unlike him. He was too busy to help her. She was going to have to go to that condo and hope someone was there.

HILLARY HAD TO DRIVE AROUND THE BLOCK THREE TIMES before she found street parking a half block from the entrance to the fifteen-story brick building. A black iron gate fronted the modest courtyard entrance to Hills Bayside. It was closed, but when Hillary pushed it, the gate swung open. Heavy glass doors leading to the lobby did not follow suit. She could see a concierge at a desk inside, bent over something at the counter. She knocked on the glass and he glanced up, frowned and looked back down at the counter. Hillary checked for a door bell or knocker but none was in sight.

A gnarled old man came thumping into the courtyard and stopped to steady himself on his silver-colored cane. He fished a laminated card from his breast pocket and waved it in the direction of the glass doors. They swung inward. The old man tucked the card back into his pocket, bowed in Hillary's direction and waved her into the lobby.

"Good evening, Mr. Hickenbottom," the desk man said, handing the old man a fistful of envelopes in assorted sizes. "Your mail, sir. And what can I do for the young lady?" He smiled at Hillary.

"Take good care of my friend." The old man ignored the proffered letters and thumped off in the direction of the spacious lobby and a bank of brass elevator doors.

Hillary straightened her navy blazer and stood tall. "I'm here to pick up some items from Number 1401."

"Ah. Is Jeffrey expecting you?"

"Yes," Hillary lied, hoping the deskman couldn't hear her heart pounding.

"Ah. One of our artist friends. Well, please, then, be our guest." He waved toward the elevator doors.

Hillary noticed there was no 13th floor button in the elevator. On the way up to the 14th floor, which was really the 13th, Hillary leaned back against the walnut paneling. She fingered her Ganesh and Mary medals. What should she say? What if no one answered?

She knocked on the dark wooden door. Knocked again. Looked around for a bell. Nothing. She pounded with her fist on the door and listened. Nothing.

She reversed her steps and knocked on the door down the hall. Waited. Knocked again. The door flew open to the sight of a young woman in a skimpy pink coverup. "Yes?"

"I'm looking for the man who lives in 1401."

"Oh, that lecher." The young woman wrinkled her nose.

"Do you know where I can find him?" Hillary felt a niggle of concern.

"Might be up on the roof garden, impressing another easy mark by pointing out the view of the City and the remodeled Bay Bridge."

"Is there a way up there?"

"What do you want from him?" The woman pulled her coverup firmly closed.

"Just to get some things from him."

"What kind of things?" She narrowed her eyes.

"My mother's clothes. She was in an accident and needs something to wear to leave the hospital." Hillary could hardly believe she was here on this strange errand, feeling distanced from her own body. Her stomach gave a loud growl. She couldn't recall when she'd last eaten.

"Ah! I hope you are taking her away from here?" The woman smiled. "That guy is a rich art collector, tries to buy the services of down and out street artists, of whatever persuasion, know what I mean?"

Taking her away from here was starting to sound like a good idea. "How do you know this about him?"

"Jeffrey thought I was a little dish he could taste, but I let him know he was not my type! We ended up neighbors. Watch each other's place when we're out of town."

"Can you let me into 1401?"

"I can if you promise you are rescuing her, yes?"

Hillary's spirits lifted. She nodded and told herself she could think later about what this might mean. Rescue her mother. The young woman invited Hillary into her condo while she changed into a black one-piece jumpsuit.

Once inside 1401, they poked around in a closet in the short hall leading from bedroom to bath. Hanging in the closet were several caftans similar to what Hillary had seen Paisley wearing in her booth near the Ferry

Building plus a suitcase with Paisley's luggage tag attached. Hillary and the young woman filled the suitcase with the caftans and other items they agreed looked like they belonged to Paisley. Hillary was zipping up the suitcase when the front door of 1401 banged opened, and she could hear a low voice.

"Is our City by the Bay enough for your artist's soul, Henry? Or do you…" The voice stopped mid-sentence, then, "…what the fuck?" A short bald man dressed in a full-length unbuttoned puffer coat turned to the young woman who'd let Hillary into 1401. "What are you up to, Cher?"

Cher smiled in sympathy at the young man, his face dotted with tattooed flowers, who followed close behind Jeffrey. "We're just cleaning out so you'll have room for Henry, my friend." She waggled the suitcase ID tag and nodded at Hillary. "This case is her mother's, and she's taking it now to help her get released from the hospital."

"The hospital? Good neighbor, I thank you." Jeffrey scowled at Paisley's suitcase. "Get her box from my basement storage, too. No need for me to ferry around treasures she thinks makes her another Georgia O'Keeffe." He smiled, patted Henry on the bottom and said to Hillary, "Tell your mother no invalids allowed around here." He bit Henry lightly on the ear.

With Cher's help, Hillary got Paisley's suitcase and another case they retrieved from the basement loaded into her Rav4. "Thank you," she said, squeezing Cher's hand. "You've been a life saver."

"I do my part to keep balance in the building," Cher said. "My kind of public service."

Hillary knew she would never understand some people, but it didn't really matter, did it? Those people weren't her concern. She drove back to the hospital, her thoughts in a whirl.

CHAPTER FORTY-FIVE

When people don't have a hopeful vision before them…
they can be attracted to violence.

-Condoleezza Rice

CHARLIE STARED AT THE GRAY RIBBON PINNED TO DOC
Rivers' white coat. The doctor stuck out his hand for a
shake and added a pat on Charlie's shoulder. For the
first time, he didn't ask which kind of news Charlie
wanted first.

He traced his finger over a spot on an X-ray hanging
on the wall light panel. "I'm afraid that we've spotted
more progression. Now it's nearer the speech center."

"Progression?" Charlie hooted a hollow laugh. "I'm
still talking, doc. Hear me?"

Doc Rivers pursed his lips and patted his gray
ribbon. "It is impossible to get every single tumor cell.

Recurrence is inevitable. We don't have all the answers yet."

"Give me the straight dope, Doc. I can take it. How long do I have?"

"It could be a matter of weeks."

"Any signs to expect?"

"Trouble speaking, some have reported difficulty swallowing." The doctor nodded gravely. "I'm sorry, Doc Bierce. Could expect problems with memory and judgment."

Charlie wasn't expecting anything better. Not consciously, anyway. Never was an optimistic man. Loved how Voltaire satirized optimism in his novel, *Candide*. Those characters had tried to change the world, but ended up tending a little garden. A modest plot of land, no projects of the urban development kind to ruin the peaceful nature of the last place they settled into.

Charlie felt the pressure of his cancer bulging against his brain, a development of the biological kind.

He and his pals had failed to persuade the city council to halt the cancerous growth Sunny planned. Now there was barely any time left to get people to pay attention to his message.

AT HOME, CHARLIE PHONED THE TV STATION. "WATCH for big news downtown on New Year's Day." He hung up before the call from his landline could be traced.

CHAPTER FORTY-SIX

Well, sometimes home is a person.

-Beth Revis

A WOOL CAFTAN CLUTCHED TO HER CHEST, HILLARY tiptoed into her mother's room, surprised to find her standing near a window, looking out in the direction of the Bay Bridge, still dressed in her short cotton hospital gown.

Hillary stood silent, watching, taking in the petite shape of this woman.

Suddenly, Paisley turned as if she sensed Hillary standing there. "Good afternoon," she said in a clear high voice.

Hillary held up the heavy caftan. "I brought you this. They said you could be released today. If you had someone to keep an eye on you."

Paisley walked over and traced her fingertips along

the narrow strip of fuchsia running down the middle of the white caftan. "Released." The woman gave a high-pitched laugh. "Back to that pervert."

She straightened her shoulders and stood as tall as her petite frame would allow. "He said I could go house sit his condo near the baseball park. Thought I caught a break, but he wants more than house sitting." She frowned and pursed her lips, devoid of lipstick.

Hillary felt sick and nervous. She was really going to have to rescue this mother who'd left her so long ago. She swallowed the lump in her throat. "I know. I went there."

"How did you know where to go?"

"My husband had a friend of his looking for you, searching for a long time. He had a couple addresses for you. That's how I happened to find you in the Embarcadero Plaza."

"Your husband?"

"Ed. He's a retired detective. His old partner put together lots of material on you."

"Ed?"

"Ed Kiffin. I'm not Hillary Broome anymore."

"You let go of your father's precious Broome byline?" Paisley started laughing hysterically and collapsed into the visitor's chair.

Hillary sat on the edge of the hospital bed and waited for her mother to stop laughing. What had happened to cause this kind of reaction? "That creepy man in the condo?" she said and waited for Paisley to nod. "He sent this," she spread the caftan out on the bed, "along with a suitcase of other clothes and a case from the condo storage. I've got them in my car."

Paisley's eyebrows lifted.

"He said to tell you not to come back. He doesn't want any invalid to take care of."

Paisley lifted her chin, and clamped her jaw to stop the trembling. "I've got friends in an Oakland art colony. Can you give me a lift over there? Maybe call it a late birthday gift?"

Hillary dragged her fingers through her hair, visualizing Walt's report and that date Hillary had repressed for decades. Her mother's birthday. It had popped right out of her mouth at the hospital intake counter. "That's right. We missed your birthday." Trembling from years of longing bursting free, she leaned towards her mother and said, "Forget about that condo. Forget about Oakland. Come home with me. Meet your granddaughter, Claire." Hillary held her breath.

Paisley stared at Hillary a few seconds, wide-eyed and wordless. She broke into a whole-body nod, her frame rocking back and forth in the hospital chair. The sound of quiet filled the room. Hillary felt as if they were acting in a silent movie from long ago, with nothing more to say. At the moment.

HILLARY PULLED HER RAV4 UP TO THE HOSPITAL entrance. There was Paisley, in a wheelchair, white hair clouded around her face like a doll's except where a small bandage remained on the side of her head. It struck Hillary how small and frail her mother looked.

"Come on, it's time to go," she said, suddenly feeling like a mother to her own mother as she bent to help her stand. "You don't need this chair." The charms on Hillary's bracelet dangled from her wrist.

Paisley reached to tap the tiny silver Ganesh. "Here's the boy who tripped me up, got me in trouble." She laughed and stepped up into the front passenger seat with ease.

As they drove by the Hills Bayside building, Paisley said, "Thank you for rescuing me from him. I'm lucky the City is storing my popup and merch."

"I've got your cases from the condo in the back," Hillary said. "This Rav4 has plenty of cargo space."

Paisley laughed. "I'm sure there are a few things in there I can bring along as fun little Christmas gifts."

Fun. Gifts. This was the mother she remembered. Always light and airy, sparkling and having fun, without a sense of the seriousness of the situation. Coloring outside any lines.

Her hands tight on the steering wheel to stop the trembling, Hillary concentrated on threading her way onto the Bay Bridge and headed home on Highway 80. Gifts. She had nothing prepared. Her call to Ed had assured her he and Claire would be home and ready to greet them. This was like no Christmas had ever been.

"Where do you live?" asked Paisley.

"Sacramento."

"The place is so different from back when we were in the suburbs. There's a lot of sweet galleries in the midtown."

"I've heard but not been there yet. We moved from

Lodi a couple years ago, and I've been busy working public relations for a community center going up in downtown. Mostly provide sports and academic support to youth in the region." Hillary realized with a jolt she'd been off the job for the past few days, occupied with this woman. What might Charlie Bierce have been up to?

"Oh? Will the center offer any art classes?" Paisley asked in a bright voice.

"We haven't got all our details settled." As she drove east on highway 80, Hillary nodded in the direction of a town halfway between San Francisco and Sacramento. "The developer Sunny Singh planned our Center to feature youth sports but also to be comprehensive, like one of those Kroc Centers." She waved in the direction of Fairfield. "There's a Kroc Center near there, for families that might find activities beyond their reach, like performing arts and health and wellness classes. We want to offer things like that, and are super excited about our four-story climbing wall." Hillary glanced at Paisley to see her reaction.

"Sunny Singh? I heard of a Sunny Singh over in Mumbai when I was running an art program over there, did you know?"

Hillary shook her head, shocked at this possible connection.

Paisley carried on. "Yes, and later when we moved to Kona, we offered sculpting and tie dye classes in our shop." She fell silent.

Hillary waited a few seconds before she asked, "We?"

"Bill. Bill and I. I'm sure you were too young to remember him. Bill Williams my art professor out at Sac State way back when."

Hillary's palms grew slippery. She took one hand off the steering wheel to wipe the sweat on her pant leg and did the same with the other hand, all the time taking deep breaths. "I do remember him. He came to our back yard one time."

"Well, Bill was laughed out of Tahiti's art community and turned into an alcoholic when Little Albert's Artworks failed in Mumbai. Without a pot to pee in, we had to move to Hawaii and live with Bill's sister in Kona. The vodka took over his life, and he took to stumbling around town, got killed when he walked out in front of a bus in downtown Kona. A tourist bus, would you believe!"

Hillary found herself unable to speak. This load of news was hitting hard. She felt connected to this woman in the way she imagined one of those little rubber balls might feel connected to a wooden paddle hitting it over and over. She breathed deep to steady herself and concentrated on keeping an eye on her rear view mirror as clouds gathered in the Bay Area.

As if she'd run out of gas, Paisley kept her bright fuchsia lips tightly pursed and her eyes closed as they drove along in silence until they reached Land Park and pulled into Hillary's driveway.

Claire wasn't out shooting baskets this afternoon. That was understandable. Maybe having Paisley here would perk up her spirits.

Hillary unlocked the front door and pushed it open.

The dogs came bounding towards them, but at Ed's loud 'Sit,' the canines plunked their bottoms on the bare hardwood entry. Paisley leaned down and scratched Daisy's head. "You didn't tell me you had labs!"

Claire stood at the tree, a tiny gold basketball ornament dangling from her fingers, her mouth hanging open at the sight of Paisley.

Ed waved them in with his spatula. "Come on in, I've got breakfast for dinner almost ready." His Denver omelets and rye toast lent a buttery fragrance to the scent of cool pine in the room, warmed by the lively flames dancing in the fireplace.

Hillary took Paisley's hand and led her near Claire. The ornament had dropped from Claire's fingers and fallen to rest on a low branch of the tree.

Hillary looked at her daughter and at her mother and back again. Each stared at the other with wide eyes, gray eyes the same shade as Hillary's own, their hair short and light in color so different from Hillary's long auburn hair. The two of them stood half a foot shorter than Hillary and gazed at each other for what felt like an hour. Then, as if hearing the same signal and with a simultaneous cry, they reached out and clasped one another in a tight and motionless hug.

Ed watched from the dining room archway, platter of buttered toast in his hand. He set it down on the table and came to Hillary's side.

When the grandmother and granddaughter stepped back from their hug, they smiled at each other, and Claire darted a look of wonder at Hillary.

Hillary took Ed's hand and held it toward Paisley.

"Mother," Hillary's heart pounded at the word, "meet the man of our house, Ed Kiffin."

"Pleased to make your acquaintance, young man," she said and then turned to Claire. "Now let's see what you've put on your tree!"

Claire pointed to the fallen gold basketball and laughed. "Most of them are basketballs and leprechauns!"

"Don't forget my shamrocks and Irish Harps," said Hillary.

"Notre Dame footballs are my favorite," said Ed.

They picked along the surface of the tree, fondling the tiny ornaments for some minutes before Ed said, "Hey, let's get into the dining room before the food gets cold."

He led them to the table and said a quick grace. Hillary's shoulders dropped and she let out a deep breath, relaxing for the first time since Paisley had fallen back into her life. Paisley and Claire cut into their omelets and forked aside the green peppers. These two, so far apart and now so close. Hillary smiled, ravenous for the first time in days.

CHAPTER FORTY-SEVEN

What you do is your history. What you set in motion is
your legacy.

-Leonard Sweet

CHARLIE SPENT A SLEEPLESS NIGHT, GOING OVER EACH
Plan B possibility, grateful for no bad dreams. He was
proud he was not a loner in this redemption work—no
Unabomber he. By nine, his friends had arrived,
bringing pastries and hot beverages. Kaz guzzled coffee
from a giant car cup, decorated with a quote from
Henry Ward Beecher: "The worst thing in this world,
next to anarchy, is government."

The quote made Charlie smile, but the coffee aroma
nauseated him. He kept his stomach calm with a second
cup of ginger tea. "My friends, to paraphrase the bard,
is it better to teach by word or by deed the folly of
outrageous fortune, devised by the collusion of govern-

ment and private enterprise. Best to offer messages or outcomes?"

"I believe we can wake the public to the danger of out of control growth by message bombing. It can be our way of telling the story, writ large," said Victor.

Charlie laughed. "Ambrose would feel validated, our battling the establishment with words, concise messages engraved on metal tags and inserted into plastic explosive." He read from the list he'd jotted: "STOP CITY THEFT OF YOUR LAND; USE YOUR TAX $ YOUR WAY; IS YOURS A CHIP OFF YOUR OWN BLOCK?"

Kaz tilted his car cup to drain the last of his coffee and then lifted the cup in an arc. "No! Got to bring down that Center, stop training youngsters to lure the masses into watching spectator sports. Let the people raise their children their way, let them run free, learn from being face to face with the natural world."

"Kaz has some good points," Charlie said and looked at KD for his comments.

"We aren't planning crimes against humanity like robbing hard-working taxpayers or throwing renters out onto the streets. Inserting pithy messages to welcome the Center Opening Day crowd with what I'm calling 'FORTUNE COOKIE BOMBS' is a great idea, in my opinion." KD laughed. "Just picture breaking open a new kind of fortune cookie and to find wisdom inside. Let's use the blank pressed board dog tags, engrave them with our message phrases." He nodded at Charlie. "It can be a set of lessons from Professor Bierce."

"The package explodes from the top of the climbing

wall at noon, just as the doors open, showering down messages on guests as they are all gathered in front of that four-story glass wall, just before they enter. Like confetti celebrating a better new year ahead. I like it!" Charlie grinned. "Let's do it."

Kaz scowled and paced the floor as others set to work with Dremels, engraving the tags with the messages.

Charlie was at peace. He would satisfy himself with warning messages delivered in the Center. Doable.

As they worked, they talked over how to make and where to place the plastic explosive, as long as it didn't go off before Charlie could set it correctly and get away before the timer went off.

Or would it really matter if the bomb took him out? He was practically a dead man walking, wasn't he?

He pinched the itchy skin under his nose, where his mustache was starting to grow back. Now he had to recall Sunny's birthdate. The ironworker had said that would be the security door keypad code number. They were both Scorpios.

What had Tiffany told him? Sunny's was a week after hers, wasn't it? She had invited him to dinner but he'd passed. What did Charlie know about signs? Nothing. Except a scorpion could deliver a deadly sting. That much he knew.

CHAPTER FORTY-EIGHT

Secrets press inside a person. They press the way water
presses at a dam. The secrets and the water, they both
want to get out.

-Franny Billingsley

THE EMPTY AFTERNOON STRETCHED OUT AHEAD OF
Hillary and Paisley, the coffee hot and the room warm
with the burst of pine scent from low-hanging
Christmas tree branches, pruned off and set on top of
the blaze in the fireplace.

On Christmas morning, Paisley had given tie dye
materials from her stash in the condo to Claire so she
could teach her the craft. They spent Christmas afternoon transforming Claire's old tee shirts into colorful
new looks, Hillary watching and feeling cozy inside
while light showers fell on the driveway.

Claire had practically fastened herself to Paisley's

side for the past few days but today was off with Keisha to Underground Books in celebration of the first day of Kwanza. Ed was downtown, helping speed up the preliminary hearing for the high school shooter who turned out to be a history teacher at a private school, fired over recruiting students into his mixed race gang.

"You started a few days ago to tell me why…" Hillary was ready to face it. "…you left."

"Yes, awful story, my dear," said Paisley. "Shocking, really, stranger than fiction. It was the late 60s, and I was seventeen, a free spirit, in love with the big strong writer who wrote about my make-love-not-war spirit." She waved her coffee spoon in the air. "Newspapers were powerful back then, not like now."

Hillary nodded, determined to not interrupt.

"He, Jake, your father, at first he was all lovey-dovey, and I was the radiant artist." She flashed a brilliant smile. "But his byline on the front page got him a swelled head, and after you were born," she gazed with squinted eyes at Hillary, "not that it was your fault…" She pressed her lips together, rubbed them back and forth, and blotted them with a napkin, which she folded into triangles, before speaking. "He started coming home late. I would walk the floor with you to sooth your colicky stomach, then sit and lay you tummy down on a wrapped warm water bottle, I would rub your back in small circles…"

Hillary found herself swaying slightly as her mother rocked and rubbed her knees as if still living in those days. "…then get up walking and watching our antique wall clock, hoping he'd be home soon to help. I watched the clock move into the early hours of morning."

Paisley drained her coffee and searched Hillary's face. Hillary nodded, remembering the times she had cradled colicky baby Claire.

"That one night he got home and there we were, the three of us in the early morning hours, you screaming, rigid with anger at the situation you were born into." Her shoulders slumped, and it was quiet a few seconds before she continued.

"After he fumbled with his key at the front door and marched in waving that *LA Chronicle* in the air, he said, 'I have to make contacts downtown, get the stories. Your art projects,' he slammed the newspaper down onto the coffee table, 'they sure the hell aren't going to feed us. The paper comes out every day, you're either in it or you're not. I got a front page story and a raise today but you were too busy at your artwork to notice.'"

Paisley nodded in the direction of Hillary's coffee table. "All the while he was talking, he was pointing at the newspaper he'd set on the mosaic tile table I created the year before in an art class." She leaned over and picked up a *Sports Illustrated* off the table. "I pointed to you, our screaming baby lying on the sofa. 'I've been stuck at home all day,' I told him. 'It's your turn!' I picked up his precious newspaper, twisted it into a log," she rolled the *Sports Illustrated* up, "and slammed the *Chronicle* against the wall, knocking our antique clock onto to the carpet."

Paisley smacked the *Sports Illustrated* against her

palm. Hillary felt paralyzed, as if under a spell as Paisley resumed her story. "Then I said, 'Your turn with your daughter. Let's see how well you do tomorrow on your beloved writing without any sleep.'" Paisley set the *Sports Illustrated* down and smoothed it flat on the coffee table before she went on. "I ran out the front door, started up his Dodge Charger and backed out of the driveway."

Paisley scooted forward, breathing deep and hard, before she continued, "We stayed together for your sake, good Catholics and all. But we weren't really man and wife anymore."

Hillary felt clammy cold and guilty as sin hearing the story.

The woman opened her eyes wide enough for white to show all around the gray of her irises. "But, I had Bill, my faithful teacher and mentor in the art world." A brilliant smile lit up Paisley's face before she stood, poked at the log in the fireplace and turned to Hillary. "And that's how your father knew," she whispered, "knew when I was pregnant again, it was not by him."

Hillary sat wordless, mesmerized by the flying sparks coming off the burning log. Did she have a sibling somewhere? A chunk of red hot wood broke away and split into coals on the bed of the fireplace. Seconds passed before she could ask, "What happened to that baby?"

Paisley's face crumpled. "That's too dreary to talk about." She turned and walked down the hall to her room. Hillary heard the lock turn. This part of the story was going to take a long, long time.

CHAPTER FORTY-NINE

LEGACY, n. A gift from one who is legging it out of this vale of tears.

-Ambrose Bierce, *The Devil's Dictionary*

AT THE KITCHEN TABLE, CHARLIE PINCHED THE SLENDER handle of his mother's favorite porcelain cup. Fingers quivering, he raised it from the saucer. A couple drops of ginger tea spilled over the edge. He set the cup down and bent to sip steaming liquid from the rim. He worked at the mouthful of tea with his tongue and his cheeks. Damn. He spit the fragrant liquid back into the flowered cup. Doc had told him trouble swallowing could be a sign. His judgement was still sharp as ever, he was sure.

It was time. Perfect timing. Tonight. New Year's Eve. Yes, he and his team would get the messages delivered.

And if something should go wrong, he was willing to die on that hill.

His papers were in order. His meager savings and his house would go to Justin. He would know how to fight to keep it out of the hands of Sunny. Charlotte was set for life with the bastard she hooked up with. Tiffany didn't need a penny, rich from that foreigner she married —might even bring her own offspring into the circle of the new establishment someday. Didn't need to leave them any monetary legacy. Charlie snorted. He planned a different kind of heritage, a more memorable kind.

Putting aside the thought of breakfast, he moved to his dining room table to craft a rough draft on his yellow legal pad, as the morning wore on. Just in case Plan B went wrong.

Let it be known my sacrifice was to provide a mirror of the larger destruction going on all around town—my life ending and this building damaged are nothing compared to the devastation from greedy powers siphoning off private land and public monies for their selfish interests. I am tormented that my daughter let herself be folded into the arms of the insatiable materialists.

HE SAT BACK AND READ IT OVER. MIGHT STILL BE TIME TO return Tiffany to his family values. He phoned her and was pleased she answered. This time. "Tiff, now's the time to repent," he said. "We haven't seen each other for a while. Come show me you care more about saving your childhood neighborhood than getting to the top of the mountain."

"What are you talking about?" she whispered. "Where are you?"

"Here in the place you belong, here asking one last time for you to respect my legacy."

"You don't sound like yourself. Are you okay?"

"My health is not the issue. It's the health of the town I care about. And you should too."

"I'm coming over." She hung up.

HE CHECKED TO MAKE SURE THE FRONT DOOR WAS LOCKED and then got out his mother's box of ivory stationary with the script B monogram centered along the top edge. He hand addressed a matching envelope to the editor of the *Suttertown News*.

He was halfway through copying his rough draft, using the elegant penmanship his mother had modeled, when the doorbell clanged its distinctive sounds. He ignored it until relentless knocking took its place.

He opened the front door to face Tiffany. "You don't even have a key to the place you grew up in anymore." He scowled at his daughter.

"Is that a crime, Daddy? Aren't you going to let me in?" She opened her coat and rubbed her belly. Was the girl sick?

"Let me in, me and your grandson. We just saw the ultra sound: Charles Ambrose Bierce Singh."

He stood, silent as a ghost, hearing the ring of the name and feeling himself filling up with sorrow.

Grandson. Never had he let himself think of this, the most ordinary of family values. He had stood alone on his narrow cliff of the present, in a fight to preserve the past. There would be a future unfurling in the sky, of course. But he would not be in it.

The tragedy of his prognosis hit him. His head drooped, and tears fell onto the round lenses of his John Lennon glasses. Imagine that, he thought.

He stood speechless a few more moments, then recovered himself and opened the screen door. She rushed into the parlor and sat in a velvet chair. Her purse fell to the carpet.

"I'm worried about you here alone, Dad."

"I'm fine, don't worry about me."

"We plan to name the baby Charles Ambrose Singh."

Charlie gasped. He never dreamed of such a thing. "What does…" he halted, not able to speak his son-in-law's name. He had to hold onto the side of the settee to keep from fainting.

"Sunny is okay with it, too. Don't you see, Dad, he supports youth of all colors and ages whether playing sports or not. And not just youth. He wants to bring generations together, let elders teach youngsters. You could even offer talks at the Center."

Charlie shook his head and couldn't find the words to express his astonishment. Joy he was unaccustomed to.

As dusk fell and the room warmed with the intensity of their conversation, Tiffany slipped her coat off her shoulders and let it fall behind her in the chair. She talked on with enthusiasm, and Charlie felt a shift in the ground of his being. "Would you like a cup of ginger tea?" he asked, and when she stood to follow him into the kitchen, he clutched the doorframe to keep from crumpling as he caught another sight of her still-flat belly. Who was this little one he would be leaving what kind of legacy to?

At the kitchen table, Charlie toyed with his cup. He didn't want her to see he was not able to swallow anymore. He worried that Kaz would arrive soon to 'get their party started' as the young anarchist called it.

While his daughter sipped at her tea, he found himself trying to explain. "We are just going to offer messages. No one will get hurt."

Tiffany set her cup down quickly. "What are you talking about? Who is 'we'?"

The doorbell clanged. "Wait," she said and placed her hand on his shoulder. "Don't answer it. What are you talking about?"

The bell insisted its urgency into the room. Charlie lifted her hand. "It's too late to turn back." He rose and made his way to the door, with Tiffany close behind.

Kaz pulled open the screen door and stepped in. The three of them stood looking at each other, wide-eyed and silent for a second. Tiffany asked, "Is this man part of your 'we,' Dad?"

"What have you told her?" Kaz fingered the corners of the silky yellow scarf knotted around his neck.

"Just the truth." Charlie turned to face his daughter. "We planned to plant a fountain bomb in the Center, timed to scatter messages like confetti just at the moment guests arrive for the Opening. No one will really get hurt, just showered with messages to save downtown."

Tiffany's jaw dropped. She clamped her hand to her chest.

Charlie glowered at Kaz. "I'm not sure this is a good idea anymore, my young friend."

"What the fucking hell!" Kaz stomped across the room and swiped the figurines off the fireplace mantle. They crashed to the hearth, glass breaking and porcelain shattering. "You can't chicken out now, old man!"

Charlie sank onto the settee. "I don't have the stomach for it anymore."

Kaz stepped behind Tiffany, grabbed one of her hands and pulled it behind her to cross the other at the wrists. "You better get yourself up for it, old man." He yanked off his yellow scarf and tied her hands. Tiffany squirmed and kicked but couldn't stop Kaz as he began patting her down. "Where's your phone?"

Charlie jumped up and pulled at Kaz's arms. "Leave her alone!"

Kaz flung him off, and he fell against the fireplace screen, then on to his knees, his glasses falling onto the stone hearth.

Kaz finished feeling for Tiffany's cell. "Must be in your purse." He pulled her along with him, picked up her bag from the carpet and pawed around inside it. He took out her phone and slipped it into his shirt pocket.

Kaz smiled and turned to Charlie, struggling to stand up. "Not to worry, Dad." He pushed Tiffany into a red velvet chair. "This little lady has a good seat for her very private New Year's party." He ripped the curtain tie-backs off the wall, reached behind her and traded his scarf for the tie-backs, pinning her tight to the chair.

Kaz picked up Charlie's glasses, helped him to his feet and held him firmly by the arm. "She'll be safe and sound, while you and I go deliver our Happy New Year messages, Mr. Postman. I just need to change the timing on your little Casio."

CHAPTER FIFTY

THE PAST, n. A moving line called the Present parts it from an imaginary period known as the Future. These two grand divisions of Eternity, of which the one is continually effacing the other, are entirely unlike. The one is dark with sorrow and disappointment, the other bright with prosperity and joy.

-Ambrose Bierce, *The Devil's Dictionary*

CHARLIE TREAD SILENTLY ACROSS THE WORN ASPHALT, ONE arm pressed tight to his overcoat, the device inside clamped against his ribs. He reached his other arm up to wipe the sweat off his brow with the back of his hand.

Close behind, Kaz whispered, "You're doing the right thing." Charlie flexed his jaw to counteract the pressure inside his skull and gave a jerky nod.

Moonbeams painted the alley in the city's oldest

residential neighborhood. Midnight. New Year's Eve. This could start something new all right. A return to the old. A surge of energy swelled through his body. He felt almost young again. Except for the pounding headache, his sore knees and the thought of Tiffany tied up in his parlor.

A skyrocket shot into the night and exploded into reds and golds. Fireworks bloomed in loud succession, signaling the end of the show. Everyone was down in Old Sac by the river, watching the New Year's Eve show in the sky. Security forces were occupied handling the drunk and disorderlies. Victor would fly the drone over undetected and lower the rectangular package onto the roof.

As they approached the end of the alley, the massive glass entry of the Center came into view, site of the Grand Opening tomorrow. Hillary had publicized the hell out of it, saying it was a place for the old and the young to learn together. For Charlie, no matter how hard his daughter tried to convince him, it stood for all that was wrong, constructed on land stripped bare of tradition in the name of what the bastards called progress. He couldn't let on to Kaz, but Charlie was almost glad they would follow through on the plan.

They walked to the back of the building. No security in sight to ward off Kaz, hulking in his denim jacket. Tonight, the man looked more impressive than ever. Charlie bent to peer at the service door while Kaz aimed the beam of his penlight at the keypad, its tiny LED blinking red.

"Regular keys not good enough anymore," Charlie

muttered. He poked 1, 1, 6, 7, 5 onto the pad, all the while keeping the trigger device immobile against his side. The LED winked red, red, red.

Kaz nudged Charlie in the back. "You sure you got the number right?"

A bead of sweat trickled down Charlie's back. But nervous perspiration couldn't set off the device clamped to his side, detonate the bomb while it was still hooked to the drone circling above. They had gone over this. Jesus.

Okay, remember Sunny's birthdate, a week after Tiff's. The two of those lovebirds were five years and seven days apart as they let everyone know in their sickening sweet, hand-holding way.

Charlie ran the old rhyme through his addled brain. Thirty days hath September, April, June and November . . . He knew for certain hers was October 30, 1980. Okay, so a week later, Sunny's had to be November 6. 1975. Okay, so give it the zero before the six. Make it six digits. He tried again.

1, 1, 0, 6, 7, 5. The red light's steady blink mocked his mental processes.

"We've got work to get started." Kaz kneed Charlie in the back of his legs, making him reach out to the wall to keep from buckling to the sidewalk.

It must be that fool Sunny had changed the code number. Maybe to Tiffany's date?

He punched in 1, 0, 3, 0, 8, 0. The tiny light blinked red once more and then shifted to green. Holding his breath, Charlie pushed the handle down to vertical. He shouldered against the door.

The door held fast for a second, then with a click, it swung open to reveal a dim stairwell off to the right, just like the ironworker said there'd be. Charlie looked at Kaz. "Text Victor, let him know we're in. Go on up, open the hatch to the roof, cradle the plastic. Real careful, don't bump it against anything. Carry it down here..." He ducked his chin toward where his arm pressed against his side. "And I'll be waiting. We can go to the front and hook up the detonator."

Kaz nodded and texted Art.

CHARLIE COULD FEEL HIS HEART PULSING AGAINST THE device pressed to his ribs as he waited for Kaz to bring the payload downstairs to the glass-walled entry.

It had turned out to be so simple—a Casio watch and a 9 volt battery. Charlie was facing the entry, visualizing the surprise of those waiting to get in, the fountain of tags bursting high and showering down, how wonderful the entry would look covered with the confetti of NOMO tags.

His back to the stairwell, Charlie barely felt the fabric slip down over his face.

Kaz gave a raspy laugh. "I've got a New Year's surprise for you, old friend. I packed a few extra goodies inside my jacket," he tightened the silky scarf against Charlie's throat, "to give our story a twist ending."

He leaned forward, cheek by cheek with Charlie. "It's going to take longer than we planned. And I'm going to have to reset the timer on that Casio of yours.

Move it an hour later when the Center will be filled up with the corrupt and the misguided. But we've got all night."

"No, we agreed not to hurt anyone," Charlie protested.

"You don't know your pronouns as well as you thought, English Professor. The 'we' you dreamed up is not what you think it is." Kaz turned Charlie's head toward the stairwell. "You and I, we are going down there. Victor found out from that ironworker, where to place our packages, in basement parking."

CHAPTER FIFTY-ONE

Winning takes precedence over all. There's no gray area. No almosts.

-Kobe Bryant

AT KEISHA'S NEW YEAR'S EVE SLEEPOVER, CLAIRE walked around holding Paisley's hand, introducing her as her artist grandmother.

Margie Ann giggled and said, "She looks just like you."

"I look like her," corrected Claire.

Hillary hugged Margie Ann's mother, finally out of the wheelchair, healed from her injuries. It heralded a truly good new year ahead with the shooter's trial to start soon.

At midnight, the girls paraded around Stacy's block, banging ladles and spoons on pots and pans and shouting "Happy New Year," the parents and grandparents watching from the front yard, laughing and clapping. Once back in the house, the girls laid out sleeping bags on the front room rug for their overnight. "They call it a sleepover, but I never see much sleepin' done," pronounced Stacy.

ALONG WITH OTHER ADULTS, HILLARY AND PAISLEY TOOK their leave. After they got settled in the car, Hillary texted Ed.

great party. we down to center now

No reply, but the Old Sac celebrations were keeping all security forces plenty busy. She was taking Paisley to the Center tonight so her mother would not have to battle opening day crowds, or what Hillary hoped would be crowds. Hillary had invited Paisley to bring along some art supplies to add to those already stocked for people not into sports. They could create tee shirts and memorabilia, practice marketing and entrepreneurship skills.

"What all did you bring?" Hillary asked.

Paisley waved toward the back seat at her tote bag. "Brushes, table easels, 4x6 canvas cards, a few pounds of clay, my favorite sculpting knives. A bare start until I see what all you've got set up already."

ZAPPING HER REMOTE AT THE PARKING GARAGE ENTRY ON the side of the building, Hillary drove down and parked on the lower level next to the elevator doors. Tonight, hers was the only car in the subterranean space, with regularly spaced columns giving the place the look of a sparse concrete forest.

She took Paisley up to the fourth floor and showed her around several program rooms and then the Art and Design Space. Paisley waved up to the ceiling. "This should have great light during the day. I'll be right at home up here. Do you remember those cherry trees back in Carmichael? I loved pitting those Bings." She held up one of her sculpting knives. "Now this one, see its tiny scoop ending?" She rotated it against her palm. "Got those pits out nice and neat in a hurry. Left my hand stained with cherry juice." She laughed, slipped it back into her tote and began lifting slim bricks of clay from her tote into a cupboard.

Hillary leaned against one of the columns and closed her eyes to savor this peaceful moment.

A sort of tapping seemed to be coming from inside the column. Was it her imagination? Her phone vibrated in her pocket. Must have been the phone.

She took it out of her pocket.

can you go check charlie's house

why?

gps alert signal. Might be nothing but we can't get away

Hillary put her hand on Paisley's shoulder. "That's enough for now. You can do the rest in a few days. Ed's asked me to drive by and take a look at something in the neighborhood."

"What kind of something?"

"Probably nothing, but he can't get away from Old Sac right now. He wants me to hurry."

"I only have a few more things left."

"Leave them, please." Hillary didn't want to frighten her mother, but it was rare for Ed to make this kind of request. "We need to go now."

She led Paisley back to the elevator and they took it down to the lower level parking.

As the doors opened to the dimly lit space, Hillary could make out two figures in the middle near the center support column. She put her finger to her lips to keep her mother quiet. "Stay here," she whispered to Paisley, and pointed to the side of her car.

Hillary tiptoed toward the two figures. As she got close, she recognized Charlie Bierce on his knees near the concrete column, with a man standing over him. Suddenly, the man turned his head and looked her straight in the face.

"What are you doing?" she yelled, closing the distance between them. Charlie looked up and then down at his hands.

"What are you doing down here?" she cried out, shocked to the core. Charlie let go of a small package he'd been holding and lifted his hands in a gesture of surrender. The other man whipped a yellow scarf off his neck, slipped it over Charlie's head and pulled it tight against his throat.

Hillary hit her remote, causing the underground parking doors to rumble open. "Leave him alone, let him go! I've called the police," she lied. "They'll be here any minute."

The stranger jerked on the scarf, ignoring her. "Get it finished," he ordered Charlie.

Charlie took hold of the package he'd dropped.

The other man kneed Charlie in the back. "Get it connected!"

Charlie set his package on top of a larger one leaning against the concrete column. Hillary saw with horror the big package sat flanked by two others the same size, connected by wires.

"You can't get away with this," she yelled.

Charlie looked up at the man pulling the scarf tight. He choked out, "Kaz... best I can..."

The man named Kaz gave a raspy laugh. "Set the timer and let's get out of here. This old lady can't stop us."

Charlie twisted suddenly and lifted his package in Hillary's direction. She darted in and reached out to grab it.

Kaz let go of the scarf and gripped her wrist. "Don't you dare. Charlie, get that connected and set the timer if you want to save this old lady."

Charlie started coughing. Hillary felt Paisley come up behind her and reach around to push something slim and cold into her free hand. A surge of recognition flowed through her. It was one of Paisley's sculpting knives.

Gripping the knife with its scoop tip facing out, Hillary swung her arm around at Kaz. He scoffed at the tiny blade and gripped both her wrists in one of his big hands, forcing her to drop the knife to the concrete floor.

He bent to the three packages at the base of the column, grabbed the small package from Charlie and set it on top of the big ones. Kaz stamped on Charlie's foot. "Get it connected, damn you."

Charlie howled in pain.

Kaz stared at Hillary, his lips twisted into a snarl.

Hillary threw an elbow hard to his jaw, knocking him down. As Kaz flung his hand back to leverage himself up, Hillary dropped to her knees and pinned Kaz's legs. She threw a heel of the hand blow at Kaz's nose. He let out a bellow. Blood gushed out.

Paisley waved the sculpting knife in the air. "You're some piece of work, mister. Like me to carve you a new look?" She scraped the tip of her knife lightly across his forehead, down alongside his eye, where laugh lines would have been, had he been the laughing kind, and drew it through the blood pouring onto his chin. "Let's outline your face in red, shall we?"

His howls were drowned out by the scream of sirens.

CHAPTER FIFTY-TWO

Failure is the condiment that gives success its flavor.

-Truman Capote

HILLARY AND PAISLEY SAT IN THE BACK OF ED'S CAR. THE Rav4 was detained in the parking garage as techs worked to clear the crime scene. Hillary ran the events through her mind, as she'd given them to the police in her statement. Those explosives had been fastened together, three of them wired around the concrete column in the middle of the parking lot. She shuddered to think of the consequences if they'd been set off.

Hillary reached to tap her mother's fingers. "Your knife saved the Center, you know."

"My favorite knife, too. Now in an evidence bag headed for the bowels of the bureaucracy."

"We'll get it replaced, don't you worry, Mother." The

word slipped out, propelled by a surge of gratitude. *Mother*.

Their eyes met and Hillary smiled at her mother.

Paisley yawned. "I like the plan for me to stay home." From under drooping eyelids, she stared out at the pink dawn sky. "Today." She nodded slowly. "I always watch the Rose Bowl parade. Those float designs are so preposterous."

Hillary closed her eyes. This was her critical artist mother. And Claire didn't even know what they'd been through tonight, how close to harm's way, both of them. Maybe best to keep it a secret? Add it to the secrets they were still keeping from each other.

AFTER A FEW HOURS' SLEEP, HILLARY WAS AT THE CENTER a little before noon. She checked to make sure the techs had finished in the basement parking lot and it was open for guests who didn't want to park on the street. In the glass-walled lobby, she went over last-minute directions with the tour guides.

As soon as Sunny Singh and Tiffany got out of the elevator, she joined them. "You look amazing," she told Tiffany. "How do you feel?"

Dropping Sunny's hand, Tiffany rubbed her belly. "I'm fine, just hope Charlie boy here is going to understand his crazy, mixed-up grandfather."

"How did you get that alert to Ed?"

Tiffany flashed an adoring smile at Sunny. "He insisted I wear this little gizmo." She dipped a finger into her scoop-necked white satin blouse and pulled out a black egg-shaped oval on a chain. "It's a GPS signal-only alert."

"But I heard you were tied up. How'd you get it to work?"

"Credit managing my teen-aged braces then years of workouts in the gym." She pushed the device back into her bra, then ducked her head down, burrowed her face between her breasts and shook her head. Hillary watched fascinated as she rose back up, the device hanging from her teeth by a tiny metal stem. She waggled it gently, then took it out of her mouth. "It helps to have pregnant boobs, too, as pushups." She laughed.

Hillary shouted, "I nominate you Wonder Woman of the year!"

WHEN THE DOORS OPENED AT NOON, PEOPLE RUSHED INTO the lobby, oohing and aahing at the height of the climbing wall. "Fly High" signs emitted tiny bubbles that floated down over the heads of the guests. Guides escorted small groups through the sports courts and workrooms.

On the indoor soccer field, tables had been set up for a Good-Luck Meal. Stacy arrived with Keisha and Claire, near the same time as most of the Tasmanian Devils and their parents.

At one o'clock, James Britto stepped onto a raised platform on the far side of the field. He picked up a microphone. "As president of NorCal Chefs, I welcome you to the Ans Botha Center Celebration Meal, courtesy of local restaurants. We consulted with community members on our menu," he pointed to a projection screen behind him, showing a list of foods named for those who'd shared recipes, "and offer you various foods believed to bring good luck, including from cultures that celebrate the new year in a different month than this."

He gestured for Stacy and a half dozen others to stand for applause. Volunteers wearing shirts printed with restaurant logos pushed carts laden with plates holding a sample of each food on the menu.

Hillary pointed at her plate and said to Stacy, "Your collard greens look like folding money. They'll bring good fortune."

Sunny flicked his fingers over his plate. "Along with the green chilies, mango and coconut in the pachadi."

Ed nodded. "Don't forget the gold in Stacy's cornbread."

Stacy's cheeks darkened in a blush. "It's what my mama served along with her black-eyed peas and ham."

AFTER THE MEAL, HILLARY WENT TO THE SECOND FLOOR for the basketball game to benefit Bring Back the Monarchs. Tiffany was coaching the Ans Botha Sprinters, calling themselves the ABS. The team was made up of females from age ten to eighty, including three Sac State Hornet players. Two team USA women joining them wore the same navy blue HOOPS FOR TROOPS tee shirts they wore at the 2016 Rio Olympics.

At the sidelines, Hillary spotted Yvonne Baker, the Olympic runner who'd stood up for Hillary back at the Women in Sports Night a couple months ago, and Hillary went and gave her a big hug.

The ABS were up against We Rock You, an all-male team of mixed ages that included the boys from Reno who'd stayed in touch with Keisha. Tiffany had convinced Old Foggy Bottom to coach the guys, scout possibilities for his men's AAU program. The game went to double overtime, and the ABS won by one point, as Claire shot a bullet pass to Keisha who slammed it down in at the last second.

Hillary watched with delight as Old Foggy Bottom walked over to the ABS bench, put his hand on Claire's shoulder and proclaimed, "I see we need you on our River City Wonders after all, young lady."

Claire flashed a thumbs up to Hillary.

CHAPTER FIFTY-THREE

Forgive us our trespasses as we forgive those who
trespass against us.

-Matthew 6:14

FOR YEARS, CHARLIE HAD PASSED BY THE SACRAMENTO
County Jail downtown, looked up at its high narrow
windows and wondered what it looked like from the
inside. Today, as he waited for Justin to enter the small
interview room, he found he no longer cared. He felt
weak. He'd had only water at the crack-of-dawn breakfast call. The smell of stale coffee nauseated Charlie, and
they didn't have tea of any kind.

Justin marched in, his eyebrows knit in a frown.
"What the hell did you think you were you doing
behind my back?"

Charlie's cheeks burned with shame. "It was just
going to be messages. I didn't want anyone hurt."

"Messages?" Justin's jaw dropped and his frown deepened.

"To wake people up. That *Anarchist Cookbook* made it sound reasonable and effective."

"Don't you know its author tried for years to get that piece of trash off the shelves? It's not logical to expect violence to stop violence. Especially not the subtle kind from gentrification."

Charlie slumped in his chair. "But I tried to stop delivery when I heard about the baby."

"Baby?" Justin was scribbling on a legal pad.

"Yes, cousin." Charlie parted his lips in a thin smile. "You're going to be a sort of uncle."

"What the hell? Bombs and babies?" Justin's pen stood poised on the page.

"Tiff's pregnant. Kaz tied her up, forced me to go through with the plan. He had more explosives hidden in his jacket. He wanted to collapse the whole Center."

"We'll let that radical anarchist sit in jail, think about it. Victor got himself released already, told me being arrested raises his standing where he's going, the University of Toronto, known for turning out anarchists. The guy is excited over their numbers rising in today's political climate. Crazy world." Justin slid his pen back into his breast pocket and shook his head slowly, as if weary to the bone. "I'll get moving on your bail. Got to get you out of here, back to your rose garden. You look like hell in orange. You're not in good shape, my friend. Be lucky to get you home, keep you out of the hospital."

Charlie felt oddly rested. He'd done his part to save

his city. There were no perfect places. Maybe it was best to accept what was, at the end of the story, like in *Candide*, and go home to cultivate the garden. In whatever time and space he had left.

He let himself be led back to his cell, lay on the narrow cot and dozed off, dreaming of teacups, roses and dark green ferns.

CHAPTER FIFTY-FOUR

Perfectionism is the voice of the oppressor.

-Anne Lamott

HILLARY LEFT THE SHOWER AND SURVEYED HER ACHING body in the bedroom's full-length mirror. Bruises on her forearms and wrists. Angry scrapes on her knees the likes of which she hadn't seen since her elementary school days. Not all that bad, considering what Professor Poison's demented pal might have done before Ed and the police arrived. The two had been taken to jail as well as a couple other of their accomplices.

Tiffany had just phoned and said her father had been found unconscious in his cell and taken to UC Davis Medical Center.

Ed came in, embraced her from behind and kissed the back of her neck. "You look like you've been knocked around by a psychopath from that shooter's gang. You should stay home and rest, Chickadee. And you've got to keep an eye on your mother."

She turned and looked at him soberly. "Stacy is coming over to keep Paisley company." It was still hard to call her Mother. There was so much more they might learn about each other, now they had time together at last. "I have to go and face Charlie Bierce. I'm not certain why, I just have to. Before it's too late."

HILLARY WAS ALLOWED INTO THE ICU, WHERE SHE JOINED Tiffany at Charlie's bedside.

"He keeps coming in and out of consciousness," Tiffany said. "Made me bring him a book he got me for my birthday. Insisted on having his glasses on so he could show me the picture of our Alkali Flat house." Tears glistened in Tiffany's eyes.

Hillary had to bite her lip not to say how awful Charlie looked, lying motionless in the hospital bed, his face like a shrunken apple doll, wearing spectacles of bent wire over his closed and sunken eyes. "Can you hear me, Professor? It's Hillary, Hillary Broome."

Charlie's chest rose and fell in jerky motions. He stirred and opened his eyes. "Battling you…" He struggled to his elbows and leaned forward. "Someone outside…to push against."

She was shocked at the piercing blue of his eyes, stabbing into hers. "Someone… to control. Like…Birdie girl."

A thunderbolt of recognition turned Hillary to stone

for a second. The old man had reached for perfection in small spaces. His face seemed to form a distorted mirror of her own in its opposition, powerful and strong.

"But…" He fell back and closed his eyes. "But never looked…in…side."

She watched him, sad that he was fading as he grasped this final lesson. His chest did not rise again. The monitor gave off a steady, flat tone. With a sob, Tiffany rushed out of the room to get help.

Hillary knew it was too late for Charlie, his time yearning to hold the past in place was over, but his battle to stop progress would be taken up by others. She must stay strong.

SHE STARTED UP THE RAV4 AND TURNED OFF THE RADIO, relishing the quiet. She reflected on what Professor Poison had taught her, after all. She'd girded up the walls inside herself. Pushing against him had forced her to break through the wall holding back her feelings. Finally she was tearing down that wall of perfection she'd erected as a ten-year-old girl.

She let go of her anger at the man, in sorrow that he had not used his life in a better way. None of the guys he thought of as his friends were with him at the end. Now her feelings were flooding her awareness, released by the battle with Charlie and jumping through flaming hoops to end Claire's suffering by finding Paisley. It was time to take on the work of truly forgiving her mother.

At home, she found Stacy and Paisley sitting around the dining room table, having tea. Keisha and Claire ran in, out of breath from playing pick-up hoops and sat down.

Claire said, "Ronnie down at the park told us his New Year's resolution was to be nicer to his little brother. What are your resolutions?"

Hillary, Paisley and Stacy looked at each other. Hillary still yearned to hear what happened to Paisley's pregnancy. Did she have a half-brother or sister somewhere out in the world? There was so much she still had to find out, try and fill in those decades her mother was gone. More than any resolution could provide.

Hillary answered her daughter with a question. "What do you want to resolve?"

"Keek said she'd come with me and set flowers on Sarah's grave. Will you drive us?"

"Now?"

"Why not?"

"We don't have any flowers."

"I made paper flowers when I went to see Dr. Bolden at school last week. She called it art therapy. I threaded the flowers into a new lei to match my tie-dyed tee shirt." She smiled at Paisley. "I'll leave my chrysanthemum lei with Sarah. She always liked it so much."

Hillary smiled and went to gather the cleaning supplies they always took to the cemetery to polish the grave marker. The five of them squeezed into the Rav4, Claire holding the faded orange lei with care.

It was cold, clear and windy at St. Mary's Cemetery. They made their way to the back section where the veterans were laid to rest. The bronze plaque lying flat at the top of John and Sarah Stoney's plot was tarnished to a dull green and crowded with grass growing in at the edges.

Hillary suggested that Stacy and Paisley go inside the mausoleum building to get out of the cold while they cleaned the grave marker. Claire set the faded lei to the side and knelt to tug at the intruding grass, and Keisha pulled at it as well. After Hillary sprayed the plaque with mild soapy water, the girls scrubbed it clean with paper towels and polished it with the sleeves of their hoodies.

As Paisley and Stacy returned from the mausoleum, Claire set the orange lei on the bright bronze plaque and rubbed her fingertips over Sarah's engraved name. "I couldn't march on Day of the Dead this year, so I'm leaving this for you now, Sarah."

Her eyes brimming with tears, Keisha looked up at Stacy. "I wish I knew if my mother had a grave." Stacy pursed her lips and said nothing.

Hillary's heart broke at hearing her daughter's friend say what Hillary had so often wondered about her own mother. "Maybe we can help you look for her," she said.

Claire put her hand on her friend's shoulder. "My mother knows how to look for missing people."

A delighted laugh burst from Paisley's lips. "Hillary found me, she did."

Hillary put the cleaning supplies back in her tote. She smiled warmly at Paisley, then Stacy, then each of the girls. "Time to go home, ladies. I think we'll be surprised at how much we all find in 2020."

THE END

ACKNOWLEDGMENTS

For inspiration and motivation for this novel, I am grateful to my late, great husband, Jerry Gillam, newsman for the L. A. Times and Dean of the Capital Press Corps, who expanded my plain white feminist self into a rabid basketball fan and gave me season tickets for the Sacramento Monarchs from the time they started in 1997 through their demise in 2009. Also, I acknowledge the Sacramento Kings being rescued from moving to Seattle by Vivek Ranedive and Mayor Johnson and KHTK 1140 radio sport show hosts and so many others in Sactown.

At the same time, I also respect groups like the Sacramento Taxpayers against Pork, who fought against moving the Kings downtown, as one among other groups and individuals who ardently oppose gentrification of downtown Sacramento. I'd like to thank Sacramento author William Burg for surfacing so much

Sacramento history, the best parts of it while making public the horrific manipulations that took place, like red lining and putting up freeways in places that ruined affordable housing for so many.

I'm grateful to the NBA, the WNBA and Black Lives Matter for their inspiring dedication to become the best they can be and their stands promoting social justice.

I bow to the patience of my writing critique buddies over the four years it's taken to bring *House of Hoops* to the printed page: Sisters in Crime, Gold Country Writers, Trinity Cathedral Writers, Elaine's Lunch Bunch and the San Joaquin Valley Writers. My beta readers improved the novel so much, as well. Thanks for the professional eagle eyed talent of Tennessee Jones, editor, and Tarra Thomas Indie Publishing Services. Most of all, I appreciate the steadfast love and support from my children: Julie, Karen, Mike and Vik.

ABOUT THE AUTHOR

Sacramento native June Gillam started out as a poet before realizing her poems wanted to become stories. Her Hillary Broome novels defy placement into traditional genres and are like the proverbial Box of Chocolates: book one is a grisly horror, the next is more soft and subtle, then on to adventurous and literary, and in Hoops there is hometown cheerleading vs keeping it all safe and small. June says her work best fits into "the social problem novel," in which various characters personify issues around region, class, race, gender, or economics to form an important part of the plot. Mostly, June loves exploring what can transform a normal person into one mad enough to kill. Visit her website here: www.junegillam.com

facebook.com/jgillam2

twitter.com/junegillam

instagram.com/jgillam700

WHAT'S NEXT FOR HILLARY BROOME?

In *House of White Crows*, Hillary finds herself awash in the chaos of 2020, hired by Clearwater College to implement a Plagiarism Prevention program and advise the student Social Justice club, coming under attack by a covert white supremacist cabal run by a mysterious Pied Piper figure.

Made in the USA
Middletown, DE
02 April 2021